FIND THE LADY!

WHEN Neville Brading, a young Canadian on holiday in London, comes upon Anna in the act of running off with his new car, he has no notion of the perilous plight into which this incident will land him, for Anna is a young woman surrounded by mystery, and is not willing to divulge much about her past.

Within a few hours of his meeting her Anna is kidnapped, and in going to her aid Brading suffers the same fate. It is here that Inspector McLean takes a hand in matters, to find himself up against an astute gang of criminals, who stick at nothing to gain their mysterious ends. The story is told with all Mr. Goodchild's inventive ability, and McLean is shown battling against heavy odds until finally he lays bare the secret of the locked box which Anna has guarded most zealously to her own great detriment and suffering.

A closely-knit, intriguing story which the reader will find difficult to lay down until the last page is reached.

Here are the exploits of the famous Inspector McLean, set out in chronological order by his creator, George Goodchild.

FIND THE LADY!

An Inspector McLean Mystery

by

GEORGE GOODCHILD

THE MYSTERY BOOK GUILD
178-202 GREAT PORTLAND STREET
LONDON, W.1

This Edition August 1956

Made and printed in Great Britain by
TAYLOR GARNETT EVANS & CO., LTD.
BUSHEY MILL LANE
WATFORD, HERTS.

THE tall, bronzed Canadian drove his big car half round the West End of London before he could find a place to park it without running the risk of being prosecuted, but at last he was able to squeeze its considerable length between two other vehicles in a back street, quite a distance from the large emporium where he had some shopping to do.

The vast store, with its many floors and wonderful array of goods, fascinated him as few things had. He, too, ran a store high up in Northern Saskatchewan, which his father had built up out of a mere trading post, and of which he was very proud, but it was as a mouse to an elephant compared with this great place, where one could buy anything from a theatre ticket to a Rolls Royce. He had been there once before and had lost himself completely, and now he lost himself again. But it was a joy to be lost amid such alluring products. For half an hour he watched a television screen, and after that was held spell-bound by an exhibit of electrically-operated gadgets from egg-whisks to washing machines. But his own immediate needs lay not in these ingenious inventions. In the china-ware department he fell for a Minton tea-service calculated to bring tears to the eyes of Aunt Jennifer, who, with his father, had emigrated to Canada forty years ago, and in the toy depart-ment he succumbed to the appeal of a clockwork train for Aunt Jennifer's mechanically-minded son. The two parcels together were a bigger load than he cared to carry to his distantly parked car, so he accepted the offer to have them delivered to his hotel.

Free of encumbrances he wandered on through the maze of departments, watching with interest the groups of shoppers, and wondering whence they all came. Then suddenly he heard an orchestra playing an air which was familiar to him, and he found himself outside the entrance to the Restaurant. He went inside and looked round for a seat, but the large room seemed packed. Finally a floor-walker came to his aid and led him to a vacant chair at a table for two. The other occupant was a frosty-looking middle-aged man, with a military cut about him.

5

A waitress came to him and he ordered tea and toast. At the sound of his Canadian drawl the stern-looking man opposite appeared to unfreeze, for his features relaxed into a little smile. But it faded out very quickly, and producing a daily newspaper from his pocket he resumed the solution of a crossword puzzle with the stump of a lead pencil. His industry in this matter was most praiseworthy, and the Canadian had finished his tea and was lighting a cigarette before the crossword solver had reached the end of his task.

"Ah !" he said. "I always do the daily crossword while I have my tea. Sometimes I finish it and sometimes I don't. But it all helps to kill time."

"Sure !" said the Canadian. "But I guess it's no problem killing time in this city."

"You like London ?"

"I'll say I do. My job is to find time to do all the things I want to do before I go back home."

"And where's home, if it isn't a rude question ?"

"A place called New Halifax, in Northern Canada. When my father went there forty years ago there was nothing there but a wooden shack where a Scot and a couple of Indians traded goods and cash for pelts, and did a bit of farming in the close season. My father went into partnership, and when the Scot died he became sole owner. It's a different place now. We've schools, a hospital, electric power, the telephone, and a couple of hotels. That old trading post is now the best store in the township, and you're looking at the proprietor right now."

"So your father's dead ?"

"Yep. Two years ago. He sure was a great person. There wouldn't be any New Halifax but for him. He was an illiterate man. It was my mother who had the book learning. She was a school teacher, and gave me my first lessons. I can remember . . . But I guess I'm talking too much."

"Not a bit. It's good to talk to someone from the wide-open spaces. Are you here on holiday, or business ?"

"Holiday. Before he died Pop told me I must come to Europe. He had a hunch it would give me a bit of culture. I'd never seen a really big city until I came here, but I'm stopping off at Paris and Rome on my way back. Guess I won't enjoy myself at those places because I only know a few words of French and no Italian. But I'll do as he wished."

6

"You'll enjoy yourself all right. Money has a way of talking all languages—especially when it's dollars."

The Canadian laughed in a deep bass voice, and then turned his head slightly to glance at an immaculately dressed girl who was carrying in her arms an equally immaculate pekinese puppy. By contrast with the pekinese her face looked almost angelic, and as she passed the table she dropped a long suède glove, which the Canadian picked up and restored to her.

"Oh, thenk yu," she said mincingly.

"You're welcome," he replied.

The older man laughed.

"Not many of that sort in New Halifax, I'll warrant," he said.

"No, our girls are mostly the working type. Isn't she on the level ?"

"Who can say ? London is a microcosm—like all big cities. She may be as respectable as Caesar's wife, and she may not. Thank God that damned band has finished."

"Don't you like music ?"

"No. It interferes with the flow of thought. There's too much noise in the world. People hate to be quiet, just as they hate to be alone. In millions of homes they switch on the wireless early in the morning and leave it on all day. They can't do anything without a background of noise. If you go out for a walk there's invariably half a dozen aeroplanes in the sky, and the new ones make a darn sight more noise than the old ones. I envy you going back to a place where there's none of this ghastly noise—where one can live a little closer to Nature. I'll tell you something Mister . . ."

"Brading is the name—Neville Brading."

"Mine is Lambertson—Major Lambertson. What was I going to say ? Ah yes—don't make that new town of yours too big. Keep it within bounds and leave no room for all the parasites that batten on big communities. Don't regard mere bigness as the sure sign of progress, or one day you may feel like going out and burning it all to the ground."

Brading smiled at his companion's earnestness. Certainly he was a man with a bee in his bonnet. The wireless was switched on and they sat and listened to the six o'clock news, the major with a cynical look on his lean face.

"All politics and war," he muttered. "And most of it a pack of lies. The Russians have exploded another atom bomb,

7

and the Americans have an even bigger one. I hope every country will have bigger and better bombs—bombs big enough to wipe out each other's country in ten minutes. Then we shall really have peace."

Before Brading could reply to this trite remark there came an announcement : 'Will Anna Westmoreland, last heard of two years ago in Bristol, go to the Princess Elizabeth Hospital at Southampton, where her mother is dangerously ill. I will repeat that message.'

"Strange world," growled the Major, "where a young woman can be separated from her mother for two years without sending her a line. Makes one despair of the human race. Well, I must be getting home. Nice to have met you, Neville Brading."

"Nice to have met you, Major."

"And if before you go home you are ever in the neighbourhood of Hampton Court look me up at the Palace. I've an apartment there. I'll have the pleasure of giving you the best glass of sherry you are likely to get in this country. Here, take my card—just in case."

He handed Brading a visiting card, and then, slipping sixpence under his saucer, took up his bill and decamped. Brading followed his example a few minutes later.

Outside there was a drizzle of rain, and the light was fading. Brading made his way to where he had left his car. Some of the parked cars had left during his absence and he could recognize the back of his own car, a little way up the narrow street. There was a woman standing very close to the door of it, and suddenly to his surprise she nipped inside and closed the door behind her. Astounded, he broke into a run and reached the car as it was moving out. He opened the rear door just in time, and entering it, clapped his hand on the shoulder of the driver. The car stopped with a jolt and a scared pale face was turned to him. It was that of a girl of about twenty-five years of age.

"What's the idea ?" he asked angrily. "This is my car."

"I—I had to," she stammered.

"Had to steal it ?"

A policeman, seeing the car stationary and half across the street, came striding towards it. The girl saw him and gave a curious little choke. He came to the open window.

"Any trouble, Miss ?" he asked.

The girl was speechless, so Brading took up the matter.

"We want to get into Sloane Street, officer," he drawled. "Guess we're a bit lost."

"Go the way you're facing, then first left and first right."

"Thanks a lot."

The girl took the cue and drove on, but after she made the first turn Brading told her to stop, and then entered the front of the car.

"Now," he said. "Why did you do it ?"

"You wouldn't believe me if I told you. Please let me go."

"Not until you've told me why you did it ? I think I've the right to know that, since I've saved you from being arrested. You don't look like a regular car thief."

"I'm not. I was having a cup of tea in that little tea-shop near where you left the car, and I heard some bad news—over the radio. It—it was about my mother. They said she was in hospital—dangerously ill. . . ."

"Say, are you Anna Westmoreland ?"

"Yes. So you must have heard the message ?"

"Sure, but I never guessed she was just round the corner. But why try to steal my car ?"

"I could think of no other way to get to Southampton. I haven't enough money to buy a railway ticket. Then I saw the cars outside. I—I resolved to borrow one, and bring it back when I had seen my mother. This car was the only one which had the ignition key in the dashboard. I would have taken a smaller car if there had been one."

Brading looked at the girl shrewdly. She might be lying, he thought. She must have heard the message, but she might be making use of it to explain her action.

"You don't believe me," she said.

"I never said so."

"Your expression said so. I can prove I am Anna Westmoreland, and that should convince you that I am telling the truth."

She delved into her handbag, and produced a letter. On the envelope was written her name at an address in Bloomsbury. Brading nodded his head.

"I'm satisfied," he said. "How far is Southampton ?"

"I don't know. About eighty miles, I think."

"Do you still want to see your mother ?"

"Yes. There are some things I must tell her."

"Can you direct me through London?"

"Yes, but——"

"I'll take you. You tell me the way to go."

He took over the wheel, and the powerful car moved smoothly through Sloane Street, thence to Hammersmith and finally out into the by-pass. From here the road was wide open, and the car gathered speed. The drizzle had now ceased and the sky became full of stars. At Esher, Brading checked his route by the map, and away they went again. From time to time his gaze would switch momentarily to the girl beside him, whose face was a soft pink glow in the reflected light from the dashboard. She was tastefully dressed, but the clothing was obviously old, and her stockings showed signs of painstaking repair. It was surprising that she should lack the few shillings necessary for the purchase of a railway ticket, and he could only draw the conclusion that she was very much out of luck.

"We're going very fast," she said, with a glance at the speedometer.

"Isn't that what you want?"

"Yes, but I've never travelled so fast before. You're American, aren't you?"

"No. Canadian."

"I never can tell the difference. But the car is British, isn't it?"

"Yes. I bought it here, two months ago. At least I ordered it and it was delivered to me at the port. I'm taking it back to Canada. Comfortable?"

"Yes, thank you."

Again there was silence for a long time, which was broken this time by Brading.

"It's a long time since you've seen your mother?"

"Over two years."

"And no letter from you all that time?"

"There were reasons, but I can't speak about them—not now."

"You needn't. Oh here's a fork in the road. See if you can read the signpost. I'll slow down."

The girl managed to read the large white board in advance of the bifurcation.

"We go left," she said. "I think it said twenty-four miles."

"Fine !"

There was a surge of power as he opened the throttle, and the bright headlights lit up a great stretch of old Roman road. The speed indicator moved steadily round the illuminated dial, and the girl gasped and gave him an appealing glance.

"Okay !" he said, with a laugh. "I've been wanting to do that for a long time, but the agent told me I mustn't till I'd clocked a thousand miles. Well, we've just done that, so my conscience is clear. Now I'll behave myself."

Very soon the lights of the big port formed a glow in the western sky, and when they reached the outskirts of the town Brading stopped and asked the way to their destination, but it took two further enquiries to bring them outside the large hospital block. He took the car through the wide entrance gate and finally brought it to a standstill in the car-park. Anna was now pale and tense.

"Cheer up," he said. "Things may not be so bad as you imagine. I'll wait here for you. No need to hurry. I shall be glad of a quiet smoke."

"You're very kind," she almost sobbed.

He got out and opened the car door for her, and then watched her walk to the hospital entrance and vanish into its vast interior. He got back into the car, lighted a cigarette and wondered what would be the outcome of this unexpected adventure. Why, in fact, had he embarked on it at all ? He could have pushed a pound note or so into her hand and taken her to the railway station. That would have been cheaper than the cost of petrol. Impulse was a fine taskmaster, and all the more impelling when it involved a beautiful young girl with tear-drops hovering on the lids of her bright eyes.

"Guess I'm a bit of a softie," he muttered.

§2

He had scarcely finished his cigarette when, to his surprise, he saw the girl emerge from the hospital and hurry down the steps. She had a handkerchief clapped to her face, and she swayed alarmingly as she walked towards the car. Quickly he went to her assistance and conducted her safely to the car, where she burst into a torrent of tears.

"Steady!" he murmured. "I guess it's bad news, but don't let it get you down."

She shook her head, utterly unable to speak, and then the sobbing gradually subsided, and she thrust the wet handkerchief into her handbag.

"I'm sorry," she said shamefacedly. "But I wasn't quite prepared for the blow. She—she died half an hour ago. But they let me see her."

"What happened to her?" he asked sympathetically.

"An accident. She was knocked down by a car this afternoon. There was never any hope, they said."

"Are you her sole relative?"

"Yes."

"Did she live near here?"

"Yes. At a place called Fenton—about three miles out of the town on the Winchester Road."

"What are you going to do now?"

"I don't know."

"Wouldn't you like to go back to your mother's house?"

"No," she replied emphatically. "It was a place of great unhappiness. I never want to go back there."

In the bright light of the lamp standard he could see her face more clearly than he had seen it before. There was an angularity about it—a rather unnatural protrusion of the cheekbones—which aroused his suspicions concerning her well-being.

"When did you last have a good meal?" he asked.

She turned her head away from him, and impulsively he took one of her hands in his. It was a shapely, delicate hand, but as undernourished as the rest of her.

"I'm starving," he said. "Let's get some food. It will give you time to think things over."

"I'm not—really hungry," she protested.

"But I am. It's past my meal time. Come on—we'll find a place."

He started the car and at slow speed they passed through the busy streets towards the centre of the town. Finally

Brading saw the neon lighting of a hotel. There was a handy car park just inside the entrance and he took the car there.

"You know I've no money," she said.

"What's money? Anyway, while you're in my car you're my guest."

On being allocated a vacant table by a somewhat moody waiter, Anna begged to be excused and vanished for some time. When she returned Brading was amazed to observe what miracles could be performed out of the interior of a handbag. She took the seat opposite him and scanned the long menu which was before her.

"What would you like?" he asked.

"I think I'll have some cold ham and salad."

"That's no meal for a growing girl," he protested. "Guess I'll have to prescribe for you. Let's make a start on the hors d'oeuvre, then Dover sole. After we've had that we can think about what follows. Okay?"

Anna nodded, and the waiter sidled along with his pencil and pad. Brading gave the order and then beckoned to the wine steward.

"Must have something to drink," he said. "What sort of wine do you like?"

"Not for me, thank you," said Anna.

"Oh come! Something very light. It will do you good. Let's leave it to the waiter, shall we?"

Anna was tired of saying 'no,' and the waiter seemed pleased to have the last word in the matter. Both food and drink were served with promptitude. As the meal progressed Anna seemed to rise above her previous hopeless dejection. She did not protest at the suggestion of roast fowl following the fish, and Brading was glad to notice that she left nothing on her plate. She took the white wine rather diffidently at first, but the waiter had done well in this respect and she permitted Brading to refill her glass. Over the coffee Brading reverted to the thorny subject of the dead woman.

"Tell me about your mother," he said.

"I can't—not now. Please don't ask me."

"All right. Tell me about yourself."

"What sort of things?"

"Are you in some sort of a job?"

"Not now. I lost my job six months ago when I had an

illness. I've been looking round for another, but have had no luck."

"What sort of a job did you have ?"

"Modelling gowns in a large store. But my illness ruined my figure temporarily and so I wasn't everybody's money. Getting back my lost weight wasn't easy when—when. . . ."

"When you weren't getting enough to eat ?"

"That and the worry combined."

"Wouldn't your mother have helped you if you had written to her ?"

Anna's silence reminded him that he was again in forbidden territory, so he switched to the immediate problem.

"What are you going to do now—stay here or go back to your lodging ?"

"I've no choice," she said.

"Wouldn't you prefer to stay here, and settle up your mother's affairs ?"

"Yes, but——"

"I know. You've got no money. That's where I come in. I'm going to book you a room here. . . ."

"But I've got no luggage, and the hotel may not——"

"I'll fix it. You stay here."

Without more ado he left the dining-room and was absent for some time. The waiter came and left the bill on the table, glancing at Brading's empty chair.

"My friend has gone to book me a room," she explained.

The waiter smiled and went away. Anna picked up the bill and glanced at the total. To her it seemed enormous. Then at last came Brading, carrying a small suitcase in his hand.

"It's okay," he said. "Number 38 on the first floor. Here's the key."

"But—but what's the suitcase for ?" she stammered.

"Solves the sleeping problem. They run a small shop here. It was closed, but I got them to open up. Better have a look inside to see if I've forgotten anything."

She opened the case and found inside a very nice silk nightdress, a pair of soft slippers, a toothbrush and a tube of toothpaste.

"You shouldn't !" she complained.

"Oh nuts ! You just happen to be out of luck, and I'm in it.

I've been in it most of my life. That's the way things go. Tomorrow you'll be able to gather up the loose ends and see what the position is. I've got to get back to London tonight because I've an old friend coming to see me tomorrow morning. But I'll run down here tomorrow afternoon, and see how things are going. I've left some money at the office. If you want any of it for anything, all you have to do is ask the manager."

She gazed at him in amazement.

"You're an extraordinary man," she said. "What's to prevent me running off tomorrow morning with the money and the suitcase ?"

"You won't," he laughed. "Sleep well, have a good breakfast, and keep your chin up. Now I ought to be starting back."

"I'll come with you to the car."

"Fine !"

He called the waiter, paid the bill with three one-pound notes, waving a big hand to intimate that he wasn't interested in any change, and then they passed through the entrance hall to the car park. In a minute or two he was away. Anna stood there as in a trance.

.   .   .   .   .

Brading motored back to London with the girl's image constantly before his eyes. There was something about her which intrigued him deeply, and much that puzzled him completely. He was certain that the meal he had provided was the first she had had for a long time, and it was some satisfaction to know that at least he had filled an empty stomach. Until now his sojourn in England had been void of any high lights. Now, out of the blue, had come this adventure, only three days before he was due to start the homeward journey, through France and Italy down to the port of Naples. Why hadn't it come earlier—much, much earlier ? How good it would have been to see the places he had seen, with Anna as his companion, instead of being alone. He knew little enough about English girls, but he had the feeling that Anna was a cut above most of them—in her deportment, her speech, and her general behaviour. True, she had been prepared to commit larceny, in fact had done so, but her need had been overwhelming. He told himself that he would have done no less in the same circumstances.

It was when he had covered about half the distance home

that he became conscious of a curious thing. There was a car in his rear which appeared to be quite satisfied to stay there. It was a fast car, because on some of the straight stretches he had put up big speeds only to find the car still behind him when he slowed down. To test out the matter he stopped at some cross-roads as if unsure of his way. A few cars passed him, but not the one which had been in his rear most of the time. He could see this vehicle well in the distance and it was stationary.

Again he went on, and very soon he was in comparatively thick traffic and not able to see what was happening behind. Mixed up with buses and taxis in Hammersmith he had no thought for anything but the road immediately ahead, and some minutes later he brought the car to a standstill outside his hotel, which had a small paved recess for the convenience of its guests.

It was now close on eleven o'clock, and he decided to have a 'nightcap' and then seek his bed. He rang the bell in the lounge and a waiter came to him with a smile.

"You rang, sir?"

"Yep. George, get me a double whisky. Oh, and ask Benson if he'll put my car away for me. Here's the key. I'm sure tired."

The waiter brought the drink, and said he had given the car key to the doorman, who would take it to the lock-up garage as soon as possible.

"That's fine!"

He was settling down to his drink when the waiter came back again.

"Excuse me, sir," he said. "But there are two gentlemen asking to see you."

"Did they give any name?"

The waiter gave a little cough.

"One of them is Inspector Willington of Scotland Yard. He wanted to know if the owner of the Humber car was here. I hope you haven't been speeding, sir?"

"Can they get me for that?"

"They can if it was in a built-up area."

"Well, better tell them I'm here."

"Very good, sir."

The two officers entered a few moments later. They were

both in plain clothes, and the taller of them was obviously the superior in rank, for it was he who opened the conversation.

"You are Mr. Neville Brading ?"

"That's right."

"A Canadian citizen ?"

"Yep."

"Did you go to Southampton this evening with a young woman named Anna Westmoreland ?"

"I did."

"How long have you known Miss Westmoreland ?"

Brading looked at the clock on the mantelpiece.

"A little short of five hours."

"How did you come to meet her ?"

Brading hesitated. The questions were put politely enough, but he did not feel that he was bound to answer them on that account.

"I don't think you've any right to ask me that," he said.

"As a police officer acting on instructions I have every right, but, of course, you are not bound to answer."

"Then I won't."

The officer smiled and shrugged his shoulders.

"It's never wise to refuse to answer questions put by an officer of the law in the course of his duty. Refusal to answer can be interpreted in a certain way."

"What way ?"

"As an attempt to shield someone guilty of a misdemeanour."

"You mean Miss Westmoreland ?"

"I haven't said so."

"Look here, officer, you knew I took that girl to Southampton. So you must know where she is at this moment. If so, why don't you question her instead of me ?"

"You must permit us to know our own business, Mr. Brading."

"Then be fair to me. What is she supposed to have done ?"

"I've not said she has done anything. I want information about her."

"Then I guess you're barking up the wrong tree. I know nothing about her, except that she wanted to get to Southampton quickly to see her mother who was dangerously ill. There was a wireless SOS and—— Ah, now I've got it ! You heard that SOS, and set a watch on the hospital to see if she responded."

"You're not far from the truth. We have been looking for her for some time."

"Well, now you've found her. Isn't that enough?"

"Not quite. Have you ever been to her lodging?"

"I've already told you I met her five hours ago for the first time."

"And you—a complete stranger—drove her all the way to Southampton."

"I did."

"Merely as a friendly gesture?"

"Yes. Does that surprise you? She was in trouble and I helped her out. Why should that shock you?"

"It doesn't shock me. But wouldn't it have been easier to have put her on the next train?"

"It would, but I was at a loose end. It was just an impulse."

"And you haven't been to her lodging in London?"

"I have not."

"Do you know where she lives?"

Brading stared into the face of his questioner. The cat was out of the bag. For some reason or other they wanted to search Anna's lodging, and they expected him to aid them. This, at the moment, he was most reluctant to do, not until he had had an opportunity of speaking to Anna.

"I'm sorry I can't help you there," he said.

"I presume you have a passport?"

"Of course."

"I should like to see it."

"You'll have to wait until I get it. It's in my bedroom."

"We'll wait."

Brading gave a little sigh of impatience, and went up to his room. When he returned with the passport the tall man thanked him and looked at the photograph and then at Brading.

"Seems to be all right," he said.

"Had you any reason to believe it might not be?" asked Brading acidly.

"No, but it is a routine matter. I'm sorry to have troubled you, Mr. Brading."

Brading said nothing, but watched them pass through the

door. Then he pushed the bell and the alert waiter was quickly on the scene.

"The occasion calls for another double whisky, George."

"Certainly, sir." The waiter glanced at the passport on the table. "I hope there's no trouble."

"Quite a bit, but not the kind I expected."

Brading browsed over the second whisky. What had the girl done that the police should take such an interest in her? She looked anything but a crook, but would the police have gone to such trouble unless they were reasonably sure that they were on the right track? But in that case why hadn't they arrested her, or at least questioned her? It was all very puzzling.

He tried to imagine just what had happened. The police had heard the broadcast SOS and had immediately dispatched a car to the hospital to see if the wanted girl turned up. They must have watched her go into the hospital, and afterwards followed her and himself to the hotel where they had dined. Later they had trailed him back to London in the hope of getting a lot of useful information from him concerning his mysterious companion, not the least important item being the girl's permanent address. Did they hope to find something there which might incriminate her?

What a tragic end to what had been to him a delightful evening! It might be that even now Anna was under arrest and that the police had concealed that fact from him. But tomorrow he would doubtless know more about the matter.

§3

HE awoke early the following morning with a new resolution. He would telephone the old friend he had promised to meet, and postpone the appointment until a more suitable date, and, after a quick breakfast, drive down to Southampton and see Anna. He put this plan into effect at once, but just prior to taking the road he rang up the hotel at Southampton and asked after Anna. There was some delay and finally the manager himself came to the 'phone.

"Miss Westmoreland is not in her room, sir," he said. "And her bed has not been slept in. Also the key of her room is missing. I don't quite understand the matter."

Brading's heart began to thump.

"Is there nothing in her room—a small suitcase, for instance ?"

"Nothing at all. There is no sign that she went there."

"All right," said Brading. "I'll probably call and see you later."

What to do next he did not know, but while cogitating on the matter he went to the garage and got out his car, and drove it into the small parking place outside the hotel. Here he lighted a cigarette, and thought hard. If Anna had been arrested the police at Scotland Yard would surely know, since the action had originated there, but would they help him, or merely send him about his business ? In any case he could foresee tremendous delay, being buffeted between one department and another until he found the right person.

Then he remembered the letter which Anna had shown him to prove her identity. He could see the thing now in his mind's eye, the name and address written in a large scrawling hand :

Miss Anna Westmoreland,
Watling Street,
Bloomsbury.

But the number ? It was either 26 or 36. It might be worth while trying to locate her lodging with a view to discovering whether there had been any message from Anna to explain her absence the previous night. Failing that, he might learn something more about the girl. From the hall porter he got instructions how to get to Bloomsbury, and a few minutes later he started off.

Despite the detailed nature of his instructions it took him over half an hour to reach his objective, for the traffic east of Marble Arch had seemed to get itself into a solid block, but after suffering the execrations of numerous taxi-drivers who wanted to earn their fares more quickly than the density of traffic permitted, he reached his destination. It was a short and rather dingy street connecting with two main thorough-fares, and he soon discovered that No. 26—or rather the place where No. 26 should have been—was just a gap in the bricks and mortar, with flowers growing from the basement floor.

"Bomb site," he muttered, and drove the car slowly along the unprepossessing façade, finally to reach No. 36. It was a slim house of four stories, and a little card in the lower window bore the legend 'Furnished Apartment To Let.' Leaving the car, he approached the front door and rang the bell. There was a considerable delay, and then an unkempt-looking woman opened the door and stared at him, and also at the car.

"Does Miss Westmoreland live here ?" he asked.

"She did, but not no more," rasped the woman.

"But she was here until quite recently, wasn't she ?"

"Until yesterday. Are you a friend of hers ?"

"Yes."

"Well I'm sorry. I had to get rid of her."

"But why ?"

"She owes me six weeks rent. Every week was the same. She'd try and pay up before another week was due, but she didn't pay, and then she tried to do the dirty on me. Yesterday morning I found her trying to get away with her suitcase. Well, I wasn't standing for that. Would you ?"

Brading had no answer to that awkward question.

"What happened ?" he asked.

"I told her that unless she found the overdue rent by the evening she needn't trouble to come back, and that I was going to keep her belongings as security, until she did pay."

"And she never came back ?"

"No. I didn't think she would. I don't suppose the stuff in the suitcase is worth half the rent, but I can't tell because she took away the key with her."

"But she was ill, wasn't she, for a long time ?"

"Yes. I wouldn't have let the rent get in arrears if she hadn't been. She wasn't a bad sort of girl," she added, soften-ing a little. "If she had given me a bit to go on with it might have been different. But it couldn't go on for ever. I've got my living to get, like everyone else."

"Of course," agreed Brading. "How much does she owe you ?"

"Six weeks at fifty bob is fifteen quid."

"It's probable she had gone to her people to get the money. I think I know where I can find her. Better hold that suitcase until I call again."

"All right. But I can't hold the flat. The first person that wants it gets it. That's fair enough isn't it?"

"Fair enough," agreed Brading. "I'll be seeing you."

The woman eyed him a little more hopefully as he turned and got into the car. The temptation to pay off that debt there and then had come to him, but now he was glad he had not acted on impulse. There had to be a limit to philanthropic acts until one was sure they were justified by facts, and the facts as he now saw them were by no means crystal clear. The one person to clear up the mystery was Anna herself, but where was she now?

He hesitated about his next step, and finally decided to run down to Southampton. He did the trip in record time and went first of all to the hotel where he found the manager much agitated by what had happened.

"I can tell you no more than I told you on the telephone," he said. "The young lady clearly did not use the room you reserved for her. By the way, she did not sign the register."

"She meant to do that after she had seen me off in my car. I suppose she did not use any of the money which I left with the cashier?"

"No. He told me about that. It's clearly a case for the police. Do you wish me to proceed in the matter?"

"Not yet."

"And am I to keep the room for her?"

"I'll tell you later. I have another call to make."

His second call was at the hospital, where he was finally handed over to the Almoner, who informed him that they were expecting Miss Westmoreland to call that morning regarding the disposal of her mother's body, but so far she had not called. Brading thought it wiser not to divulge what he knew.

"Has anyone else called?" he enquired.

"Yes. The dead woman's solicitor. He had heard the bad news and wanted to get in touch with the daughter. I told him we would inform Miss Westmoreland when she arrived."

"Who is the solicitor?" asked Brading.

"Mr. James Moffat. His office is in Charles Street—Number 12."

Brading then went in search of Mr. Moffat, and found him in his office surrounded by deed boxes and dusty-looking tomes. He peered over his goggle glasses at his visitor.

"I understand you wish to see me about the late Mrs. Westmoreland?" he asked.

"Yes, but more especially her daughter Anna."

"I know little about the daughter, not having seen her for years. But are you a relative?"

"No, only a casual friend. I brought her down here last night in my car to see her mother."

"Indeed. Then you may know where she is staying?"

"Last night she intended to stay at the Talbot Hotel. I left her there about half-past nine. But she didn't stay."

"Why not?"

"I don't know. I rang her up this morning from London, and was informed that her bed had not been used and that she was no longer in the hotel."

The solicitor stroked his long jaw for a few moments.

"Can you think of any reason why she should not stay there?" he asked.

"None at all. I booked the room for her myself, and bought her a few things which she lacked."

"That is rather extraordinary behaviour. I think I will ring up the hospital."

"There's no need. I have been there. They were expecting her this morning, but she did not turn up."

"Mr. Brading, may I ask what is your interest in Miss Westmoreland?"

"No interest—except sentimental. We met by accident and she told me that her mother was dangerously ill, and that there had been an SOS over the wireless. She had no money and was in a fix. That's all there is to it. When she arrived and found her mother dead it knocked her to pieces. I believed her to be almost starving so I took her to the hotel and made her eat. It was the least I could do. Then I got a hunch she was in great trouble, and so I decided to hang around for a bit to see if I could help."

"That is good of you. I must admit I am in a dilemma. It seems premature to get in touch with the police, unless you have reason to believe that the girl is in some sort of danger."

"She didn't say she was, but look at the facts. She was

23

grateful when I booked her a room and bought her a few toilet things. These were in a small suitcase, and she was holding the case, and her handbag, when she said good-bye to me outside the hotel. She appears not to have gone back to the hotel at all after that, and she wouldn't have gone for a walk with the suitcase in her hands. There were a number of other cars in the car park. She could have been taken away in one of them, couldn't she?"

"Why should she be?"

"Could there be any connection between her disappearance and a will left by her mother?"

The solicitor shook his head.

"That, I think, is out of the question. Mrs. Westmoreland had no money of her own. She was in receipt of an income provided by a distant relative on the death of her husband ten years ago. She lived in a furnished rented house. The income terminated at her death, and the few personal items which remain are of no value. There are, in fact, some debts which I shall have the greatest difficulty in meeting. To the best of my knowledge there is no will, and if there were it would be useless."

"All the same, something should be done."

"I intend to do something, but I will give Miss Westmoreland another twenty-four hours before I bother the police. If I hear from her I will tell her of your visit here."

It was clearly the end of the interview, and Brading left the office more bewildered than ever. He wondered now whether he had acted wisely in withholding from the solicitor the matter of the police enquiry, but until he saw Anna again he did not feel like publicizing allegations which might turn out to be false.

With his mind full of conflicting thoughts he drove back to London. With but two days left of his holiday it seemed foolish to pursue this matter, but Anna Westmoreland was not a person to be lightly dismissed from his mind. She had impressed him as no one else ever had, and he hated the thought of leaving England without solving the mystery of Anna's disappearance.

On the following morning he telephoned the solicitor, and was told that there had been no news of the girl and that the solicitor was taking up the matter with the police. Sitting over a drink in the hotel lounge he came to a new decision. There was no real reason why he should hurry back home. He could cancel his air-ferry passage, and re-book at a later date. A telegram to Saskatchewan would remove any anxiety at that end. Without more ado he dispatched the telegram, and then went to the agency where he had booked his passage and cancelled it.

After that he felt much better, and resolved to do something about Anna's lodging. He went along to Watling Street and the same untidy woman answered the door.

"Oh," she said. "It's you."

"Yes. Miss Westmoreland wishes to retain her room."

"Sorry," she said. "I let it an hour ago. Has she sent the money she owes me?"

"As a matter of fact she has," he lied.

"That's good. I'm sorry about this, but a gentleman called and wanted the room at once. She can't expect me to turn away good money."

"I understand."

"Well, if you'll give me the money you can take away her suitcase."

"Couldn't you keep it for her?"

"No. I want to finish with the matter."

"Very well."

Brading took out his wallet and handed her the notes. Then she excused herself for a few minutes and came back with a fairly big suitcase. Brading took it from her and was soon back in his car.

§ 4

Two days passed and no news came to Brading. He telephoned again to Moffat, the solicitor, and was told rather crisply that the police had the matter in hand.

"Which police?" he asked.

"The police here and at Scotland Yard. It is possible you may receive a visit from them."

Within an hour that prophecy came true. Brading was in his bedroom changing his shirt when he was informed over the telephone that Dectective-Sergeant Brook wished to see him. He thought it might be the man who had accompanied Inspector Willington on the previous visit, and said he would see the officer in his room.

A few minutes later there came a rap on the door and a big deep-chested man entered.

"Mr. Brading?" he asked.

"That's me. Is it about Miss Westmoreland?"

"Yes. We have information from Southampton that you saw Miss Westmoreland a few days ago."

"That's true. I took her down to Southampton and left her at a hotel there."

"You know that she vanished that evening?"

"Of course."

"Will you tell me how you came to meet her?"

Brading stared into Sergeant Brook's big face.

"Are you not from Scotland Yard?"

"Yes."

"But I've told you already. At least I told Inspector Willington."

"I don't quite follow. Who is Inspector Willington?"

"One of your own force. He and another officer called here and asked me questions about Miss Westmoreland."

"I'm sorry, sir, but I can assure you that there is no such Inspector at Scotland Yard."

"But——!" Brading stopped short.

"You were saying. . . ?" asked Brook.

"I guess I've been a darned fool. Gee, I fell for a cheap trick. But how was I to know? They asked me questions about Miss Westmoreland, particularly about her lodging in London. I stalled about that because I was led to believe that the police had been searching for her a long time. The girl had had a bad break and I didn't feel like spilling the beans."

"Suppose you spill them now," said Brook. "So far as I know, we have nothing on the girl. We merely wish to locate her because Mr. Moffat, her mother's solicitor, is under the impression that something may have happened to her."

So Brading told his story without omitting anything, and the Sergeant made a few notes regarding times and places.

Finally Brading brought the story up to date by telling him of the visit to the girl's lodging, and the handing over of the solitary suitcase.

"Have you opened the case?" asked the Sergeant.

"No. I couldn't if I wanted to. It's locked and she has the key."

"Where is it now?"

"In the wardrobe. I didn't know quite what to do with it, but the woman forced it on me."

"I think I shall have to take possession of that, Mr. Brading."

"By all means, but. . . ."

"But what?"

"I've been fooled once. . . ."

The Sergeant laughed and then produced his warrant, to dispel Brading's very obvious doubts.

"Sorry," said Brading. "I'll get it for you."

He went across to the big wardrobe and opened the left side of it. Where the suitcase had stood there was nothing but bare board. He opened the other side of the cabinet, but saw only his personal belongings.

"It's gone!" he gasped.

"When did you last see it?"

"Last night. I haven't opened the wardrobe since. I put the suitcase in there yesterday morning."

"At what time did you see it last night?"

"Eight o'clock. It was raining outside and I kept a mackintosh in the wardrobe. I left it downstairs when I came in."

"So you went out after eight o'clock?"

"Yes. I went to a cinema and came home about eleven."

"Did you leave the key of your room at the desk downstairs?"

"Yes, and it was on the hook when I came back."

Brook stroked his big square jaw.

"I'll have to make enquiries downstairs," he said. "It looks as if some unauthorized person borrowed the key when no one was looking. Not very difficult to do that."

"The spurious inspector?"

"Could be."

"But how did he know I had the suitcase?"

"I expect we shall find he discovered where the girl had

27

been living, and went there only to hear that you had taken possession of the suitcase."

"But the woman didn't know where I was staying."

"She could have described you. That might have been enough."

"Yes, you're right. But I still don't see how he could have got the suitcase out of the hotel without being questioned."

"He could have got it out easily if he booked a room here and had some luggage of his own. I think it was someone who booked in late last night, and booked out early this morning. We'll go into that later. Now, can you tell me what kind of clothes the girl was wearing when you last saw her?"

Brading thought for a moment and then gave the Sergeant a fairly detailed description of Anna's dress, surprising even himself in this worthy effort.

"No photograph of her I suppose?"

"Good heavens, I was only with her an hour or two!"

"Well, what was she like?"

Again Brading reflected. He could see her face now as he had done across that table at which she had eaten a belated meal.

"About average height," he said. "Lots of light brown hair, done in a sort of halo. Lovely eyes—hazel I should call them. A straight little nose, and prominent cheekbones. Very slim—almost fragile, but that was due to semi-starvation. She told me as much, though not in so many words. Very sad expression, until she smiled. I guess that's all."

The Sergeant closed his note-book, and put it back into his pocket.

"Are you staying on here, Mr. Brading?" he asked.

"Yes—for a time, anyway."

"If you should see that spurious inspector again, or Miss Westmoreland, I should be glad if you would give us a ring. This number will get you through to the right department."

Brading took the card bearing the telephone number, and the next moment Brook was gone, leaving Brading breathless and relieved. At least Anna's stock had gone up a little, though she still remained tantalisingly mysterious. That she had been kidnapped seemed fairly obvious, for it was impossible to account for her disappearance in any other way. But what part did that battered old suitcase play in this

28

sinister business ? His excitement at being projected into this affair changed to sober reflection when he was brought to realize that the interested persons had succeeded in finding Anna's lodging. It seemed to him they must have got this information from Anna herself, and that suggested measures far removed from gentle persuasion. But what was she hiding, and for what purpose ?

When at last he went downstairs the man at the reception desk, where the key of his room was normally kept, was still smarting under the collar from his interview with Sergeant Brook and with the manager.

"I'm sorry about the suitcase, Mr. Brading," he said. "But a man's only human. I can't be expected to stand here twelve hours a day without spending a penny, if you know what I mean. That Scotland Yard chap talked to me as if I was a kid. Did I ever leave the keyboard unguarded ? Seemed to think I had nothing else to do but sit and watch those damned keys. I hope the loss isn't great, sir ?"

"I don't know what was in it. You see, it wasn't mine. I was holding it for a friend."

"That's a bit awkward. Have you told the manager that ?"

"Not yet."

"Well, take my tip and don't, or there may be some trouble with the insurance company if you make a claim."

"I guess it's best to stick to the truth. But the police may succeed in getting it back."

The receptionist shrugged his shoulders. He seemed to have a lower opinion of police efficiency than Brading. But he was reduced to silence as the manager, coming through the hall, saw Brading and hurried to him.

"I'm sorry, Mr. Brading, about this unfortunate business," he said. "Such a thing has never happened before. It's quite incredible that anyone should have had the audacity to purloin a bedroom key with felonious intentions. I assure you we shall do our utmost to recover the missing article."

"I'm sure you will," replied Brading.

A little later he was on the busy pavement wandering somewhat aimlessly towards Marble Arch, and so immersed was he in his own thoughts that he found himself lost in a maze of streets and crescents almost entirely composed of stately Regency houses, some still bearing the scars of Hitler's bombers, others bright and gay in their new paint. He wished there were someone who could put him right about these lovely memorials of the past—their builders, and the people who had lived in them. He had heard vaguely about the Regent and those rollicking days of sin and depravity before the young queen had come to the throne to change the 'sorry state of things entire' and to set England rocketing to the very summit of prosperity and power.

But again, inevitably, his thoughts turned to Anna—that sad-faced beautiful outcast, who had jumped into his life for a few blessed hours, and out again. Where was she ? What was happening to her ? And why couldn't he do something about it ? But to these questions there were no immediate answers, and ultimately he found himself in a street which he knew.

§5

At Scotland Yard Inspector McLean had been listening to Sergeant Brook's report of his visit to the hotel. He had expected something very brief, for such excursions on Brook's part were seldom exciting, but Brook made the most of his story and dwelt dramatically on the matter of the visit of the spurious police officer, and the subsequent theft of the suitcase.

"There's no doubt about Brading's surprise," he said. "I've never seen a man so dumbfounded. All the same, it's queer that he should pay the girl's back rent. He's either up to his neck in love with her or is trying to pull a fast one on us."

"He could be in love with her," said McLean. "Such things have happened."

"But he admits having been with her only a few hours in all, and then he paid for her room at an expensive hotel in Southampton and left some money. . . ."

"Yes, I know about that. But tell me more about the man Drummond, who booked in at Brading's hotel late last night, and left early this morning. Wasn't the hall porter able to say whether he took out more baggage than he arrived with ?"

"No, sir. It was a different man. The only other person to book in last night and leave this morning was a woman, and she carried only a very small case."

"What address did Drummond write in the hotel register?"

"Ransome Street, Manchester. I've since found out there is no such street. That's mighty significant."

"How was he described?"

"Very vaguely. All I could get was that he was built on the large side, and of dark complexion. The woman at the girl's lodging was equally vague, but she confirmed his bigness."

"What reason did he give for wanting the suitcase?"

"He said he was the girl's father, but we know she hasn't any father. The landlady told him that he was too late and that a young man with an American accent had come along, paid the rent, and taken the suitcase. She didn't know where the young man came from."

"But presumably the other man knew, and lost no time in booking himself a room at the hotel and getting away with the suitcase. The obvious thing is to find the girl, but the suitcase comes very clearly into the picture."

McLean gave the matter some thought. It seemed a little premature to assume that the girl was genuinely missing. She might have her own reasons for keeping out of the limelight and for avoiding the further attentions of the obviously amorous young Canadian who had befriended her. That she had not communicated with her own mother for two years tended to back up that view. Yet the stealing of the suitcase suggested that she was mixed up in some kind of conspiracy in which certain audacious persons were involved, perhaps to her detriment.

"I think we'll find out a little more about Miss Westmoreland," he said to Brook. "We'll run down to Southampton and see Mr. Moffat, the solicitor who managed her mother's affairs."

Mr. Moffat, having been warned in advance, welcomed his two visitors in his usual dry and unemotional way. Since he had communicated with the county police he had heard nothing from Miss Westmoreland. The body of Mrs. Westmoreland had been interred that morning and he had hoped that the daughter would come and pay her last respects to her mother, but she had failed to do so, and he was bound to say that he took a serious view of her silence.

"Does she stand to benefit from her mother's estate?" asked McLean.

"No. Her mother lived for years on an income provided by a distant relative who died some time ago. Under that deed the income ceased on her death."

"Had she no assets at all?"

"Nothing worth mentioning. The house she lived in was a rented one, and the proceeds from her personal effects are unlikely to meet some outstanding claims. I am arranging for an auction sale very soon."

"What do you know of the family?"

"Not a great deal. Mr. Westmoreland appears to have been a peculiar man. Some fifteen years ago I arranged a judicial separation, under which he agreed to pay his wife seven hundred pounds a year for the support of herself and her two children. He was a mining engineer—a brilliant man, but a drunkard. He died in Bolivia ten years ago, leaving his wife nothing. She managed to carry on for a year or two, and was on the verge of bankruptcy when her brother-in-law died, leaving her an annuity of five hundred pounds for life. With a biggish house on her hands, and two children, she managed to struggle along. Then suddenly her son left home, and within a few months the girl left too. I have had occasion to see Mrs. Westmoreland recently. Despite the fact that she had no longer to support her children she was in debt, and was trying to raise a loan to pay off pressing creditors. I did what I could, but the bank wasn't helpful. They knew a little too much about Mrs. Westmoreland."

"In what way?"

"She was drinking heavily, and was in a poor state of health. All she had to offer as security was her annuity. It was scarcely a business proposition. When she was hit by a car and killed she was undoubtedly under the influence of drink, and the car driver was exonerated from blame. It almost looked as if she deliberately ran into the car."

"What happened to the son?"

"I don't know. She wouldn't discuss her two runaway children. But once when I saw her, in her cups, she referred to them as ungrateful rats."

"Was the son older than the daughter?"

"Yes—by three years."

"What did you think of them yourself?"

"I found the boy—Derek—intolerable. He sorely needed a father to give him a good thrashing occasionally."

"And the girl?"

"An enigma. Most difficult to describe. Physically she was most attractive, but between her and her mother there appeared to be a barrier of steel. I had the feeling that they hated each other, and would go on hating while both lived."

"You do not know what caused this friction?"

"No."

"Is there a photograph of the girl available?"

"I know of none, but there may be one at the house. I haven't had time to go through the place."

"Where is the house?"

"At Fenton—only a few miles from here."

"Have you the keys?"

"Yes."

"Might I borrow them?"

The solicitor was quite agreeable, and a few minutes later McLean and Brook were on their way to Fenton. It was little more than a hamlet, in a beautiful setting, and they had little difficulty in finding Greystoke, for Mr. Moffat had given McLean very precise directions. It was a large, early Victorian house lying back in grounds of some three or four acres, in which Nature had obviously been allowed a free hand for a considerable time. The house, like the garden, was in a sad state, with some of the upper windows almost obscured by thick ivy and the paint peeling off the front door.

"What a shame!" said Brook.

"Don't blame the poor owner," replied McLean. "Blame the Rent Restriction Act, which is putting most of them in the workhouse. Ah, that's better!"

At last he found the right key, and opened the door. Immediately inside was a large hall, with threadbare carpets on the floor and sundry items of huge furniture along the right-hand wall. Centrally placed was a broad staircase of polished oak, but the polish had long since vanished. A number of doors led from the hall to various rooms, and McLean opened the nearest one and stepped into a large room that was somewhat scantily furnished. This room, like the hall, exuded a musty smell, and McLean went to the bay window and opened one of the sections to let in fresh air from the garden, and also additional light, for the window panes were covered with grime.

"Impoverished gentility," he said, as he gazed around at faded decorations and tattered chair covers. "Must have been a nice home at some earlier date. Can the gentleman with the walrus moustache be the late Mr. Westmoreland?"

Brook gazed up at the large portrait over the mantelpiece.

"Looks like that chap in *Faust*," he said.

"Mephistopheles? Yes, you're right. It's that upwards tilt of the dark eyebrows."

On the grand piano were several photographs in stand-up frames. One of them was undoubtedly the original of the oil painting, taken some years earlier. Others featured a boy and a girl at an early age, and were useless from McLean's point of view, presuming they were the two children mentioned by the solicitor.

"We need something much more recent," said McLean. "See what's in that desk."

The desk revealed nothing of interest except vast numbers of old bills, many of them for whisky and gin, and some bearing a slip asking for immediate payment.

"Six bottles at a time," said Brook. "The old lady was a bit of a soak. Caught it from her husband, no doubt. Shall I try that corner cupboard?"

McLean nodded and Brook turned the handle of the cupboard and pulled hard to no effect.

"Locked," he said.

"That's impossible. There's no keyhole."

Brook pulled again, and the handle came off in his hand. McLean sent him out to the car for some tools, and finally the door was levered open. Inside was a jumbled mass of children's toys, old juvenile books, and games. Amongst the books was a photograph album, obviously going back many years, and displaying all the members of the Westmoreland family, sometimes together, and sometimes separately. Despite lack of dates, one could follow the vicissitudes of the family by the changes in the two younger members. The collection started with Derek in long clothes being held in his mother's arms,

34

with his father—young and handsome—looking over his wife's shoulder. Later the girl came into the pictures, and the father vanished. It was noticeable that afterwards the good-looking young wife suffered the ravages of time. She no longer smiled, and a hard cynical expression took the place of her dimples. The boy grew more and more like his father, but Anna was like neither of them. She had her mother's earlier good looks, but appeared to be a more vital personality. The last snapshot of her was taken when she was about seventeen and clad in a school sports outfit, with a hockey stick in her hands.

"I think this will suit our purpose," said McLean, "if, as I presume, she is Anna Westmoreland. But Moffat can settle that point. Slip out the print and put the album back."

Before leaving the house McLean went through the other rooms, and found ample evidence that in her later years Mrs. Westmoreland had been a drunkard and a slut. Many of the rooms contained no furniture at all and were in a filthy state. In the kitchen was a cupboard full of whisky and gin bottles, and even the room she slept in was like a pigsty.

"No wonder her children ran away," said McLean. "Yet at one period it was a happy family. I wonder what happened to bring about this state of affairs ? Where did the blame lie ?"

After locking up the house McLean drove to Southampton to hand back the keys to Mr. Moffat. He was shown immediately into Moffat's office.

"Ah !" said Moffat. "I'm glad you're back so soon. I have to go to court, but I have some information for you. I've heard from Miss Westmoreland."

"You mean—a letter ?"

"No. She telephoned just after you left. She told me she is quite all right and will call on me in a day or two."

"But did she explain her strange disappearance from the hotel ?"

"Partly. She hinted that the young Canadian—Brading—was pestering her, and that at the last moment she decided not to accept the accommodation which he had offered her. She had some urgent business to attend to up north, and hopes to be back in a few days."

"Did she not give her present address ?"

"No."

"Can you be sure it was Miss Westmoreland who was speaking?"

Mr. Moffat looked quite surprised at this question.

"I—I had no reason to doubt it," he said.

"But do you know her voice sufficiently well to recognize it over the telephone?"

"No. I haven't seen her for some years. But she knew all about the situation and——"

"Other persons may know a good deal about the situation. Was it a long-distance call?"

"I don't know. She was put through to me by my secretary, who takes all the incoming calls. Just a moment."

He pushed a bell and in a few moments a young woman entered the room.

"You rang, sir?"

"Yes. Miss Whibley, you remember the telephone call from Miss Westmoreland about an hour ago? Was it a local call or long distance?"

"It must have been long-distance, for it was the operator who spoke to me first."

"Thank you. That is all."

When she had left the room McLean asked to use the telephone, and then spoke to Enquiries. He wished to trace the call, and as it was a long-distance one he presumed there would be no difficulty. He was told he would be rung back as quickly as possible.

"While we are waiting," he said, "you might settle a small point, Mr. Moffat. Is this a photograph of Miss Westmoreland?"

Moffat gazed at the print which McLean produced and nodded his head.

"A very good likeness," he said. "I haven't seen her for two years, but she was very much like the photograph then, perhaps five or six years older."

"I think you told me that you arranged a judicial separation between Mrs. Westmoreland and her husband about fifteen years ago."

"Yes. He died five years later."

"Can you tell me the reason for that separation?"

"No. All I know is that the marriage wasn't a success. It may be that the husband's long periods of absence from home

36

contributed to the breakdown. His work took him to places where it was impossible for his family to live."

"Was it he who took the initial steps for a separation ?"

"No. They came to see me together. There was no difficulty in arranging terms. In fact both of them behaved most sensibly in the matter. Unfortunately the arrangement lasted for only five years, when Westmoreland died, leaving practically nothing."

"I think you told me that later she inherited money from her brother-in-law."

"Yes. He was a rich man and a widower. He married Mrs. Westmoreland's sister."

"Have you any idea what became of the son Derek ?"

"None at all, but since Mrs. Westmoreland asked to see her daughter when she was dying it seems quite likely that the son is dead."

A little later the telephone bell rang. It was from the telephone supervisor, and McLean listened for a few moments, then thanked her and hung up the receiver.

"That call from Miss Westmoreland came from a public call-box at Stepney," he said. "I think it was a spurious call, made with the object of holding up action on our part."

"But couldn't she have been on her way north when she made the call ?" asked Moffat.

"That alleged urgent business up north need not have prevented her seeing you this morning. I don't believe a word of it. And the statement about mistrusting the intentions of Brading rings equally false. She certainly accepted his invitation to dinner. Why jib at the booked room when she knew perfectly well that he was going back to London that night ? I am going to act on the assumption that she was kidnapped immediately after Brading left in his car."

"Yes, I think you're right," said Moffat reflectively. "But it doesn't seem to make sense. You intend to publish the photograph ?"

"Yes. What is the girl's full name ?"

"Anna Maria Westmoreland."

McLean thanked Moffat for his services, and then he and Brook drove back to London.

37

IT was in the evening of the following day that Neville Brading, entering the vestibule of his hotel, bought an evening newspaper and took it with him into the cocktail bar. The alert bar-tender reached for a glass and looked at his regular customer.

"The usual, sir?" he asked.

"Yep. Make it a double."

The bar-tender poured out the drink, and cast a sly look at the newspaper which Brading was carrying. Brading sipped the drink before he realized the significance of the bar-tender's glance.

"Oh, that horse you tipped me," said Brading. "Did it do any good?"

"You look at the Pontefract results—the three-thirty race."

"I forget the name of the darned thing. What was it?"

"Frosty Morning."

"Sure! Here we are—Pontefract three-thirty. Wal, if it didn't come in first—at eight to one. How much do I win?"

"Eight pounds for the win, and two for a place. Ten quid in all. Better than a kick in the pants."

"Walter, you've missed your vocation. You're in on this—fifty-fifty."

"Oh no, sir."

"Yep. If I had used my own judgement I'd have backed the favourite and lost. Shall we take our winnings or put the whole lot on a horse tomorrow?"

"There's a saying about a bird in hand, sir."

"There's another about casting your bread upon the waters. Let's give the bookmaker a chance."

"They don't need any chances. But I'm willing to have another bash. See if they give tomorrow's runners."

Brading was turning to the sports page when suddenly his whole attention was transferred to the photograph of a pretty

38

girl bearing the caption 'DO YOU KNOW HER?' Underneath was a paragraph to the effect that Scotland Yard was anxious to trace Miss Anna Maria Westmoreland who disappeared on the eighteenth of May, and would be glad of any information leading to her whereabouts. Followed a description of the girl and her dress, which he recognized as that given by him to Sergeant Brook.

"Can't you find the runners?" asked the bar-tender.

"Runners? No. You'd better have a look."

The bar-tender found the list and started to expatiate upon the merits and demerits of a number of entries, but Brading's interest in that mundane matter had almost vanished. The announcement meant that the police were of opinion that Anna's disappearance had a sinister significance. The hunt was on, and he felt keenly his own helplessness.

"I'd go all out for Blackcap," said the bar-tender. "Just the age and weight for the two-thirty. Forecast odds a hundred to eight. It's a long price, but that's because he failed in the mile and a half. This is just his distance. Shall we do it? A fiver each way?"

"Sure!" said Brading, with a complete lack of enthusiasm. "If you think we——"

"No. Put the money on."

The bar began to fill up, and he left it and went to his room. There he sat and stared at the photograph for some time. How beautiful she was in her health and youth, obviously full of the joy of life and without a trace of the sadness which he had seen in her eyes. Why had she been spirited away? What was the mystery which surrounded her?

After a bath and a change of clothing he cogitated whether to have a rather dull evening meal in the hotel or go out and seek some livelier place where he could sit and watch the human menagerie, a form of relaxation which never failed to interest him in this huge city. But before he could make up his mind the bedside telephone rang. He picked up the receiver and was told by the hotel switchboard operator that a lady wished to speak to him who wouldn't give a name.

"Put her through," he said.

There was a mechanical click and a soft voice spoke.

"Is that you Mr. Brading? It's Anna speaking."

"Gosh!" he ejaculated. "Where are you?"

"In London—not far away. I thought you might have seen the police announcement in the newspapers, and be wondering what happened to me."

"I'll say I'm wondering."

"It's so difficult to explain. I couldn't stay in that hotel. Someone needed me urgently, and now I need your help. I know I've no right——"

"Cut it !" he said. "Where are you ?"

"At a friend's house, but I don't want the police to know—not until I've got a certain matter settled. Can I see you for a few minutes ?"

"Sure ! How do I reach you ?"

"The address is Miss Alice Coverton, Tangley House, Sheen. It's a house that abuts on Richmond Park. Get a piece of paper and a pencil and I'll give you details how to reach it."

"I've got paper and pencil right here."

"Good !"

He wrote down the details at her dictation, and finally read them back to her.

"That's it," she said. "You can't mistake the white gates. Oh, come soon."

"I will."

Within five minutes he was in his car, threading his way impatiently through the dense traffic, but once across the river he made better going, with his heart thumping at this unexpected release from comparative boredom.

With the little direction chart stuck on the dashboard he had little difficulty in taking the numerous turnings mentioned by Anna, and in the dusk of evening he approached his objective. But now he made his one and only mistake, passing the final turning in the fading light. This was later corrected by a pedestrian who told him he would have to go back and take the first turning on his left. This he did, and finally, in a secondary road, in which there were several large houses lying well back in extensive grounds, he saw a pair of white gates invitingly open, with a signboard on the green verge bearing the name Tangley House. He turned the car into the drive, and finally brought it to a stop outside a wide porch, where he got out and pushed a bell button. A few moments passed and then the door was opened by a well-dressed woman of about thirty years of age.

"You must be Mr. Brading ?" she said.

"Sure ! I had a telephone message. Are you Miss Coverton?"

"Yes. Please come in. Anna is resting, but she told me to call her when you arrived. This way."

She conducted him along a well-furnished hall to a door on the right, which gave access to a commodious lounge, brightly illuminated by many wall lights. By the electric fire was a low table bearing a box of cigarettes and an ash-tray.

"Do sit down," she said. "I'll tell Anna."

He sank into a comfortable chair and helped himself to a cigarette. All the furnishings were exquisite, and he was a little surprised that down-and-out Anna could lay claim to such an obviously opulent friend. But England was a strange place, he ruminated. You never knew quite what was going to happen next. In his own country people were more forthright. He wished he were able to understand them as he did his own people.

His reflections were cut short by the entrance of a big bearded man, with bushy eyebrows and a moustache to match. He was quite the hairiest man Brading had ever seen, and he walked with the aid of a thick stick. He dropped rather than sat into the chair opposite Brading, and rested the stick against the arm of the chair.

"I am a friend of Anna's," he said. "She has told me about you, and I should like to ask you a few questions."

"I should prefer to see Anna first," said Brading.

"It would be better if you listened to what I have to say. Anna is not very well, and there are certain points which should be cleared up as a preliminary. Recently you went to her lodgings and took possession of a large suitcase. Is that correct ?"

Brading looked at him fixedly.

"I came here to see Anna at her request," he said. "I cannot discuss Anna's affairs before I see her. Why should there be any difficulty about that ? She certainly wasn't unwell when she spoke to me."

"It is greatly to Anna's advantage that you should answer my questions."

Brading didn't like the way the conversation was going, nor the expression in the dark eyes. He had the feeling, too, that the beard and moustache were far from genuine.

"Before we go any further—who are you exactly?" he asked.

"I was a friend of Anna's father before he died, and I am now acting in Anna's interest. My name is Edwin Grogan, and it is possible she may have mentioned me to you."

"She did not."

"Well, it makes no difference."

"It makes all the difference, Mr. Grogan. I'll say nothing until I see Anna herself."

"You will not see her until you answer my questions."

"In that case I'll bid you good evening," said Brading, and stood up.

The sitting man reached out with his stick and pressed a bell button beside the fireplace. Brading heard it ringing outside, and then suddenly the door opened and two men slipped into the room, closing the door behind them. Both wore hats pulled well down over their foreheads and black crêpe masks reaching from their eyes to their chins.

"Is this some sort of a game?" asked Brading angrily.

"On the contrary it is strictly business," grunted Grogan. "I have not the slightest wish to cause you any inconvenience, but unless you change your mood I am afraid you are going to be very unhappy in the near future."

"So the telephone message was a fake," growled Brading. "Someone impersonated Anna to induce me to come here—possibly the woman who let me in. Wal, I sure fell for that, which shows I'm not up to your standard of trickery. But I'm learning."

"Now be sensible," said Grogan ingratiatingly. "There's no reason why we shouldn't get together. No doubt you think Anna is an innocent little creature, eh? No doubt she told you a tearful little story about her tragic past. But there's another side to it——"

"Shut your trap!" said Brading, "and call off your watchdogs, because I'm in a hurry to get home."

"So you won't play?"

"Not with a bunch of thugs."

Grogan glowered at him, and then nodded to the two men. Instantly two pistols appeared in their hands, but simultaneously Brading picked up a small but solidly built marble-topped table and drove at the nearer of the two men. Two of

42

the legs pinned him against the wall, but not before he let off the pistol, the bullet from which hit the wooden underside of the table, but was stopped by the thick marble surface. In a flash Brading turned on the second man, but there was no time to treat him as he had treated the agonized first man, for he had moved away and was getting a line on Brading's uncovered legs. With an enormous effort Brading flung the table at him. He saw him drop, and then turned on the first man who was reaching out for his fallen pistol. Brading's arm went back like a piston, and the big clenched fist went forward and upwards. There was a resounding crack and the fellow sagged at the knees and crumpled up like a deflated concertina.

Brading snatched up the pistol and turned to see what Grogan was doing. He was but a fraction of a second too late, for Grogan was on his feet with a long, slim, shining rapier in his right hand. Before the pistol could be got into action there was a lunge and the needle blade was buried in Brading's biceps. The pain was agonizing and his numbed fingers let the pistol fall. Grogan kicked it across the room, and drew back the rapier so that its bloody point stayed over Brading's heart.

"One more movement from you and it will be your last," he said. "I thought you might turn out to be a reasonable man. I find you are only a fool. Jan, pick up your gun. Leon, stop that damned noise and get on your feet."

His two battered cronies obeyed his orders, but not until they had the situation completely in hand did he push the rapier back inside his hollow stick.

"That's better," he grunted. "Jan, get some rope, and be quick about it. This animal is dangerous."

Brading, bleeding profusely, and feeling faint, sat down in a chair, covered by Leon's pistol. It seemed madness now to resume the struggle, for he had no doubt that Leon would like nothing better than an excuse to use the weapon.

"Do you propose to let me bleed to death?" he asked Grogan.

"That mightn't be a bad idea, but I still have hopes of knocking some sense into you. I may be more successful when you have lost a pint or two of that hot blood."

Brading said nothing. He was staring at Leon, who had apparently damaged the right side of his face, and in rubbing it with his free hand he disturbed the crêpe mask and revealed momentarily a little scar that was shaped like a crescent. Brading stored that information in his mind. Then came Jan with what appeared to be an old clothes line. Grogan tested it in his hands.

"That should do," he said. "Rope up his legs, and then I'll attend to his arm."

When Jan had done the roping very efficiently he was sent to get warm water, a swab, and a bandage. Grogan's subsequent bandaging was as efficient as Jan's roping, and Brading felt a little more comfortable despite his saturated shirt and coat.

"What do you expect to get out of this?" he asked.

"Only what is due to me. You are now about to take a nice ride, but don't blame me for that. Blame yourself. All right, Jan, you can now tie his arms. After that you can untie his legs. It will save having to carry him to the car."

Brading submitted because there was nothing else he could do. Bitterly he reproached himself for having walked into this trap with all the innocence of a trustful child. Why had he not suspected the voice on the telephone? Why had he not communicated with the police and told them that he had heard from Anna? The answer was a simple one. He had wanted to help Anna off his own bat, not to sit still and leave the matter to the police, and his present unhappy predicament was the price of his conceit.

§7

McLean's press announcement, with its accompanying photograph, brought a number of replies, but none of them proved to be of any use in tracing the missing girl. In the majority of cases it was a matter of mistaken identity, and in two others the persons had known Anna before she was missing and had no information concerning her which McLean did not know already.

44

Then, later in the day, came a telephone message from the manager of the hotel where Brading had been staying. McLean was in conference when it arrived, and Sergeant Brook wrote down what was told him and waited anxiously for McLean to return. When he did so Brook handed him the message.

"A new development, sir," he said. "It came over the telephone about eight minutes ago."

McLean read the message and arched his eyebrows.

"So Brading is missing now! One can't overlook the significance of that. I think we had better run over to the hotel and get all the information available. It may be a coincidence, but I doubt it."

A little later they were in the hotel manager's office, where the manager himself sat, looking quite distressed at this new blow to his reputation. To lose a suitcase from the bedroom of a guest was bad enough, but to lose the guest himself was shattering to his professional pride.

"He left the hotel last evening at about seven o'clock," he said. "The doorman saw him get into his car which was parked outside. It was this morning when the chambermaid reported that his bed had not been slept in. I thought he might have had trouble on the road, and perhaps was unable to telephone us, as he did on a previous occasion when he decided to spend the night somewhere else. But in view of the mysterious theft from his bedroom I thought I ought to let you know."

"You did quite right," said McLean. "I presume you took steps to find out if his car is back?"

"Oh yes. The car is also missing."

"Can you give me the registration of the car?"

"Yes. I have it here."

He referred to a slip of paper and read out the number which Brook recorded.

"Do you know if he received any kind of message during the evening?"

"Yes. I was coming to that. The telephone girl told me that a few minutes before he went out there was a local telephone call for him. It was a lady who would not give her name. The girl asked Brading if he would take the call and he said he would. According to her the line was engaged for quite a long time."

"Did he take his bedroom key with him?"

"No. He gave it to the porter before he went out. I hope I haven't acted prematurely, Inspector. We have had guests who make a habit of staying out all night, but not Mr. Brading. He wasn't that sort of person."

McLean finally left the hotel convinced that Brading's absence was involuntary, and that the immediate thing to do was to try to locate the car.

"What do you make of the telephone call?" asked Brook.

"It could have been the Westmoreland girl, but since we have good reason to believe that she was impersonated in the telephone call to Bournemouth, that impersonation may have been repeated here."

"To lure Brading to some place?"

"Of course."

"But why?"

"It may be that Brading is in possession of some information useful to certain persons, or it may be that those persons only imagine that. Let's hope we have some luck with the car."

Particulars of the car were sent out to all police stations immediately McLean returned to his office, and for two hours nothing came in. Then came important news. It was that Brading's car had been found on Putney Heath by a patrol constable. It was empty and undamaged. McLean gave instructions that the car was not to be touched until his arrival, and then he and Brook hurried to the spot.

Ultimately they found the car, well-shielded by a group of trees and guarded by two police patrols. The doors were not locked and the ignition key was in position. On the left side of the front seat was a dusting cloth which had apparently been taken from a cubby hole in the dashboard, the cover of which was open.

"Used to wipe the steering wheel," said McLean. "Not much hope of finger-prints, I'm afraid."

"You don't think Brading left the car here?" asked Brook.

"Would you leave your new car here to be used by anyone who might take a fancy to it? And why leave it here—half a mile from the main road?"

"Must have been here all night," said Brook. "It's still wet, and the only rain we have had for days was a heavy shower early this morning. It woke me up."

McLean searched diligently for any sign of blood on the

cushions and elsewhere, but found none. Lying up under one of the pedals was a flimsy square of paper which had clearly been trodden on. Brook retrieved it.

"Blank, sir," he said.

McLean turned it over and peered through the layer of dust which he had gathered from the floor.

"A small item overlooked in the darkness," he said. "It's a rough plan in pencil. Here's Sloane Street, Hammersmith Bridge, and Sheen, near Richmond Park. There's something written here. Looks like Tangley House. That appears to have been the objective—the outcome of that telephone call. We seem to be in luck."

He gave instructions to the two constables regarding the disposal of the car, and then got back into his own vehicle and directed Brook, who took over the wheel. In a very short time they were on the route inscribed on the sheet of dirty paper, and from this point there was no difficulty in following the plan. Finally they came to the two white gates of Tangley House. These were now closed, but Brook got out of the car and opened them.

Several rings at the front door bell brought no response, and McLean observed that all the windows were closed. He walked round to the domestic quarters and found that the door there was locked. He peered through the barred kitchen window and saw that the interior was quite tidy, with not a sign of a living soul. Away to his left there was a casement window fronting a lawn. He moved towards it and examined the two doors. Down the centre there were unmistakable signs of a jemmy or similar tool having been used, and when he put his weight on the doors the right-hand one opened and revealed the fact that the rather slim bolts had been torn away.

"That tells a story," he said.

"You mean the house was empty and used by some unauthorized person?"

"I can't imagine the owner or tenant smashing his way in with so little regard for the property."

They passed through the small room and into a passage which brought them to the main hall. McLean looked into the first room he came to. It was clean and tidy, and very cold. The next room was obviously the dining-room and full of beautiful furniture and valuable paintings. Like the other

47

room, it was spotlessly clean. But the big lounge in the front of the house told a different story. Here there was the smell of stale tobacco smoke and two ash-trays containing cigarette ash and stubs. A Regency table with a marble top had a broken leg, and when McLean examined it he found a bullet embedded in the wood under the marble.

"This is evidently where it all happened," he said.

"Brading came here and met a rough house?"

"That's pretty obvious. Look at that damage to the wall. The table must have been flung there. For it to have been hit by a bullet on the underside suggests that Brading used it as a shield. Finally he flung it, and was subsequently subdued."

"By a bullet?"

McLean made no reply. He had noticed a stain on a cretonne-covered chair, and another smaller one on the floor carpet. In both cases some attempt had been made to remove the stain, but with little success.

"Blood undoubtedly," he said. "It was after this gory affair that Brading's car was driven away. Quite a neatly-planned business and one which may cause us quite a lot of trouble."

"You think the owner of the house will know nothing about the matter?"

"I'm certain he won't. There's a cunning brain behind this mystery—quick to think and act. There's just one hope. One doesn't enter and use an unoccupied house without certain knowledge that one will not be interrupted. We must try to find out what persons knew the family were temporarily absent. See if that bureau is locked."

Brook went to the bureau indicated by McLean and found he was able to pull down the flap, which came to rest on two supports to form a writing surface. Inside were several pens. notepaper and envelopes. At the back was a series of pigeon-holes in which were numerous papers.

"Some bills here, sir," he said. "Made out to Mr. Malcolm Browning. Oh, here are some letters."

McLean scanned the bills and then took the letters, and looked through them hastily. One of them caused him to halt. It bore the heading of a hotel at Hove, and was dated a week previously. It begged to inform Mr. Browning that a double bedroom had been reserved for him for two weeks from September 20th, at the inclusive charge of £12 per person per week, also a lock-up garage at an extra charge of 2s. per night.

"So he, and presumably his wife, must have left here three days ago," mused McLean. "I think we'll try to get him on the telephone."

The call was put through, and after some delay Mr. Browning was heard on the line. McLean informed him that he was speaking from Browning's house, and that the place had been entered the previous evening. Browning gave a little gasp of surprise, and asked anxiously if anything appeared to be missing. McLean told him that robbery did not appear to be the motive, and suggested that he should come back at once and check up on his belongings. This Browning promised to do without a moment's delay. He had a fast car and calculated that he would be at the house in about an hour.

"We'd better go and get some tea," said McLean. "I think he's a little optimistic about doing the journey in an hour, but no doubt he won't waste any time in the circumstances."

It was exactly an hour later when they returned to the house to find Mr. Browning getting out of a long limousine parked outside the front door. He was a man in the early thirties, dressed in a sports coat and beige trousers, and he wore a very worried expression as he waited for McLean and Brook to leave their car.

"Inspector McLean ?" he asked.

"Yes. I'm sorry to have to bring you back from your holiday."

"I'm sorry to have to come. This is the first time I've had this experience. I persuaded my wife to stay where she was. She hates fast driving, and it was no occasion for dawdling. Shall we go in ?"

McLean nodded and Browning produced some keys from his pocket and opened the front door. He gazed round the nicely furnished hall.

"It looks just as we left it," he said.

"Yes. The trouble occurred in the lounge. Elsewhere the place is in perfect order."

Browning opened the door of the lounge and stepped inside. Very quickly he saw the broken table and the damaged wall. It was when he went to look at this damage that he noticed the bloodstain on the cretonne-covered chair.

"What's this ?" he asked.

"Blood."

"Good heavens ! What does it mean ?"

"We have every reason to believe that some person, or persons, used this house as a rendezvous, and that a fight took place here. I have an idea that your possessions are safe, but you had better have a quick look round."

Browning did this and was back in a few minutes.

"The silver has not been touched, and my wife's jewellery—not very valuable—appears to be intact. I don't think anything is missing. But the casement window is broken."

"Yes. They got in that way."

"What an astonishing business !"

"Yes, it is. Now, Mr. Browning, can you tell me the names of such persons as knew that you and your wife would be away at this time ?"

"Very few indeed. We made up our minds suddenly. I told the woman, who comes in daily. Her name is Mrs. Welcome, and she lives in Ryder's Lane, quite near here. I think it is Number 15. We stopped the daily papers, the milkman and the baker's man. Oh, yes, we filled in a form at the post office for the re-direction of any letters."

"Anyone else ?"

"I'm trying to think. We had a bridge party after we had booked our rooms at the hotel. It consisted of my sister and her husband—Mr. and Mrs. Wayland—and a friend who was staying with them. I think his name was Toovey. My wife didn't play. I think I told my sister that we were going to Hove for a few days."

"Where does your sister live ?"

"Over at Richmond. No. 63 Grove Road."

"Is that all ?"

"Yes. I think that covers everyone."

"What about your wife ?"

"I'm pretty sure my wife didn't gossip about our prospective holiday. She is rather the secretive type. But I will question her on that point when I get back and let you know."

"Did you perhaps mention the matter at your place of business ?" asked McLean.

"I have no business, except an occasional flutter in the stock market. Until a year ago my father and I were in

50

business in Rangoon. But he died and I was glad to sell out and come back here with my wife, who had never liked the climate of Burma."

Before they left the house Sergeant Brook managed to make a temporary repair of the casement window, for which Browning expressed his gratitude. McLean handed him a card with a telephone number on it.

"Don't trouble to ring me if your wife is satisfied that the list of persons you have given me is complete," he said.

Mrs. Welcome was McLean's next witness. She lived in a terrace of small cottages, and was clearly amazed and somewhat terrified to receive a visit from the police. In reply to McLean's questions she said she was a widow with two children, and that she had been employed by Mrs. Browning for nine months, from the time the Brownings came to live at Tangley House. Mrs. Browning had told her a week before that she and her husband were going away for two weeks, and had agreed to pay her her wages while they were away.

"Did you tell anyone they were going away?" asked McLean.

"No, sir. Only my children."

"Isn't it possible that you might have told someone else in conversation?"

Mrs. Welcome swore positively she had not. "As a matter of fact," she confided, "I'm not keen that my neighbours should know I go out charing."

McLean saw no reason to doubt her emphatic denial, and went on his way to Richmond, where he found Mrs. Wayland in an attractive house overlooking the river. She bore a strong resemblance to her brother and looked as if she had just emerged from a beauty parlour. Unlike plain and homely Mrs. Welcome she appeared to welcome her unusual visitors.

"I'm sorry my husband is at business," she said. "But he should be home at any moment now. Please come in."

McLean and Brook followed her into the sitting-room which had a lovely view up the river towards Petersham. One of the first things which McLean noticed was a large portrait of Mrs. Wayland in an obviously stage costume of a Hawaiian girl, which displayed her admirable legs to advantage, and Mrs. Wayland, catching McLean's glance, nodded her head.

"Yes," she said. "I used to be on the stage before I met my husband. Now the only thing I see of the theatre is from the other side of the curtain. My husband is rather old fashioned and thinks the profession is a sink of iniquity. But please tell me the reason for your visit."

"Your brother's house was entered last night."

"Golly!" she gasped. "You mean burgled?"

"That would appear to be the object," replied McLean, preferring not to go into details. "We think it possible that the housebreakers knew that the house was temporarily unoccupied, and we are working on that supposition. It seems that very few persons were aware of that fact, and by a process of elimination we may be able to get on the track of the culprit. I believe that you and your husband knew that your brother and his wife were taking a holiday?"

"Oh, yes. Malcolm told us when we went there to play bridge. But you don't think that we went there and burgled the place?" she asked, with a smile.

"No, I don't. But you had a friend with you."

"So we had. He's a friend of my husband with the incredible name of Lancelot Toovey. He left yesterday morning for Bournemouth, where he lives in some deadly hotel. He was bored stiff, so we invited him here for a week. As he was crazy to play bridge and I couldn't get a fourth, I rang up my brother. He wouldn't come here, so we all went there. He's quite a charming man, and I can't see him breaking into anyone's house."

"I'm not suggesting anything like that," said McLean. "But did you mention your brother's intention to take a holiday to anyone else?"

"No. I don't know anyone who would be interested. Ah, I think that is my husband."

McLean heard the arrival of a car outside, and a minute or two later a burly red-faced man entered the room and stared at the company.

"Oh, Ralph dear," said Mrs. Wayland. "These gentlemen are from Scotland Yard. Would you believe it, poor Malcolm has been burgled."

"That's bad," he said. "Did he catch——? Oh, of course he is on holiday. What a rotten thing to happen. When did it take place?"

"Last night," replied McLean. "I have since seen Mr. Browning. So far he has not found that anything is missing."

"That's a bit strange, isn't it ? Malcolm has a lot of very fine silver. Were the burglars interrupted ?"

"Their business there was not burglary, but I don't wish to go into that. My object in calling was to find out what persons knew that house was unoccupied. Your wife has assured me that she told no one."

"I don't see why she should. Malcolm is always taking holidays. In fact, his life is one long holiday. His father left him a ton of money and forgot that he had a daughter."

"Ralph, dear !" expostulated his wife.

"Anyway, Malcolm's plan to take a holiday was not of sufficient interest for us to go shouting it around. I had forgotten all about it. Certainly I have not told anyone."

"What about your late guest—Lancelot Toovey ?"

"Toovey ? Oh yes, he was present when Malcolm told us about his prospective holiday. But you can wash out Toovey. He's a very rich client of mine and can make money much easier than breaking into people's houses."

"May I ask what your business is ?" asked McLean.

"Certainly. I am a stockbroker."

"On the Stock Exchange ?"

"Not yet. I am an outside broker."

"And you can't help me any more ?"

"I wish I could. If there was a leakage of information which resulted in my brother-in-law's house being entered couldn't it have come from one of the regular tradespeople, or even the post office if Malcolm had his letters re-addressed to him ? Some post office employees are not saints."

"Thank you for the suggestion," said McLean. "But that possibility had not escaped us."

Wayland seemed to resent the tinge of sarcasm in McLean's voice and looked up at the clock as if to hint that the passage of time was of some importance to him.

"Well, thank you for your help," said McLean. "I think you said that Mr. Toovey lived at Bournemouth, Mrs. Wayland ?"

"Yes. The Glendower Hotel," replied Mrs. Wayland. "He is interested in some property in the neighbourhood."

"Then I won't keep you any longer."

"Haughty kind of person," said Brook, as they got back

into the car. "Likes to air his theories, too. But it doesn't get us much further, does it ?"

"It may do yet. I think it might be worth while looking up Mr. Toovey. I have yet to be convinced that the break-in was a mere haphazard affair. We'll run down to Bournemouth in the morning."

§8

IN the meantime Neville Brading had suffered an unforgettable experience. With his arms bound he had been marched through the hall of the house to the place where he had left his car. But in the place where it had stood was another vehicle, a large closed utility car, with double doors at the rear and two long seats inside. He was pushed inside and was followed by Jan, who now carried the pistol in his side-pocket, since there was now little to fear from the helpless prisoner.

"Sit down !" growled Jan. "Over there !"

Brading sat on the long seat, and Jan took up a position opposite him. The interior was lighted with a tiny roof light, and the driver—Leon—could just be seen through the small glass panel at his back. The engine was started, but before the car moved Grogan put his bearded face through the rear door.

"Watch him !" he said. "I'll lock the rear door in case of accidents."

"Okay !"

The doors closed and Brading heard them being fastened. Then, after a few moments, the car began to move. He looked at the glass panel, but the road ahead from his point of view was completely obscured by the driver's shoulders. Quickly the car gathered speed and was soon moving rapidly through the darkness. The flash of headlights could be seen at intervals as oncoming cars passed, but these flashes grew less frequent as they penetrated deeper into the country.

Brading, sitting on the uncomfortable bench, winced from time to time as the jolts of the swiftly moving car were transmitted to his wound. Where he was being taken he had not the slightest notion, nor was the purpose very clear, unless it was to submit him to further punishment in the belief that he would give them certain information. But what information? If they were responsible for the removal of Anna's suitcase from his bedroom they must know what it contained. Did they imagine he had opened it and removed some valuable item? Might not it have been wiser to have listened to Grogan, since he knew nothing about Anna which could have been the slightest use to the gang? But his mind revolted at the idea of co-operating with them in any way.

Jan, sitting immediately opposite, with most of his face still concealed by the ridiculous-looking mask, seemed to be finding the speed scarcely less uncomfortable than Brading, for he moved uneasily from time to time.

"Feeling those bruises?" asked Brading.

"Shut your mouth!"

"A little while ago you wanted me to open it very wide. Shall I tell you something?"

"No."

"I'll tell you all the same. It will help pass the time. You can't get away with this. D'you know why?"

"No, and I don't want to."

"Oh, but you do. No guy running from the police can be quite so indifferent as you pretend to be. Maybe you think I was just a sucker to be taken in by a fake telephone call. You see, Anna never knew where I was staying, and couldn't possibly have known where to telephone me. I wasn't alone in that car when I called at the house. Think that over, sonny boy."

This thumping lie, which Brading had been thinking up, was not without effect, for Jan's body seemed to stiffen, and Brading saw his hands close involuntarily.

"You're a liar," said Jan, after a pause. "Another word from you and I'll smarten you up."

"Beat me up, you mean. But your boss wouldn't stand for that. He likes to do the smartening up himself. Now how comes it a guy like you gets himself mixed up in a racket like this? Maybe you were quite a nice sort of kid before the rats got at you. And now you're going to end up in jail. Just goes

55

to show how you never know what's hanging over you."

"It's nothing to what hangs over you," retorted Jan. "If you think you're on a joy ride you've got another think coming. You can't bluff your way out of this."

"I don't need to. I'm sitting quite pretty."

Jan said nothing. He seemed to be reflecting on the cocksure attitude of the prisoner, which quite obviously puzzled him. A few moments passed and then, through the narrow glass window at the top of the double doors, a ray of light flooded the somewhat dim interior. It was clearly the headlights of a following car, making a speed at least equal to the van. On bends the light vanished, only to re-appear on straight stretches. Brading deliberately kept his gaze on this, and conjured up a cunning smile. That smile did not escape Jan's observation, and soon he, too, was watching the persistent ray from the rear.

"Now who's a liar ?" asked Brading.

Jan now did exactly what Brading hoped he would do. He stood up with the object of taking a look through the rear highly-placed glass panel, and as he took his first step Brading's foot shot out like a battering ram and caught him on the knee of his hindmost leg. He gave a cry of agony and fell heavily to the floor. Brading rushed at the door and rained blow after blow on it with his foot in the hope of bursting it open and attracting the attention of the following car. But his efforts were fruitless, and the next moment the butt end of Jan's automatic fell on his uncovered head with a dull thud.

Brading lay on the floor for some minutes with his eyes closed. He was quite conscious, but dazed and sick from the heavy blow. A little later he heard the scream of a honker, and soon realized that the following car was now overtaking the van. The ruse had failed, and now he was in no fit state to start further trouble.

Opening his eyes, he stared up at Jan, who sat with the pistol now held the right way in his hand and with his legs up on the long seat.

"Help me up," he said.

"Help yourself up. You chose that position, not I."

Brading struggled into a sitting position on the floor and tried vainly to raise his body on to the seat. He was halfway up when he collapsed. Jan laughed at his helplessness.

"Not so cocky now, eh ? You'd better try to get to sleep. We've a long way to go."

Brading made no further appeal. The suggestion seemed a sensible one, for he was tired and exhausted, and no good purpose would be served by keeping awake since he could see nothing from his present position and had not the slightest idea in which direction the van was heading. Time passed and he dozed at intervals, to be bumped into semi-consciousness by occasional bad stretches of road. The journey seemed interminable, and now the van seemed to be in hilly country, for there was much changing of gear and slow grinding up steep inclines.

By pushing his arm through the tight binding he could just manage to see the dial of his wrist-watch. It gave the time as 2.30. It meant that he had been in the van for nearly four hours, and in that time it must have covered at least a hundred and fifty miles. Again he dozed, and the next consultation of his watch showed that yet another hour had passed, and still the van rattled and jolted through the darkness.

It was shortly after this that Jan rose from his seat and went to the glass partition behind the driving cab to rub off some mist which had formed on it and to peer between the two heads on the other side. He gave a little satisfied grunt and came back to his seat.

"Get up !" he said to Brading.

Brading glared at him.

"You're not even funny," he said. "Only stupid."

Jan reached out and lifted him on to the seat.

"We're nearly there," he said.

"Nearly where ?"

"You'll find out—if you're lucky."

The van was now climbing steeply, but soon the noises from the gear-box ceased and it ran smoothly over some flat land, but with diminishing speed, until forward movement stopped altogether. There came the sound of voices from the front and then the rear door was opened and Grogan and Leon were seen.

"Out you get !" said Jan.

Brading rose on his stiff legs, staggered along the van and stepped out. They were all in a big garage, the main doors of which were now closed, but away in the corner, up a few steps, was a small door, obviously leading into the main building. Grogan led the way, with his two hirelings bringing up the rear. On the further side was a narrow passage, on the left of which were two doors. Grogan passed these and stopped at a single door on the right. He pressed a switch on the wall, and then opened the heavy door. Brading saw a flight of steps going downwards.

"This will do," said Grogan. "Hurry up. I want to get some sleep."

He followed the party down the steps, where Brading found himself in a big stone chamber which looked as if it had once been a coal cellar, but there was no coal in it now, and the only means of ventilation was a small grill high up in the wall. In the centre was an old deal table, a chair and a long couch. Under the grill was a pile of junk from deck chairs to garden seats.

"Quite cosy," said Grogan, looking round. "I regret the lack of toilet facilities, but we may put that right in time."

"Do you propose to keep me here?" asked Brading.

"Not longer than is absolutely necessary. In a few days perhaps you will be a little more co-operative."

"In what way exactly?"

"I'll tell you in the morning. At the moment I am dead tired. You, too, look as if you can do with some sleep."

"Sleep! How can I sleep with my arms bound and numbed?"

"I'll make a concession. Jan, untie his arms. Go on—are you deaf?"

Jan produced a knife from his pocket and cut the rope in two places. Brading tried to raise his arms, but found them almost dead from restricted circulation.

"Thanks for everything," he said. "But you've made a big mistake tonight."

Grogan shrugged his shoulders, and then the trio mounted the steps and a few moments later Brading heard the door close and the sound of a turning key. He sat down in the chair, rubbing each arm in turn with the other hand, and feeling the blood return. Finally he stood up and marched round and round the chamber, reflecting on the situation and easing his cramped muscles.

It was clear that his captors believed him to be in possession of information of vital importance to them, and that they —or rather Grogan—believed he could be induced to talk in due course. That this business was closely connected with the kidnapping of Anna was beyond question. It was ironical that his innocence was to his disadvantage, for if he knew anything at all about Anna's past and the mysterious suitcase which figured so largely he might have told them some cock and bull story and led them up the garden path. And what of Anna herself ? To what extent was she involved ? Was she the conniving adventuress which Grogan made her out to be ?

He rested from his perambulations and lighted a cigarette. Then suddenly the light went out, and he realized that the switch was outside the door and that there was nothing he could do about it. He finished the cigarette in the darkness, and then groped for the couch and stretched his body on it with a sigh. Never in his life had he suffered so many physical and mental worries at the same time. His head ached, the wound in his arm nagged persistently. He was hungry and thirsty, and the bug of mistrust had got under his skin. Was it for this he had cancelled his passage home ? And where would it end ?

On the verge of sleep, in the intense stillness he heard sounds from above him which jolted his brain into full consciousness. They were like the cries of someone in pain or in a wild nightmare. But now all was silence again. He turned over and thought that he might have been dreaming, but after a minute or two the sounds were repeated. Now he sat bolt upright and found the petrol lighter in his pocket ; a flick of his finger produced a tiny flame, and with this to light him he crept up the stone steps to the locked door and placed an ear close to the keyhole. For a few moments there was no sound and then suddenly there was a cry of terror which chilled him to the marrow. It was a woman's voice and it came from somewhere above him. Now there seemed to be hurrying footsteps, and a little later a slamming door.

"Anna !" he muttered.

It was the one probability which made sense. They had got Anna as they had got him—a prisoner in that house—and were trying to wring from her what they were hoping to wring from him if all else failed, by what means he dare not attempt to imagine. Frantically he put his weight against the door, but quickly realized the futility of it, for the door was of real old-fashioned solidity. Even a break-through would have availed him little in his present condition. Without some sort of a lethal weapon he would go like a lamb to the slaughter. This was a situation which called for cunning more than brawn.

Finally he crept back to the couch, with all ideas of sleep swept from his tortured mind. From time to time he looked at the luminous dial of his watch, to curse the slowness of the passing minutes. But inevitably the darkness was eased by the reluctant approach of the dawn through the iron grill in the stone wall, and he got up and went to the corner where the seats and other jumble were piled up in disorder. He delved into it, but found no useful weapon. Under a deck chair was a pile of old newspapers. He looked at them and found they were all old issues of the *Western Morning News* and this was enlightening. Clearly he was somewhere in the West of England, and this was in accord with the long car journey. The only other discovery of interest was an old petrol can. By the weight of it he judged it was about a quarter full, but then came the thought that it might contain water. He removed the cap and smelt the contents. It was petrol.

The germ of an idea entered his mind, but it was not the sort of idea that could be exploited at that time of the day. In the dead of night it might be possible to put it into practice. It was worth thinking about. He piled up the chairs again, concealing the petrol can completely from view, and then waited for what was to come next.

§9

ANOTHER hour was to pass before Brading's impatience was rewarded. The electric light came on to supplement the poor illumination through the small grill, and then down the steps came Grogan followed by Jan. It was significant that Jan did not approach the table with his chief, but stood well back, with one hand in his jacket pocket. As before, he wore his silly little mask.

"Now," said Grogan, "we can talk."

"You talk," retorted Brading. "I'll listen."

"I'm hoping this will be a two-way conversation, not a monologue."

"It depends upon what we are to talk about. If the subject is food I'm interested."

"Indirectly it is food and your early freedom. In the first place I am sorry I had to resort to violent action, but you forced that on me by your conduct."

"Don't make me laugh," growled Brading. "But have your say, I'm listening."

Grogan took a cheroot from a case and lighted it, blowing the smoke towards the ceiling before resuming.

"How long have you known Anna ?" he asked.

"What's that got to do with you ?"

"Quite a lot. You see, Mr. Brading, I knew Anna years ago, before she left home and married a man who was in my employ. His name was Besterling, and I trusted him. He repaid my trust by robbing me of certain documents which would be of the greatest value to certain people. Also he took money. When he was arrested the money was found on him. but not the documents. He was charged and convicted and sent to prison for two years. At the same time Anna disappeared, I had every reason to believe that those documents were handed to Anna against the day when Besterling would be released. I tried in vain to trace Anna, but failed. Then, only a few days ago I heard an announcement on the wireless, asking for Anna to go to her mother, who was seriously ill in hospital at Southampton. I went at once to the hospital and saw Anna arrive—with you."

"Go on," said Brading grimly.

"I saw you take her to the hotel, where you had a meal, and I waited there until you left in your car."

"And took her by force ?"

"I had to. She started to scream."

"What then ?"

"We drove her back to London to question her about the documents. She swore she knew nothing about them, but I knew she was lying. When we asked her about you she refused to say anything. But finally she told us where we could find you."

"And then some of your friends came to my hotel posing as police officers?" said Brading scornfully.

"They merely wanted to find out where Anna was living, because she had refused to tell us that."

"Well, you didn't find out."

"No. But we did later."

"How? Did you beat her up?" asked Brading angrily.

"No. There were other ways. You know what happened after that, don't you?"

"Yes, you discovered that I had already taken away the suitcase containing Anna's belongings, and you stole it from the wardrobe in my room."

"Correct. But when we opened the suitcase the documents were not inside."

"Did you expect to find them there?"

"Yes. Anna had sworn they were there."

"But you told me just now that she denied all knowledge of them."

"That was earlier. Finally she confessed. I told her I would release her with a sum of money if she would tell me what she had done with the documents. She refused."

Brading thought for a moment or two. The story did not ring true in all its details. But how much was true? He found it difficult to believe that Anna was married, and in his heart he hoped that that part was a lie. Grogan might use such a falsehood to undermine his—Brading's—trust in the girl. One had to go warily with such an obvious scoundrel.

"Just where do I come in?" he asked.

"Only one person could have taken that parcel from the suitcase, and that is you."

"But the suitcase was locked when I took it."

"It was a trumpery lock which could be opened with any useful tool."

Brading gave a short laugh.

"Suppose I did—what then?"

"The documents could be of no use to you. Without the key you could not even open the heavy metal box which contains them."

"You really think so?"

"I'm positive. Now, be reasonable. Return the box and I'll set you free and pay you handsomely for the inconvenience I have caused you."

"How much does handsomely stand for ?"

"Five hundred pounds in cash."

"You think that will compensate me for a hole in my arm, a painful bump on my head, and a night of absolute misery ?"

"You forget that I hold all the cards."

"All except the aces. And there's something else you have overlooked."

"What ?"

"Anna's wishes in the matter."

"I told you that Anna was willing to give up the documents."

"You told me, but I want Anna to tell me that."

"That is impossible at the moment."

"Why ?"

"Anna is hundreds of miles away."

"Oh no, Mr. Grogan, you can't put that one over. I know where Anna is. I heard her screaming in the night."

"That was Leon's wife. They were having a quarrel."

"No. I'm not such a simple fool as not to know a cry of anguish from a quarrel. Take me to Anna and if she is agreeable to your having the parcel I'll fall in with her wishes. Otherwise I stay put."

"Staying put can be very uncomfortable. Why this regard for a cheap little thief, who doubtless told you a pack of lies about herself ?"

"Why are you so reluctant to let me see her ?"

"I'll answer no more questions. Perhaps tomorrow you will be more amenable. If, in the meantime, you should change your mind you have only to bang on the door three times. Then I will come down to you."

"It is you who must be more amenable, or you will never see your precious parcel again. I suggest you start by giving me some food and drink."

"I'll send you some water, but food is another matter. You've got to earn that."

He went off, followed by Jan. Some minutes passed and then Brading heard the door open and close again. He climbed up the steps and found an enamel jug full of water and an old cup. He carried these to the table, and after slaking his thirst washed his face and hands, drying them with his handkerchief. Sitting, reflecting over the conversation which had passed, certain things became clear. Anna had lied about the mysterious package, and he could only conclude that she had done so under the pressure of physical punishment. But that must have been prior to the stealing of the suitcase from his bedroom at the hotel. Why had the punishment been continued ? Had they tried to make her confess that she had told him—Brading—about the package, and had she in the last resort lied again, not dreaming that she would put him in this predicament ? Did she, in fact, know anything about the missing package, or had she already taken steps to remove it to a safer place ?

What were these documents that were so vital to Grogan that he was prepared to commit almost any crime to lay hands on them ? And what sort of a man was this who could call to his aid gunmen and thugs ad lib ? He spoke like a well-educated person, but there was something in his speech which suggested a foreign origin. Leon, too, could be foreign, for it was significant that so far Leon had not uttered a word. Jan was the only obvious Englishman of the trio. There was never any doubt about his bitter sneering speech.

As the hours passed, Brading gave up all hope of any change in Grogan's attitude, for no sound of any sort came from above, except on one occasion the noise of a car engine. Brading used two piled seats to look through the grill, but all he could see were massed shrubs blocking out everything else. Then, at last, came darkness, and this, added to his gnawing hunger, emphasized the need for desperate remedy. But not yet was the time ripe, for his watch gave the time as nine o'clock. He dared not try out the plan in his mind, nor even prepare it, lest Grogan should put in an appearance and ruin everything. At least three hours must pass, and to make life more unendurable his supply of cigarettes were reduced to two.

It was slightly before midnight when an unexpected ally came to his aid. The pitch darkness was reduced by a ghostly light which filtered through the grill and enabled him to see things dimly. It was the indirect light of the moon, and he prayed it would continue and thus obviate the use of his almost exhausted petrol lighter. He crept up the steps and

64

listened at the door. Not a sound came to him. As a check-up he rapped on the door three times, rather softly. Then much louder. He waited some minutes, ready with a plausible excuse in case anyone came. But there was no response, and then he decided to go forward with his desperate plan and risk the outcome.

Returning to the dump, he tore some rotten canvas from a deck chair, saturated it with petrol and wiped it all over the door. Then, breaking the chair frames to pieces, he built a fire against the door, until he had used all the available inflammable material available, with the exception of the heavy garden seats. On this he sprinkled the remainder of the petrol. The question now was—would the whole thing go off with a bang and arouse the people upstairs, or would it burn comparatively silently ?

With the fire ready for ignition he came halfway down the steps with a piece of saturated canvas tied round the end of a long piece of wood. Now was the moment, and his heart thumped as he produced the petrol lighter, flicked it into a flame and laid it on a step above him. The torch burst into flame at the moment of impact. He picked up the lighter and then propelled the flaming torch into the bonfire. There was a dull boom and the red angry light licked up the face of the door. He ran back to the bench under the grill, and stood on it, with his face close to the bars.

The flames roared like a furnace, and very soon he saw through the smoke that the door itself was well alight, and being assisted by the paint of ages. But how long would it take for that barrier to freedom to be reduced to a state which would permit a break-through, and how long for the occupants of the house to be aware that something was undoubtedly wrong ?

Despite the fresh air which came in through the grill the smoke nearly suffocated him and caused his eyes to stream. He made one premature attempt to get to the door, but recoiled before the heat and fumes. The plan had succeeded even better than he had hoped for, but he feared at any moment to hear cries of alarm from above and to find himself cut off. Anxiously he watched his bonfire being reduced to a heap of glowing ashes, but the door continued to burn, and at last he resolved to make the supreme effort. Taking off his coat, and placing it over his head so that only a peep-hole was left, he mounted the steps, hesitated a moment on the edge of the wide top step, and then attacked it with the sole of his shoe. To his great joy his foot went almost through the timbers. He struck again and again, and now a whole plank gave way, covering his leg with sparks. Breathlessly he attacked the second plank, and that, too, went down. But simultaneously there came a shout of alarm from above him.

He squeezed through the gap and ran down the passage. Someone was shouting "Fire !" He turned left, but quickly realized that it would be folly to continue as far as the big garage. That was almost sure to be locked on the outside. He tried the first door on his right. It was a big kitchen, with an old-fashioned barred window, but to the left there was another passage, and at the end of that a door. He reached the door and found it secured by two heavy bolts. Quickly he drew the bolts and staggered out into the open air.

What air it was, too, after the suffocating fumes of his late prison ! Overhead the sky was full of stars, through which a half-spent moon was pursuing her course, and all around him were ancient trees heavy with foliage. Slipping on his coat, he moved round the big house to where he believed the entrance drive to be, but as he was about to turn the corner along the wide paved terrace he saw a man emerge from a basement window with a gun in his hands. He slipped back to the cover of the high wall.

"No one here," the man called.

Grogan's rasping voice came back.

"Go up the drive—hurry ! I'll get the car out. He can't have got far."

With the drive cut off, Brading had to think quickly. To stay where he was would be dangerous, for the moonlight was no longer his ally. Leading down from the terrace was a flight of steps. He leapt across and ran down the steps to the lower garden where there was shelter in the form of flowering shrubs. As he looked back he saw, through a gap, a man appear on the terrace only a few yards from where he had recently stood ; and beyond the house he saw the headlights of a car moving between the tall trees which fringed the long drive. His gaze followed the moving headlights until they were obscured from view, and then he concentrated his attention on the man on

66

the terrace. He walked the whole length of it and then came back and descended the steps very cautiously. As he advanced, Brading retreated, deeper and deeper into the wilder part of the grounds. From a point of vantage behind an outcrop of rock he saw the man turn in a wide circle, and walk back towards the house.

He, too, moved closer to the house in order to see the route taken by the car, for it seemed to him inadvisable to leave the cover which the thickly timbered grounds afforded until the car had come back, and also the man with the gun. But here he made a bad decision, for suddenly he heard voices in his rear, voices that grew louder every moment.

"He can't have got out of the drive. There hasn't been time. He's hiding up somewhere, and we've got to get him. You go round to the left. Use the whistle if you spot him. But take care. He's a dangerous fellow."

Brading felt dangerous at that moment. He crept away to the right, but soon realized that he was in a trap, for the land sloped away in that direction, leaving a high wall between him and the terrace. To reach the steps down which he had come he would now have to cross an open part of the garden. But the situation was momentarily eased by the moon entering a thick patch of cloud. He turned like a hare and raced towards the steps over a grass verge. Reaching them while the darkness held, he made the terrace and peered round the corner to see if the way was clear in that direction. But there was the man with the gun coming towards him. His brain worked quickly. There was no time to get to the further end of the terrace, for the black cloud was passing, and in a matter of seconds the man with the gun would be at the corner. Close to him was a casement window. He tried the handle and it opened. Silently he slipped inside and put down the latch.

It was obviously the dining-room, for in the centre was a large mahogany table, and along the wall facing the curtained windows was a sideboard carrying some plated dishes, a large silver salver, and some odd articles. The lights were off, but a door leading to the hall was ajar and let in sufficient light to enable him to see things clearly. The thing he saw most clearly was a telephone, and it caused his heart to bound. He went to it and read the number on the dial. It was *Upford* 2347.

After a moment's thought he went to the door, took the

key from the outer side, and locked it on the inside. Then he crept to the telephone, got his petrol lighter into action and dialed '0'. There was a little delay during which he could hear the double ring at the other end. Then the operator spoke.

"I want Police Headquarters," he said. "Quickly please. This is very urgent."

There was more delay and then to his great relief he heard a deep masculine voice informing him that he was connected with Falmouth Police Station, and asking him what he wanted.

"My name is Neville Brading," he said. "I am speaking from a house whose telephone number is Upford 2347. I was kidnapped in London and brought here. I believe the missing girl Anna Westmoreland is also here. Sergeant Brook of Scotland Yard will corroborate. But in the meantime I am in danger of being recaptured. Can you send help at once?"

"Surely. Repeat that telephone number please."

Brading did so, and added that he had locked himself in the dining room of the house.

"Have you no idea where the house lies?"

"None at all."

"All right. We'll find out. Hang on there and we'll send help at once."

Brading breathed a sigh of immense relief as he hung up the receiver. This was better than roaming about the country-side in the darkness. It shouldn't take the police long to find out the owner of the telephone number, and after that Mr. Grogan was going to get a very nasty surprise.

§10

On the following morning Inspector McLean arrived at his office to find Sergeant Brook in a very excited state.

"Something happened during the night," he said. "I found a message here from Superintendent Rawlings of the Falmouth police, asking me to ring him as soon as possible. That surprised me quite a bit. I rang him up just now, and he asked me what I knew about a man named Neville Brading, as he had a message purporting to come from Brading. I told him that Brading was missing, and that you had the case in hand. He then asked to speak to you and I said you hadn't arrived yet. He wouldn't tell me any more, but asked me to ring him as soon as you were available."

"I'm available now," said McLean. "Get me through to him."

In a minute or two McLean was speaking to Falmouth. It was a lengthy conversation, McLean making notes on his pad as he spoke, and asking questions. Finally he hung up the receiver.

"An echo of the Sheen affair," he said. "And a very loud echo. It seems that at one-fifteen this morning the police at Falmouth received a message from a man who said he was Neville Brading, and that he was held prisoner in a house with the telephone number of Upford 2347. To make his story good he mentioned your name, and stated that he believed Miss Westmoreland was also in the house. Rawlings traced the place through the telephone exchange. It is an old stone-built house about four miles out of Falmouth, named Pengarron. He rounded up some men and they went to the place, arriving there at one-fifty."

"Not very quick off the mark," complained Brook.

"No. But he had to get the address and also the men for the job. Anyway they found the house unoccupied."

"Didn't they enter it?"

"Give me time, Brook. Yes, they did enter it, but found no sign that anyone had been there recently. Yet the operator at the telephone exchange confirms that a call did come from the house at about one-fifteen. The owner of the property is a man named Hugh Templeton, believed to be abroad. Rawlings is attempting to find his present whereabouts. That's the extent of my information."

"It must have been Brading," said Brook. "Who else would mention my name in that connection? It was bright of him to think of that. What do we do about it?"

"There's only one sensible thing to do, and that is to run down to Falmouth. I'll look through my mail and then we'll get on the road."

"The cheek to work the same trick twice!"

69

"It may not be the same trick—only a variation. But it's no use speculating in this curious case."

They were on the road within half an hour, in one of the Flying Squad's fastest cars. Exeter was reached in record time and there they halted for about twenty minutes to snatch a drink and some sandwiches. Then on again through ever more beautiful scenery until at last, late in the afternoon, they came to the broad waters of the enchanting Fal. A few minutes later McLean was shaking hands with Superintendent Rawlings in the latter's very comfortable office.

"Any further developments?" asked McLean.

"Unfortunately, no. I've tried the Post Office in case the owner of the house left instructions there for the forwarding of letters, but he had not."

"What do you know of the owner?"

"Very little. He bought Polgarron six months ago. The house is in a bad state of repair. It had been in the market for years, and finally the late owner decided to put it up for auction. It fetched only two thousand pounds. Templeton, the man who bought it, put in some old furniture, but did practically nothing about the dilapidations. He is described as a swarthy fellow, round about fifty years of age. He doesn't appear to have used the place much. Perhaps he bought it merely for holidays. The grounds slope down to the sea, and there's a little cove which is almost covered at high tide."

"What about servants?"

"No details available. If you're ready to see the place I'll come with you now. But I'll take my own car, because I have an appointment in half an hour, and you may want to stay on a bit."

He led the way through the town and towards the Helford River. It was lovely unspoiled country, giving occasional views of the beautiful estuary on the one hand and the blue Atlantic on the other. Finally he turned his car into a drive, halting a moment to make sure that McLean was behind. A turn in the timbered drive brought the big stone house into full view.

It was obviously very old, and ivy-clad at one end. McLean noticed that the slated roof was in a bad state of repair, and that the built-on garage was a comparatively recent addition. The expansive grounds, except for the part immediately under the terrace, were a wilderness.

The Superintendent stopped his car just short of the terrace and got out. McLean and Brook followed his example, and then walked with him to the back door, where the Superintendent produced a large key.

"We removed this from the inside after one of my men entered through one of the bedroom windows which was open. He had to climb over that lower roof to do so. I didn't want to be held responsible for any damage," said the Superintendent. "Here we are !"

McLean and Brook followed him through the kitchen out into a passage.

"What's that other door ?" asked McLean, looking back.

"It leads to the garage. There's nothing inside it."

He turned in the other direction and soon came to a wide entrance hall, with a staircase in the centre and some doors on either side. The whole place smelt damp and musty, and what little furniture there was was dirty and mildewed. In the large sitting-room there was no sign of any very recent occupation and McLean could write his name in the dust on the mantelpiece. The windows there were firmly latched.

But the dining-room told rather a different story, for McLean quickly discovered that the door had been forced and part of the lock torn away. But this had been roughly repaired.

"No proof that that was done last night," he mused. "Ah, there's the telephone !"

He examined the receiver and found that, unlike most other things, it was completely free of dust.

"It looks as if Brading did telephone from here," he said. "And that shortly afterwards he was recaptured. Suspecting that he might have telephoned for help, the gang lost no time in getting away."

"Yes, it's the Sheen affair all over again," said Brook.

The Superintendent looked at his watch and expressed his regret at having to go back to Headquarters at once. He handed McLean the key of the back door before he left.

McLean then went upstairs, where he found a whole array of bedrooms. In two rooms the beds were made up, and in two others the blankets were folded up. The rest of the bedrooms were void of furniture.

"It's curious," said McLean, as they came down the staircase, "but there's a smell of burning everywhere."

"I thought it was just plain honest-to-goodness dirt," said Brook.

"No. There must be a basement in a house of this sort, but so far I haven't seen any entrance to it."

"May have been bricked up in the past," replied Brook. "I noticed a coal-shed outside, near the kitchen door."

McLean went along the passage towards the kitchen, still sniffing hard. Along the wall was a huge high-backed settle, with a long box seat. It seemed a curious place to have such a piece of furniture, which was more suitable for the entrance hall.

"Pull that out, Brook !" he said.

Brook heaved the settle away from the wall. Behind it was what had once been the door to the cellar, but now little more than a charred frame. McLean went to it and found the steps still wet with water and blackened with fire.

"I think that settles the matter beyond doubt," he said. "Brading succeeded in burning the door. We'll have a look down below. There's the switch."

They descended the steps and came upon pools of water. Near the table was an empty petrol can, and an enamelled jug and cup.

"Our local colleagues were singularly unobservant," he said. "Perhaps the Cornish people suffer from defective olfactory organs. Let's get some fresh air."

They went upstairs and out on to the long terrace, from which glimpses of the sea could be seen through small gaps in thick timber.

"Marvellous spot !" said Brook, sniffing at the salt laden air.

"Brading didn't find it marvellous, imprisoned in that airless place. Question Number One is why did they bring Brading all this way ? The obvious answer is that they wanted information from him, which they failed to get at the Sheen house. They dared not stay there long, and Brading presumably was either unable, or unwilling, to oblige them. But the obvious answer isn't always the right one. They may have had others eggs to fry."

"What sort of eggs ?"

"They may have reason to believe that Brading and the girl share a secret, and having discovered that neither of them

72

can be persuaded or bludgeoned into divulging it, they may have struck the not very original idea of torturing the one to loosen the lips of the other."

"And the one would be the girl?"

"It could work either way. But let's have a look round the garden."

They descended the steps which led from the terrace and were soon almost lost amid overgrown bushes and broken-down pergolas. Nowhere was there a sign that any work had been done there in years, and the once-cultivated beds were fighting a losing battle with Nature. But there was a fascination about the wildness, for many of the garden plants had self-seeded in nooks and crannies away from their normal home, and some of the trees were prodigious. There were hedges of fuchsias six feet high, engaged in silent battle with entangling convolvulus, and hydrangeas as large as dinner plates.

"Could be wonderful, given time and human sweat," said Brook. "Here's a path going downwards. May lead to the sea."

"We'll see," said McLean.

The narrow track wound through giant ilex trees, and finally through a narrow gorge, where some natural springs trickled over the bare rock. Finally the gorge opened and a flight of steps hewn in the rock led down to a sandy cove, with the dazzling blue Atlantic stretching on either hand.

"What a sight for sore eyes!" said Brook.

McLean made no response, but walked forward almost to the edge of the foaming sea. There, just above the high-tide mark, was a deep impression in the fine sand which the steady wind had not succeeded in obliterating, as it had any foot-prints which might have been between it and the stone steps.

"A boat was pulled in here—and quite recently," he said.

"So that's how they got away."

"Obviously a small boat, and probably a tender from a larger vessel."

"But they had a car. Why didn't they use that? Surely it would have been quicker?"

"No doubt they had good reasons. We'll go back to Fal-mouth and try to learn what vessels left there during the night."

"Not easy," said Brook. "The Fal is always full of shipping. I lived there for some years when I was a kid."

"We can but try."

They walked across the sand to the stone steps, and McLean was about to mount them, when he saw a small piece of paper driven into a crevice by the wind. He stooped and picked it up. It was an elaborate cigar band which was broken at its narrowest part. Across the oval face was embossed in gold the word 'Estella.'

"Indicates a gentleman with expensive tastes," he said, and slipped it into his note-book.

By the time they got back to Falmouth the sun was low in the west and the long day was drawing to a close. Superintendent Rawlings was still in his office, and McLean quickly summed up the results of his investigation.

"Ships?" he said, on learning McLean's requirements. "You can't count the ships which come and go every day. Of course there's a check on the larger vessels, but the place is teeming with smaller craft. This is almost the height of the holiday season, and there are hundreds of cabin cruisers, yachts and what not. Isn't it possible that someone may have landed in that cove just for a pleasant picnic?"

"All things are possible," agreed McLean. "I am in the position of a starving man snatching at a crumb, and I can't afford to ignore the smallest possible chance of making some progress in this case. What men have you to spare?"

"Precious few. But of course I'll help all I can. I'll put on a couple of men tonight, and another one tomorrow morning. It's impossible to guarantee a hundred per cent check, but I'll do my best. Where can I get in touch with you in case of need?"

"The Ferryboat Inn."

"Good! I'll get things moving at once."

McLean and Brook went to the small hotel along the waterfront where they managed to secure accommodation. Having had little to eat all day, they were glad of a full meal, and the Ferryboat was not lacking in that respect. From the sitting-room on the first floor one had a splendid view of the busy waterway, with its moving and stationary lights, and McLean could well appreciate the difficulties of Superintendent Rawlings' task.

"I think I'll turn in early," he yawned.

"Me, too," said Brook. "This soft air makes a fellow sleepy. What time in the morning, sir ?"

"Seven o'clock, and I mean seven o'clock. I'll go and tell the head-waiter we want breakfast at seven-thirty sharp."

They were at breakfast the following morning when a boy came to McLean's table and told him he was wanted on the telephone. He hurried to the public box in the hall and heard Rawlings on the line.

"Hell of a job you gave me !" he complained. "We're not half finished yet, but there's one bit of news which sounds promising. I thought you'd better have it at once. At about half-past one the night before last a biggish motor cruiser named *Rob Roy* left its mooring way up the river and went out to sea at a good lick. It's run by a fellow on holiday, and he and his friends sleep aboard. A man who has another boat saw it move off. It was trailing a tender. This man says that its departure was preceded by the arrival of a man in a car, who went aboard and then left in the car."

"Where is it now ?"

"That's the interesting part. It hasn't returned."

"Do you know who owns it ?"

"A man named Toovey. No one knows much about him."

"Thanks !" said McLean. "I think you can call off the search. Tell you more later."

McLean went back to his breakfast.

"Any luck ?" asked Brook.

"Quite a bit. A large sea-going motor cruiser left its anchorage up the river about a quarter of an hour after Brading made that telephone call. It is named the *Rob Roy* and was towing a tender. So far it hasn't returned."

"That sounds promising."

"But there's something else more promising. Remember the man who was a guest of the Waylands in the Sheen affair, and whom we tried to find at Bournemouth with no success ?"

"Mr. Toovey ?"

"Yes. Mr. Toovey happens to be the owner of the *Rob Roy*."

Brook signified his extreme satisfaction by giving vent to a long, low whistle.

THE summer home of Lancelot Toovey was in the opinion of his scattered neighbours a dream of a place. It was modern and of quite modest dimensions, but it embodied every kind of luxury known to man. Its situation was in keeping with its domestic perfection, for it lay high in the woods above the beautiful Helford River and commanded unimaginable views of the South Cornish coastline. The garden was a special feature of the property, for Toovey had introduced many subtropical plants which, in the mild climate and rich soil, seemed as happy and healthy as they would have been in their native terrain. He was a great man for masonry, and with ample means to indulge this whim he had built wide terraces and paved ways to match the well-dressed Bath stone of his immaculate dwelling. It was all in good taste, for he had employed an excellent architect and the best master mason in the West of England. He called the place The Sanctuary, and in the wall over the main entrance was a beautiful porcelain plaque of Italian origin depicting an angel brooding over an injured hind.

The man himself was an enigma. He joined no clubs, took no part in social activities, and was seldom seen outside his huge saloon car, which was sometimes seen filling the narrow lanes which led to The Sanctuary and driven by his 'man' who was reputed to be variously a Frenchman, a Spaniard, and an Arab. In appearance Toovey was ageless. He could have been a comparatively young man dissipated by immoderate living, or a much older man who had managed to retain most of the attributes of youth.

On this particular evening he was sitting in his beautifully appointed study, with the curtains half-drawn to shut out the sunlight, and his new toy—the best television set which money could buy—in full operation. Considering his geographical situation the reception was remarkably good, far better than the programme itself, which was deplorable. He was making some impolite comments, *sotto voce*, when there was a tap on the door and his chauffeur-cum-butler entered, neatly attired in a short black satin coat and a bow tie.

"Excuse, sir," he said with an unlocatable accent. "There are two gentleman call. One say he is Inspector McLean from Scotland Yard. Are you in, sir ?"

"One is always in to police inspectors. I shall be delighted to make their acquaintance. Show them in."

A few moments later McLean and Brook filed into the room, to find Toovey relieving the place of its semi-darkness. The figures on the large screen became like ghosts and then vanished completely as Toovey switched off the current.

"Excuse my childish amusement," he said, with a smile. "And now, Inspector, what can I do for you ?"

"You are Mr. Lancelot Toovey ?" asked McLean.

"Yes."

"I believe you have some friends named Wayland at Richmond, near London ?"

"That is so. I stayed with them a short time ago. Mr. Wayland is a stockbroker, and occasionally I place a little business his way."

"While you were there did you go to the home of Mrs. Wayland's brother to play bridge ?"

"Yes. It was a most enjoyable evening."

"During the bridge did you hear Mr. Browning remark that he and his wife were about to spend a few days at Hove ?"

"I really can't remember. There was a good deal of chatter between the hands. No, I'm sorry, I don't remember that. But is it of any importance ?"

"Yes. Mr. Browning's house was entered during his stay at Hove, almost certainly by some persons who were aware of his absence. I am anxious to have a complete list of the persons who knew that the house was empty at that time."

"I wish I could help you, but am afraid I can't. I hope Browning didn't lose much. He had some rather nice things in the house."

"Do you own a motor cruiser named *Rob Roy* ?"

"Yes. I have no fit anchorage here, and the boat is normally on a mooring up the Fal."

"Is she there now ?"

"I can't say. You see, I let the boat to some people for the month of July, and they come and go as they please. The only restriction I made was that they should confine their cruising to British waters. I didn't want them crossing the Channel and possibly having trouble which might result in the boat being taken to a foreign port and putting me to no end of trouble."

"Who were the people who hired the boat?"

"A Major and Mrs. Kelly from County Cork. I met them at Bournemouth where I stayed a week or two, and liked them very much. The matter of boats came up and I happened to mention that I had a motor cruiser which I sometimes let out in the Summer. They were as keen as mustard and we did a deal there and then."

"Was there any kind of written agreement?"

"No. The Major and his wife came down to see the boat, and I satisfied myself that he knew how to handle it. To save waiting for a cheque to go through he paid me the two hundred pounds in cash, and I gave him a receipt. I think he said that two other persons would be joining them."

"Were they to live aboard?"

"Yes. There is sleeping accommodation for six. But I must say I am a little bewildered by these questions. Are they guilty of some misdemeanour?"

"Not necessarily, but I am interested in the movements of the boat."

"I can't help you there. But why not go and ask them? The mooring is——"

"I know where the mooring is, but the boat left in the early hours of Wednesday morning and has been away ever since."

Toovey reflected for a few moments.

"They may have gone on a longish trip round the coast," he ruminated. "I can't believe they would ignore my restrictions. You don't suspect smuggling?"

"At the moment I have an open mind. But I should like some more details about Major and Mrs. Kelly. Did they give you their full address in County Cork?"

"I think it was a place called Inneskeen, or something like that."

"Where did you meet them exactly?"

"In the concert hall in the first instance, and after that in a bar where I used to go for an aperitif in the mornings."

"Do you know where they were staying in Bournemouth?"

"With some friends, I think."

"So you really know little about them ?"

"Well—not a great deal."

"Yet you had no hesitation in letting them your boat ?"

"Not when they agreed to my terms and paid me in advance."

"Where were you yourself staying at that time ?"

"At the Glendower Hotel."

McLean said nothing, but he knew this was untrue, for he had taken up this matter previously and had been told by the hotel manager that they knew nothing of Mr. Lancelot Toovey. A little later he and Brook got back into their car and drove away.

"So he's a liar ?" said Brook.

"Yes. In regard to his stay at Bournemouth. It's curious that he should have told his friend Wayland that he was staying at that address."

"More curious that Wayland, who did business with him, apparently didn't know he had a permanent home here."

"He may have found it convenient to lie to Wayland, just as he lied to us most of the time."

"You think the story about letting the boat isn't true ?"

"Does it ring true ? Can you see a man with a five-thousand-pound boat letting it to people whom he met by chance, and if, as Wayland stated, he is rich, why should he bother about letting his boat at all ? This man needs careful watching."

"And what about the boat ?"

"We'll take some steps about that at once. If the boat is in a British port it shouldn't be very difficult to locate it. We'll put out an SOS to all port authorities to have the boat and its occupants apprehended."

The message was sent out, and the local harbour master in particular was instructed to keep a close watch for the return of *Rob Roy* and to notify police headquarters immediately. But no news came either that night or the following day. It was early the next morning that McLean was informed that the *Rob Roy* had returned during the night and was lying at her old anchorage. That she had not been observed entering the river was due to a great amount of drifting mist in the early hours.

Within a matter of minutes he and Brook were in the car moving swiftly towards the higher reaches of the river. There were innumerable craft swinging on the heavy tide, and it was not easy to identify the *Rob Roy*, despite the very detailed description which Superintendent Rawlings had furnished. But at last, after a few enquiries, they came upon the powerful-looking boat lying off a little headland. Beached on the headland was a tender, also bearing the name *Rob Roy*. As there was no boatman in the vicinity McLean decided to make use of the tender, and Brook set it afloat.

Brook's muscular arms soon had the tender under the hull of the parent ship, where he fastened the mooring rope to a short flight of steps which gave access to the deck. He and McLean then went aboard. McLean rapped on the door of the centrally-placed saloon, but there was no response of any kind. Finally he opened the door and entered the saloon. It was a lavishly equipped place capable of accommodating half a dozen persons, and the long benches on either side of the teak table bore soft and colourful cushions. Beyond the table was a small writing room-cum library, and then another door which led to the sleeping quarters, which comprised six bunks with sliding doors. The bunks were all empty and the beds unmade. Nowhere was there a sign of any baggage or clothing.

"They've gone !" blurted Brook.

"Yes. That was why the tender was on the beach. Presumably they had no wish to be questioned."

"You think they knew we were waiting for them ?"

"I do."

"But they could have abandoned the boat, and not risked bringing her back."

"I think they probably didn't know until they made port, and then someone tipped them off."

"Toovey ?"

"That's a fairly intelligent deduction."

"Tricky, isn't it ?"

"Everything in this case is tricky. If we go to Toovey and tell him that his trusted friends have absconded he will merely express amazement, but may be ready to admit that he was mistaken about their integrity. If we were to go Kelly-hunting in County Cork no doubt we should find many of them, but not the ones in whom we are interested. I doubt if we shall find here the slightest trace of the late occupants, or of Brading and the girl. But we can try."

The subsequent search bore out this prognostication. Nowhere was there the slightest clue to the boat's recent movements. The magazines and newspapers were all British, and there was not a single thing aboard to prove that the boat had ever left British waters.

"This changes the situation a bit, doesn't it?" asked Brook. "You might now get a search warrant on Toovey's house."

"To what end? Even if I were successful in getting the warrant, which I doubt, do you imagine that Toovey is the sort of man to harbour incriminating articles or documents? At the moment we have nothing against him but the fact that his boat was used for unlawful purposes. We can believe or disbelieve his story of letting the boat to the mysterious Major Kelly, but at the moment we cannot entirely smash it."

"But we can prove he lied about his stay at the hotel in Bournemouth."

"I don't want to prove too much against him at the moment. Nothing would be more detrimental to our investigation than to issue a daily bulletin of our small but quite valuable discoveries. The way to cook Toovey's goose is to let it run a little. And talking of the devil, there he is in person."

Brook, rowing with his back to the headland, turned his head slightly, and saw the man they were discussing standing at the open door of his car, staring towards them. He came to the beach at their point of landing and then waited for McLean to step out of the boat.

"I heard that the *Rob Roy* was back," he said. "In view of your call I thought I'd come and see what the Major had been up to."

"You're a trifle late—as we were," said McLean. "There is no one aboard, but definite signs that they have left for good."

"Gone! But that's incredible. They hired the boat for a month and have only had her for ten days."

"That appears to have been long enough for them to have completed a certain undertaking."

Toovey looked at him sharply.

"You must mean smuggling. It is the only thing which makes any sense."

"Yes, it is about the only thing that makes any sense. You have been hoodwinked, Mr. Toovey."

"But couldn't they have gone away for a day or two, with the intention of returning ? I mean, have you any definite proof that the boat was used to transport contraband ?"

"No proof at all. One can only draw fairly obvious conclusions."

"You may be wrong, Inspector. I still believe they will come back."

"If they do you had better communicate with Superintendent Rawlings immediately, as he will have charge of the matter at this end. I hope your optimism may be rewarded, but at least you have got your boat back."

"Yes. I think I'll go aboard to see the state of things there."

"You'll find it all very tidy. Well, I'll bid you good day."

As they left in the car Toovey was seen pushing the tender into the tideway.

"Did you mean what you said about Superintendent Rawlings ?" asked Brook.

"No. We'll change our lodgings and hang around for a bit. I should like to observe Mr. Toovey's future movements. For that we shall need more help, for Toovey is the sort of man who may be quite active in the dark hours."

§ 12

IN the meantime Brading's series of misadventures had continued, and at the moment when he believed he had turned the tables on his captors. He had scarcely hung up the telephone receiver, after speaking to the police, when to his dismay there came a penetrating double ring from the hall outside the room. He almost leapt to the telephone and lifted the receiver. Immediately the bell stopped ringing, and a voice said sweetly :

"Have you finished your call to Falmouth?"

"Yes," he replied in a soft voice, and waited for the sequel.

It came in a matter of seconds. There were footsteps outside the door, and the handle squealed as it was turned in vain.

"That's funny," growled a voice. "It's locked on the inside. Now, how the hell. . . !"

There was whispering, and then dead silence. Brading sensed the meaning of that. The room was now a trap, and the sooner he got out of it the better. Unlatching the casement window, he looked out. Everything was bathed in moonlight, and the terrace was clear. He made a dash towards the steps with the intention of taking shelter in the lower garden, but suddenly he heard a voice in his rear.

"Stop! Or I'll shoot."

He turned his head and saw, within twenty yards of him, the man with the gun. The barrel was levelled at his back, and the marksman was squinting along the sights. Then from the opposite direction came two more men, running, one of whom he recognized as Grogan.

"Hold him!" yelled Grogan. "Shoot if he moves!"

Having no doubt that this order would be joyfully obeyed, Brading turned round, breathing heavily.

"Put down the gun," he said.

"I'll put you down if you move a finger. You've caused enough trouble already."

Grogan now reached Brading, very much out of breath from his exertions. He stood for a few moments with his hands on his broad hips, glaring at the prisoner.

"Very clever, Mr. Brading," he said. "But you won't get another opportunity like that. I presume you rang up the police?"

"What would you have done?" retorted Brading.

"Had you accepted my proposition you might have been free by now."

"I don't like your propositions. Hadn't you better do something about it? The police may be here at any moment."

Grogan gave a snort of contempt.

"Take him into the dining-room," he said. "Hurry!"

The man with the gun came round to his rear and pushed the hard barrel into his back, and he was hustled into the room he had just left, and pushed into a chair.

"I want a rope and a large pillow case," snapped Grogan. "Jan, see to it."

"So it's Jan again!" said Brading. "Quite a useful fellow."

"Cheap sneers are rather childish in the circumstances. You got yourself into this mess by your stupidity, when by a little co-operation you could have avoided it. I can't guarantee that your future will be comfortable unless you change your attitude."

"Brave words, but it might pay you to think a little about your own future. I guess you can't be very certain how that will turn out."

Jan was back very quickly with the pillow case and a length of rope. Brading put up a tremendous resistance, more with a view to wasting time than with any hope of spoiling their intentions, but in the end they had the pillow case over his head and his arms tightly bound to his sides. The pillow-case let in just about enough air to prevent suffocation.

After that all was confusion. He lived in a world of sound and was aware of great commotion in the house. From outside he heard the sound of a car, and for a moment believed that the police had arrived, but this proved to be but wishful thinking. Then finally he was led out into the open air and down the steps from the terrace. From there his progress was downwards all the way, then over some hard rock and on to a patch of sand, where he was permitted to sit down. For a time there came only the sound of waves breaking on the sand, but some time later he heard another noise—the deep throb of powerful engines. Then silence, until a new sound entered his little world. It was the unmistakable noise of oars moving in rowlocks, and finally the scraping of a keel pulled up on sand quite close to him. The significance of this was plain enough.

A few moments later he was hauled to his feet and helped into a small boat, where he barked his shins against two seats before he found a resting place. Then there was a delay.

"Cutting it fine," muttered Jan's voice. "Shall we get across and come back for the others?"

"No," snapped a voice. "Orders were to wait here."

There was silence for a few minutes, and then one of the men uttered a sigh of relief.

"Here she comes!"

"S—sh!"

84

Brading pricked up his ears. Who could 'she' be but Anna? So his conjectures had been right. It was Anna who had cried out in the night, and now she, like himself, was being removed to a safer hideout. There were plodding footsteps on the sand, and for the first time since he had left the house he heard Grogan's voice.

"Steady! Get her more amidships. That's better, but there's not room for all of us. Get the boat over quick and then come back. Lend a hand here."

The boat was pushed slowly off the sand, and finally floated. There was splashing of water, and the sound of oars and the gentle rise and fall of the craft. The journey was short, and then commenced the difficult task of getting aboard the larger vessel for a man with no arms to aid him. All the time he was listening intently for Anna—if it was Anna—to make a sound, but no such sound came. Once on deck he was seized and hustled down some steps and through a narrow passage, and finally down another step where he fell with a crash on to a hard floor. A door was slammed behind him and latched on the outside. Unable to regain his feet, he lay there breathing with the greatest difficulty, and cursing his bad luck.

A quarter of an hour must have passed before the powerful engines started up and the vessel began to move forward, gathering speed every moment. In his bad condition the heavy vibration and the movements of the vessel brought on sickness. But relief came some time afterwards when the door was opened, and someone entered and cut the bonds which held his arms and the pillowcase. He blinked in the pale light of an electric lamp, and saw Grogan with a knife in his hand regarding him closely. He stood up on shaky knees and sat down on the bunk close to him.

"Your little trick didn't work," said Grogan. "Now we are bound for a more convenient place."

"I think you're mad," said Brading. "You may be keeping one step ahead of the police, but they'll catch up with you."

"For your sake I hope they don't," retorted Grogan. "For then I might be compelled to dispose of you permanently. But why should we talk in this strain? We have in fact a common interest."

"I'm sick," said Brading. "I don't want to talk to you."

"The sickness will go. I can help you in that respect. A couple of these tablets will put you right in half an hour."

He produced a little phial from his pocket and tipped out two white tablets which he placed on a shelf above the bunk.

"Take those and have a nap. You'll feel better afterwards. This will prove they are innocuous."

He took two more tablets from the phial and swallowed them at a gulp.

"In my early days I was a medical student," he said.

"Until you took to crime."

"Until crime took to me. I am a victim of social conditions. You seem to imagine I have no virtues at all."

"If you have you haven't displayed them. What are you going to do with Anna Westmoreland?"

"That depends largely upon you. But of that more anon. Better take those tablets. Then we can talk. Now I'm going to snatch some sleep."

He went out latching the door behind him. Brading passed a hand across his swimming head, and then reached up and took the tablets in his hand. He hesitated for a moment and then swallowed them. Within ten minutes he was asleep.

It seemed only a few minutes later when he woke up, and to his surprise saw light streaming through the very small porthole. The sickness had passed and he felt immeasurably better. A glance through the porthole showed only a great expanse of sea, with no land visible in that direction. But he could not see the sun itself and could form no idea of the direction in which he was travelling. Opposite the bunk was a tiny wash-basin and a towel. He got up and washed as well as he was able, for the injured arm was still stiff and painful.

Grogan's attitude puzzled him. Now he was more conciliatory despite the fact that his—Brading's—action had hounded him out of his late retreat. One would have imagined that it would have increased his hostility and brutality, but the contrary was the case. What lay at the back of that cunning brain? Brading, with his hostility by no means lessened, was in no mood to be deceived by one kindly act. That something big was at stake there could be no doubt. There were at least half a dozen persons involved in this mysterious business, probably more, and it all boiled down to some kind of package which they believed to have been in

Anna's suitcase. Only Anna could explain that package, and here he was, as innocent as a new-born lamb, suffering one misfortune after another because Grogan was convinced he was the king-pin of the whole thing. The ironical thing was that if he told the truth they would refuse absolutely to believe him.

He was still wrestling with the problem when the door opened and a man he had not seen before, so far as he knew, entered with a tray, on which were two eggs and two rashers of bacon, some bread and butter, and a pot of coffee and a cup.

"Mr. Grogan's compliments," he said.

"Very kind of him. Put it on the locker."

The fellow grinned and did as he was bade. He went out, latching the door behind him, and Brading sat down before the welcome meal. Wonders never ceased. Undoubtedly Grogan was becoming humanized, but for what reason ? Was there some new factor in the game which favoured this distinct change of heart ? If so, it would doubtless emerge before very long.

He ate the meal and then stared through the porthole at the changing lights on the surface of the heaving sea and the slow movements of the heavy cumulus clouds high up in the blue. Then he tried to open the porthole to let in some fresh air, but it refused to budge. It was about an hour later when the door opened again and Grogan entered.

"You're looking better," he said cheerily.

"I'm feeling better."

"Good. Like me to take a look at that arm of yours ?"

"No. If you've got something to say—say it."

"Some time ago you said you would be more communicative about my stolen parcel provided you saw Anna first."

"Well ?"

"Anna is ready to talk to you."

"Alone ?" asked Brading suspiciously.

"Yes."

"So you lied when you said she was hundreds of miles away ?"

"I had my own interest to protect. I hope now we shall be able to clear up this matter to our mutual satisfaction."

"All right. Take me to Anna."

Brading thrilled as he followed Grogan into the passage.

Whatever the outcome, it would be good to see Anna again. He had not far to go, for Grogan tapped on the door of the next cabin but one, and then opened it. Lying in a bunk, fully dressed, and partly covered by a rug was the girl he had last seen outside the hotel at Southampton, when she had waved him good-bye. Her face was pallid and her eyes staring.

"Push the bell when you want me," said Grogan, and vanished.

Brading closed the door and latched it, before he went to the bunk, and pressed one of Anna's slim hands. The drawn cheeks and the sunken eyes alarmed him.

"Anna, are you ill?" he asked.

"No. Not ill. They told me you were here, but I couldn't believe it. You shouldn't have come. You shouldn't have tried to find me."

"I wouldn't have found you but for Grogan. I was kidnapped and taken to a house on the coast. I escaped and got in touch with the police, but before the police could act I was recaptured. Didn't you see me in the small boat when they brought you to the ship?"

"I—I've been unconscious for some time. My head's all muddled still. They've been giving me drugs to make me talk —pentatol, or something like that. It has the effect of making you tell the truth. It's easier to tell the truth than make up a lie. I had to fight it, and it's been hard."

"So you've told them what they want to know?"

She shook her head.

"No. I beat the drug. I had to. I made a promise. But Neville, I've dragged you into this trouble without meaning to. You told me you were going back to Canada, and I didn't think it mattered what I said."

"I don't get it. What did you say about me?"

"I gave them to believe that you had the package they were after. No, that isn't quite true. Oh dear, it's all so complicated!"

"Don't hurry things," he begged. "Take your time. Don't tell me anything if you don't want to."

"But I do. You were kind to me when I needed a friend, and that evening with you at the hotel was the happiest I had spent for a long time, despite the shock of my mother's death. I didn't want to talk about my mother then, but I can now.

88

She was a strange woman, with no motherly instincts, and she drank heavily. When in drink she could be horrible. It was no sort of a home, and five years ago my brother left for good. I had two letters from him and then no more. What became of him I don't know."

She stopped and stared past Brading as if she were quite unconscious of his presence. Then her gaze shortened, and she resumed her story.

"Life became even more unendurable after my brother had gone. My mother's enmity towards me increased, and I knew that sooner or latter we must part. The end came one evening when I came home from a restaurant where I had a temporary job. It was my pay day and my mother had asked me to bring her a bottle of gin. I pretended to have forgotten about it, and she flew into a rage and called me filthy names. I was tired and overwrought, and gave her a piece of my mind. It was then she told me something which stunned me, and she did it gleefully. She—she told me that I was illegitimate, but that her husband didn't know because he died before I was born. The next day, when she was in a better mood, I asked her if what she had said was true, and she told me it was. That night I packed a bag and went to London."

"How long ago was that?" asked Brading.

"Three years. In London I managed to support myself by going as a waitress, but I grew tired of the hard work and long hours, and finally managed to get a start in dress modelling. It was while appearing in a dress show that I met a man named Harold Besterling."

Brading gave a little start at the name, for it looked as if Grogan's statement was, most unexpectedly, going to be confirmed.

"Do—do you know him?" asked Anna.

"No, but Grogan mentioned him to me."

"They were friends—strange friends. Harold was some years older than me, a gay and engaging person. He liked music and so did I. We had many things in common. He said he had been trained as an engineer, but had a private income. Within three months we were married."

Brading's mouth twitched, but he made no comment. Anna pointed to a glass of water on the table and Brading held it to her lips. As she drank it her eyes regarded him wistfully.

"I should have told you that before," she said.

"That's okay. It makes no difference. Were you happy?"

"For a time. I needed happiness—I had had so little. But soon I was bewildered. We had been living in good style, Harold spending money freely, but suddenly his money seemed to come to an end. We moved to cheaper lodgings and debts began to pile up. I begged him to get a regular job, and finally he got one. It was with Grogan. I don't know exactly what he did, but it kept him away from home sometimes for weeks on end. On occasion he went abroad. Secretly I discovered that Grogan had an office in Fenchurch Street. It had a plate outside inscribed 'Toovey & Toovey—Exporters'. I said nothing to Harold about this, but I was troubled in my mind. Then, one night, after Harold had been away for two days, he came back to our flat in a state of great excitement. I asked him what was wrong. He opened a bag which he was carrying and took out a parcel wrapped in a kind of waterproof material.

"'I'm in trouble,' he said. 'In a few minutes I must go. If anyone should call you are to say you haven't seen me for days. Tonight you must leave here and take this parcel with you. For God's sake don't ask me any questions now. There's something you must do for me. As soon as you have got yourself fixed up in a lodging take the parcel and dispose of it as instructed in these directions. All being well I will get in touch with you at Post Restante, Charing Cross Post Office.'

"He handed me an envelope and told me to read the contents later. I asked him what was in the parcel, but he refused to tell me. I then asked him if he had stolen it and he swore he hadn't. When I lifted the parcel it was extraordinarily heavy. Again I asked him what was in it, but he would not tell me. I had never seen him so serious as he was then. He got a Bible and asked me to swear on it that I would never divulge to a living soul where the parcel was until I saw him again. I—I swore, and he was satisfied.

"Ten minutes later he was gone. I packed up everything we possessed, including the heavy parcel, called a taxi and drove to Paddington Station where I deposited everything until I could find a place to stay in. Finally I got that room in Watling Street, and I collected my suitcases from the railway station. The next day I carried out Harold's instructions and tore up the letter containing them. The next day I called at the post office at Charing Cross, hoping to hear from Harold, but there was no letter, and it was the same every other day. I was short of money and tried to get my old job back, but I failed. Then I was taken ill, a very mysterious sort of illness, perhaps due to worry. I had to sell most of my personal belongings to pay the rent. One day I saw in the newspaper that Harold had been on trial for theft. The action had been brought by Grogan, who swore that Harold had robbed the office of fifty pounds. They were new notes got from the bank that day, and the numbers were recorded. Some of them were found in Harold's pocket. He was sentenced to three years imprisonment."

"Grogan told me that," said Brading. "I thought he was lying. But was no mention made at the trial of some documents which were stolen with the money?"

"No."

Brading thought for a moment. It seemed clear that the 'documents' were none other than the parcel which Anna's husband had brought to her, and that Grogan had very good reasons for keeping that item out of the case. But were they really documents?

"And now what is the position?" he asked. "Do you propose to tell him where the parcel is hidden?"

"Yes."

"But why?"

"Because of you. I owe it to you to get you out of this trouble, since I got you into it."

"What about your sworn promise to your husband?"

"I didn't know then what trouble I should bring you. If I remain silent there is no knowing where it will end. He wants that parcel so badly that he will commit murder for it."

"I don't think so. Anything short of murder, perhaps. So long as he thinks he can get the truth from one of us he will keep us alive. No, Anna—you keep your promise and——"

There was a rap at the door, followed by Grogan's rather impatient voice.

"You've had enough time," he said. "Open the door!"

"Give us another minute or two," said Brading. "It's quite all right."

"Two minutes then."

Anna waited until the footsteps vanished.

"What—what can we do?" she asked.

"How much have you told him?"

"Only that when I last had my one remaining suitcase the parcel was inside."

"Did he ask you if I knew you had the parcel?"

"Yes. I said I might have mentioned it in conversation. He asked me how long I had known you, and I was deliberately vague. I really wanted him to think that you had the parcel. I never dreamed he would be able to harm you. . . ."

"That's all right. It's better he should think that. Anna, let me deal with this matter, and don't be surprised by anything I may say. Is it a deal?"

"If you think it's best."

"Good! He mentioned a bell. Oh, there it is."

He crossed to the bell button and pushed it. Then he went to the door and unlocked it. A minute or two later footsteps were heard approaching and Grogan entered. He had changed his sober attire since Brading had last seen him, and now sported an immaculate linen coat and grey slacks.

"Well?" he asked. "I hope you've come to a decision."

"We have," replied Brading. "Anna is willing that I should tell you what I did with the parcel, but there are conditions."

"What are they? Don't make them too impossible."

"We want some compensation for pain and suffering, as the lawyers call it."

"What sort of compensation?"

"A little while ago you offered me five hundred pounds. It's not enough. I want a thousand when you are in possession of the parcel."

"Are you in a position to dictate terms?"

"Are you in a position to decline them? You can't continue hiding us in borrowed houses for ever, and murder is not a nice alternative even to a guy like you. Is it a deal?"

Grogan hesitated for a moment.

"It's a deal," he said finally. "But I must continue to hold you both until the deal is completed. That's understood?"

"Not exactly. What do you mean by holding us? The last time you held me was in a filthy cellar. As for Anna, she's ill and needs a doctor."

"You're mistaken. There is nothing seriously wrong with Anna. A few days of sunshine and good feeding will put her right, and I know just the place. We are, in fact, on our way there. You will both receive every attention and comfort until the package is in my possession again, when you will be permitted to go where you please."

"With that thousand pounds ?"

"Of course. But on handing you the money I shall want a letter from you exonerating me from any inconvenience which you may have suffered. Now let us get to the crux of the matter. Where is the parcel ?"

Brading gave an appealing glance at Anna.

"You are still agreeable, Anna ?" he asked.

"Yes. I want to be free of all this worry."

"Very well," said Brading. "Here is the dope. I handed the parcel to a Canadian friend of mine. He is the London representative of the *Toronto Sentinel*, and lives at Graham Mansions, Maida Vale. His name is Charles Winterton. Wait a moment, I think I have his card."

He took his wallet from his pocket, and finally handed Grogan a professional card, which Grogan scanned.

"Will he hand over the parcel ?" he asked.

"He will if I write him a note. Can you get me a sheet of notepaper and a pen ?"

Grogan went to the table beside the bunk and finally produced both articles. Brading used the top of the table as a desk and then penned a note to his friend requesting him to hand the parcel to the bearer.

"That should do the trick," he said, and gave the note to Grogan. "The sooner you get that into Winterton's hands the better I shall like it. Satisfied ?"

"Up to a point."

"What point ?"

"The point of actually getting the parcel."

"You'll get it. Now I want to talk to Anna—about the future."

"All right. We shall reach our destination late evening. In the meantime I can't give you the run of the boat. Is there anything you want ?"

"Yes—some cigarettes and a bottle of beer. Tell me one thing. Where are you landing us ?"

"That's the one thing I prefer not to tell you. But you shall have the cigarettes and the beer."

Brading gave a little sigh of relief as Grogan went out and closed the door behind him. But on this occasion he did not latch it on the outside.

"It worked," said Brading. "At least we have gained a little time, plus better treatment."

"But I don't quite understand," said Anna. "Very soon he must discover that you lied to him."

"Not very soon. When I last saw Winterton, just before I met you, he told me he was flying back to Toronto in a couple of days to talk business with his chief. It's improbable that he will be back yet. That means that Grogan will find it impossible to check the truth of my statement and must wait for Winterton's return. In the meantime I'm going to make an effort to contact the police. If I succeed they may be able to nab the person who takes that note of mine to Winterton, and that may lead to the arrest of the whole gang."

Anna reflected for a moment, and it seemed to Brading that her eyes were now brighter and her cheeks less bloodless. She then asked him to open the porthole wider, and finally to give her the hand mirror. Peering into the latter, she made a grimace.

"I look ghastly," she complained. "But you've made me feel much better. It all seemed so hopeless before. I dreaded that he would keep on injecting that horrid drug and finally compel me to tell the truth. Look !"

She rolled back the sleeve of her blouse and exposed the puncture marks left by the hypodermic syringe.

"The swine !" he ejaculated. "He told me he had been trained to be a doctor. But what a doctor ! Have they given you any food lately ?"

"Yes, but I couldn't eat it. . . ."

At that moment the man who had brought Brading's breakfast arrived with a packet of cigarettes, a large bottle of beer and a drinking glass.

"Wait !" said Brading. "Miss Westmoreland wants some food. What have you got ?"

"I must ask Mr. Grogan."

"Never mind about Mr. Grogan. What have you got ?"

"Eggs and bacon, ham, and some cold chicken."

"Make it chicken and ham, and there's five dollars if you bring it quick."

94

"Okay."

Ten minutes later Anna was sitting up and taking a little more notice of things. Brading sat and watched her getting through the simple but excellent meal, and it brought to mind that night when he had last seen her, and when her body needs were little less than they were now. She looked up at him and smiled.

"You're a marvellous man, Neville," she said. "Why didn't I meet you years and years ago?"

"Perhaps Browning had the answer. Wasn't it he who said 'Never the girl, the place and the time together,' or something like that?"

"I must read Browning one of these days," said Anna.

§ 13

It was at three o'clock the following morning that Madame Frontenac was awakened by unmistakable thumping on the door of her remote abode. She switched on the electric light, generated by a small petrol engine, and then shook her snoring spouse by the arm.

"Gaston—wake up!"

Gaston opened his eyes and blinked at the light.

"What's the trouble?" he growled.

"There's someone at the door."

"Nonsense! You've been dreaming. It's only the wind on those loose window-frames."

"No. There—listen!"

Gaston himself now heard the noise, and not only the thumping but the sound of his own name, repeated in a gruff voice with some impatience.

"You're right," he said, and went to the window, which was immediately above the main doorway.

"Who's there?" he asked.

A figure emerged from the cover of the portico.

"It's me—Grogan. My boat's lying offshore. I want to see you on important business. Come on down."

Gaston closed the window and slipped on a dressing-gown. Madame Frontenac gazed at him anxiously. She had heard the name, and it obviously gave her no pleasure.

"What can he want, Gaston?" she asked.

"Who can tell?"

"Well, be cautious. A little of Grogan goes a long way. The last time——"

"For God's sake don't start recriminations," he interrupted. "Where are my damned slippers?"

"Where you put them—there under the chair. Get rid of him as quickly as you can."

Gaston put on his slippers and went down to the front door where Grogan was waiting. In silence they passed through the timbered hall and into a large lounge which was full of old Breton furniture and strange maritime articles.

"Now," said Gaston in French. "What's it all about?"

"I've got two passengers who are in need of a change of air. I propose to dump them on you for a while."

"Who are they?"

"A man and a woman. I want you to hold them until I come again."

Gaston stared at him.

"You mean against their will?" he asked.

"We needn't go into that. I want to know they are safe here for a few days until I complete a certain deal."

"My wife will object."

"Is your wife in command here?"

"I have to consider her."

"I will pay you five thousand francs for every day they are here, with ten thousand now on account."

"Not enough. You'll have to do better than that if I'm going to get my wife's approval."

Grogan stared into Gaston's shifty eyes.

"You can get your wife's approval by telling her about a man who was once a prisoner on Devil's Island until he miraculously escaped and got back to France. I believe there is still a reward available for his capture—dead or alive."

"S—sh!" said Gaston, flapping his hands.

"Then be reasonable. Tell your wife now that she is going

to receive two charming guests, and that she had better get two rooms ready at once."

"Two rooms !"

"Yes. The man might be willing to share one, but the lady happens to be someone else's wife, and I am the last person to aid and abet any unseemly goings on. Hurry ! I want to bring them ashore."

Gaston shuffled away, and then from above came the sound of bickering, but in a short while there was silence and Gaston came back.

"It's all right," he said. "Louise is getting the rooms ready."

"Good ! Here are the ten thousand francs. With any luck I shall be back in four days."

Gaston counted the notes with great care and thrust them into the pocket of his dressing-gown.

"Now listen," said Grogan. "I saw a small motor boat in the cove. Has it got any oars ?"

"Yes."

"Then remove them and empty the fuel tank. What about passing ships ?"

"They never come closer than four miles, because of the dangerous reefs."

"Any fishing boats ?"

"I've never seen any within miles."

"Good ! Now I'm going back to get your guests. Your wife had better come down and welcome them. No reason why this shouldn't be a friendly business."

It was about a quarter of an hour later when Grogan came back with Brading and Anna, the latter leaning a little heavily on Brading's supporting arm. Brading had nothing but what he was wearing, but Anna had a suitcase which Grogan was gallantly carrying—the same suitcase which Brading had removed from her lodging and which had subsequently been stolen from his bedroom.

Gaston's wife was now downstairs, doing her best to look charming and innocent. She had a mass of fair hair pinned up in a dozen places, and she looked about ten years younger than her dark husband.

"Here we are," said Grogan, dumping the suitcase. "These are my friends, Monsieur and Madame Frontenac. Gaston, meet Mr. Brading and Mrs. Besterling. They are in need of a change of air, and should benefit from a short stay here."

"Pleased to meet you," said Gaston in quite good English. "I hope you will be comfortable. Are the rooms ready, Louise?"

"Quite ready," said Madame, with a dreadful accent. "You must be ver' tired. I take you up now, yes?"

Anna nodded and went off with Madame, who turned her head and told her spouse to bring the suitcase.

"Guess I'll turn in, too," said Brading.

"Wait!" said Grogan. "I hope for your sake you are going to play fair?"

"The same applies to you," replied Brading. "I only have your word that you will come back here when you have got the package. You could vamoose with that thousand pounds."

"You must trust me."

"The same goes for you. This may be a healthy sort of place but I shall be glad if you will come back without a moment's delay. I want to get back to Canada, where I have work to do."

"I shall waste no time."

"Good! That suits me."

He went upstairs and found Gaston on the landing. He was shown into a small but comfortable room, with a window which framed a patch of moonlit ocean. There was even a wash-basin, and a reading lamp on the bedside table.

"Very nice," he said. "But can you fix me up with a razor of some sort. You see, I have no baggage."

Gaston went into his own bedroom and came back with a safety razor and a toothbrush in a sealed package.

"I keep spares," he said, "as I go to the mainland very infrequently. We have breakfast here at eight o'clock—English fashion, not *petit dejeuner*."

"Suits me. Where is Mrs. Besterling sleeping?"

"Two doors along. My wife is getting her some warm milk. It is our own milk. We keep a couple of cows. Now I will wish you good night."

"Good night!" said Brading.

Inviting as the bed was, he sat by the window for some time staring out at the sea and browsing over the events of the past day. So far as he could gather, they had been cruising almost due south the whole time, and he believed that the land which he had seen shortly before sunset was France. After that all he had seen was the periodic flashing of a lighthouse far away. What this rocky islet was he had no notion, but it seemed almost certain that Frontenac and his wife were the sole inhabitants, for that particular set-up was the only one that would suit the cunning Grogan.

He was about to turn in when there came a gentle tap on the door. He went to it and found Anna outside, clad in an old but quite attractive dressing-gown.

"I saw the light from under your door and thought you might be up," she said. "My room is so stuffy. The window is almost closed and I can't open it. Can you help me?"

"Of course—unless it's screwed up."

"I don't think so. It's just jammed."

He followed her into a room that was similar to his own, but rather better furnished. The window was an old-fashioned push-up affair, and was open at the top a bare inch. He put his hands to it and succeeded in pulling the top section down about a foot. Beyond that it refused to go. The bottom half was completely immovable.

"Will that do?" he asked.

"Yes. Oh, the fresh air is marvellous! Now I shall be able to sleep."

"Good. You need it."

"Don't go yet," she whispered. "I've had no chance to talk to you since we left the ship. What do you make of all this?"

"It looks just like a variation on an old theme. Here there is no need to lock us up, or Grogan would have done it. I think we shall be treated quite well until Grogan discovers that I told him a pack of lies. Then he will come back here and give us hell."

"But there was a boat afloat in the cove where we landed."

"Yes, but don't imagine Grogan overlooked that. He had a talk with the Frontenacs before we landed. Trust him to deal with the more obvious loopholes."

"What about the Frontenacs? Couldn't we win them over?"

"Grogan wouldn't have brought us here if there was the slightest chance of that. Did you notice how Frontenac quailed before him—like an office boy before the general manager?"

"Then it means just a few days of comparative freedom, and then the rack?"

"I hope not. But tomorrow we shall get a better idea of our position. I am sure we are near the French coast, and there may be ships about, or pleasure boats."

"Isn't that a little inconsistent with your previous remark about Grogan's thoroughness?" she asked with a smile.

"Yes, but we mustn't give up hope so soon. Let's see what tomorrow brings."

" 'Tomorrow and tomorrow'," she quoted. "But you're right, Neville, and I'm not complaining. Bless you for your kindness to me. I shall never forget it."

"Nor shall I forget you, Anna. You are the most unforgettable thing in the whole of this cock-eyed world. Now good night, and sleep well."

"Good night, Neville!" she murmured.

Brading awoke at the crack of dawn and got up immediately. He went to the window and gazed out at the calm blue sea, tinged by the roseate light of the rising sun. The path which led up from the beach ran between rugged rocks, but on either side there were isolated green meadows, and he caught a glimpse of one of the cows mentioned by Frontenac, already placidly grazing. A little curving promontory almost encircled the cove in which he had landed the night before, and there was the small motor boat moving gently on the swell, and attached to a long mooring line which terminated in an anchor half buried in the sand. But the sea in that direction extended to the horizon, over which lingered the smoke of a vessel hull down.

He shaved and washed, and then donned the few articles of clothing which he had shed. A minute or two later he was outside filling his lungs with cool invigorating air. The house was bigger than he had expected, and built entirely from the local roughly-hewn reddish rock. At the rear of it was a pleasant little garden, and beyond that some timber sheds. From this side he was able to have a long view to the south. There was light mist on the sea, but he could clearly distinguish land in the distance. On passing the sheds he came upon Frontenac milking the second of his cows.

"Good morning, Mr. Brading," he said. "You're up early. Wasn't the bed comfortable?"

"Excellent, but the sunshine drew me out."

"Yes, it's a nice day. Just right for fishing, but I'm clean out of petrol until I can get to the mainland again."

Brading was quick to see the significance of that remark and did not pursue the subject. He walked down the path and past an enclosure where a score of pullets were scratching for what they could find, and finally he came to the cove. From here only the top part of the house could be seen, and since Frontenac had only just started milking the cow he pulled on the mooring line of the motor boat and slowly brought her close to where he stood. Taking off his shoes and socks, and turning up his trousers, he waded to the craft and looked inside. There was some fishing tackle and a boathook, but no sign of oars. He pushed the boat out again and waded back. Yes, Grogan had had the sense to cut off that means of escape.

He crossed the promontory and came upon a lovely little beach, backed by high rocks, in which were many caves which at high tide were full of water, but which now contained pools full of shrimps and other small creatures. He continued along the beach and in a very short time was back where he started. The whole island was but a few hundred acres.

But now the slight mist had cleared and the mainland came up like a view in a crystal globe. It looked so near, and yet he guessed it was at least four miles away to the nearest point. Nowhere could he see a sign of shipping, and the coast itself seemed void of buildings.

"Neville !"

He looked round and saw Anna approaching him. Her head was bare, and her mass of hair glinted in the sunshine. To his surprise her hitherto pallid cheeks were aglow.

"Is that complexion manufactured or natural ?" he asked.

"What a rude question ! And I considered you the most gallant of persons."

"Well, you look miles better."

"I feel better. You look better, too. Is that due to having a shave, or is it your natural beauty ?"

"Now we're quits. I've had a walk round the island. It's about the size of a pocket handkerchief, but quite lovely."

"What about the boat ?"

"Ah, the boat ! Frontenac told me quite casually that he

would like to go fishing, but alas, he has run out of petrol. Now isn't that a coincidence."

"It could be true."

"Could it ? If he has really run out of petrol how is he going to get to the mainland to lay in new supplies ? There are rowlocks in the boat for oars to be used in emergency, but the oars are not there now."

"Hm !" said Anna. "How bright they are in some matters!"

"It was only to be expected. Well, we've got to think of some other plan, and think quick, too, because I don't want to be here when Grogan returns. What was that ?"

"It sounded like a bugle. Oh, I've got it. It's to tell us that breakfast is ready. Come on, I'm famished."

Brading was relieved to find that the meal was served in a separate room from the Frontenacs. Madame shoved it through a hatch which connected with the kitchen. There were lashings of fat bacon and eggs, and the coffee was all that could be desired. Frontenac came in for a moment to ask if they had everything they wanted, but Madame kept her distance.

"I wonder if he can be bribed," mused Brading. "I've got about a hundred pounds in British and Canadian currency in my wallet."

"If you tried and failed he would know that you are contemplating escape, and would become extra vigilant. A better plan would be to try and locate the petrol, or the oars."

"Not easy with Frontenac in the offing. But let's go for a walk. No doubt you would like to see the rest of the island ?"

"Yes."

"Can you make it ?"

"Oh, yes. Don't treat me as if I were an invalid. The effects of that beastly drug have worn off."

He conducted her over the headland to the beach which he had visited earlier. The tide was now coming in, and the whole scene was enchanting. In view of the circumstances it was remarkable that Anna could be so high-spirited. He thought of the husband serving a prison sentence, and wondered what he could be like to have won the affection of this lively and fascinating creature who was skipping round the pools like a child, and trying to catch elusive shrimps in her bare hands.

"I almost envy the Frontenacs, with all this to themselves," she said. "Their needs are so few. They produce their

102

own milk, eggs and cheese, grow their own vegetables, kill a fowl now and then, and fish in the sea. Find me an island."

"But Madame doesn't give me the impression of being contented. Maybe there's a skeleton in the domestic cupboard, and it's a safe bet that your friend Grogan knows all about it. He wouldn't have entrusted us to anyone but those whom he had good reason to believe he could rely on. Now come and see this cave, before the tide reaches it."

He took her inside the eerie but beautiful place, which went in so far that the end part was almost completely dark. Here there were shells, strange seaweeds, and many pitfalls. Anna was balancing herself on a thin ridge of rock when she lost her footing and fell against him. To save her from the deep pool he caught her and held her close to him. The desire to continue to hold her, when the danger was past, was overwhelming.

"Oh, I nearly got a ducking !" she gasped.

"Well, don't do it again," he said, and hoped desperately that she would.

They made their way out into the bright sunshine and continued along the beach. After that Brading was very silent. It was dawning upon him that this interest in Anna's welfare which had prevented him from going back to his own country had passed the bounds of true altruism. Innocently, perhaps, she was weaving a spell about him that grew in intensity every minute.

"Neville, you're very quiet," she complained.

"I was thinking."

"About ways of escape ?"

"Partly."

"What else ?"

"You'd be surprised. Look, there's the mainland, and not a ship in sight. That must be a big headland which juts out there. To think that only a few miles away are shops, hotels, police-stations, and here we are almost helpless. There's little time to spare, Anna. I've a good mind to try what appears to be our only chance of beating Grogan."

"What chance do you mean ?"

"At the moment conditions are most favourable. A warm calm sea, and good visibility."

"But the boat. . . !"

"I wasn't thinking of the boat. I was thinking of swimming."

She looked at him in astonishment.

"But it's miles—five or six perhaps."

"I've swum as far as that in a lake."

"But this is the sea, with all sorts of unknown tides. No, Neville, please. Not that way?"

"It may be the only way, and I've got to make up my mind quickly, in case there is a sudden change in the weather. There is an alternative, but it doesn't appeal to me."

"What is it?"

"To copy Grogan's technique. Tie up Frontenac and his wife, and give them no food until they tell us where the petrol is hidden. Don't look so disgusted. I would rather try my luck with the sea."

"But, Neville, we haven't even tried to find the petrol. At least let us make a search."

"It would take too long, and we could only hope to do that during the night. I can't afford to wait until then, for the weather might change."

"But even if you reached the mainland you couldn't get back to England without a passport," she protested.

"I had thought of that. I could go to the nearest British Consul and get him to telephone Scotland Yard and tell them that Grogan, or one of the gang, will probably try to contact Winterton. Even if that failed I have money enough to induce someone with a good boat to make the trip back here with me and get you away."

"And if you got drowned?" asked Anna.

"You wouldn't be any worse off than you are now. The worst thing that can happen to us is to be here when Grogan returns. You can see that, can't you?"

But Anna was dead against the perilous plan. In this wonderful air and sunshine she was regaining her health amazingly. She wanted the present situation to continue, at least for a few more days.

"Why not try to bribe Frontenac?" she pleaded. "It couldn't make matters any worse. A hundred pounds to him might be a fortune, and he could pretend to Grogan that we had found the petrol without his aid and got away in the night."

"I'm certain he won't play."

"Then try Madame. I'm sure her heart's not in this. Let

me make the approach. Would you be willing to give her, say, eighty pounds if she told us where we could find the petrol?"

"Sure!"

"Then I'll tackle her as soon as her husband is out of the way. He is bound to milk the cows this evening. That will be the best opportunity. Agreed?"

Brading nodded, and Anna breathed a little sigh of relief. At the mid-day meal Anna made herself particularly pleasant to Madame, complimenting her upon her cooking and upon the cleanliness of the house, at which Madame's habitually grim face broke into a smile.

"But it must be very lonely to stay here always," said Anna.

"One get use to it," said Madame, with a thick accent. "But sometime I go vit my 'usband to the mainland to get— what you call it—groceries. Always I am sick if the sea is rough."

"And now you cannot go because you have no petrol," said Brading.

"That is so—the engine which make the electricity use it all up. But Mr. Grogan promise to bring us a bidon when he come back."

"Then how do you run the plant?" asked Brading.

"We 'ave storage battery. It last a fortnight."

"She certainly knows all the answers," said Brading later. "No doubt her husband has told her what to say to awkward questions. You won't get much change out of her."

"She doesn't yet know the price we are willing to pay for her co-operation. Anyway, I am now in her good books."

The afternoon was passed in a little sandy cove, where Brading finally broke all conventions by undressing behind a rock and plunging into the sea naked. Anna saw him swimming with the ease and grace of a fish, but had not the courage to emulate his example. Later, clad only in his short pants, he came and sat beside her. It was then she saw the bandage on his arm, which had survived the sea water.

"What have you done to your shoulder?" she asked.

"A souvenir from your friend Grogan. I think I'll get rid of the bandage now. It serves no purpose."

She watched him strip it off, and saw the thin blue puncture in the bulging muscle, now thoroughly sealed.

"What do you mean about Grogan ?"

He told her of his first encounter with Grogan at the house at Sheen, and Anna expressed her astonishment.

"Why didn't you tell me before ?" she asked.

"We've had so many other things to talk about. Anna, tell me more about your husband."

"Why ?"

"I like to hear about people who have been luckier than me."

"Luckier ! And him in prison !"

"Lucky to the extent that he has got you to come back to. Anna, be frank with me. Do you still love him ?"

Anna stirred uneasily, and her gaze appeared to be focussed on some spot far beyond him. Then her gaze shortened and met his.

"I don't know," she said. "I wish I did."

"Yet you carried out his instructions to the letter."

"What else could I do ? I was his wife. Isn't there such a thing as loyalty ?"

"You've got me there. Of course I oughtn't to ask these questions. Forget it."

"You, too. Already I've brought you so much bad luck. In a short while you'll probably be on your way back to Canada. That's how it should be."

"I cancelled my booking days ago."

"That was foolish, Neville. If you had gone, all this could have been avoided."

He looked at her intently.

"You really wish I had caught that plane ?"

"For your sake, yes. But for my sake. . . . No, I don't want to pursue the subject. My job is to wait until the man I married comes out of prison, when perhaps he will be able to prove to me that my misgivings are false."

Her tone was one of absolute finality, and Brading had the good sense to say no more. He left her for a while and came back fully dressed. Tea was non-existent in the Frontenac *ménage*, and so they passed the time meandering between the rocks and sandhills, coming back when the sun was well in the western sky. Anna noticed at once that the two cows were absent from their grazing.

"I believe they're being milked," she said. "Let's go in through the yard."

There was Frontenac on his little stool, patiently hand-milking one of the cows, while the other, as yet unmilked, was standing by. She gave Brading a glance, and Brading, taking his cue, began to talk to the milker.

"I'm going in to have a rest," said Anna. "See you later."

Anna entered the house by the yard door and found Madame preparing the evening meal in a very strong atmosphere of garlic. Madame did not appear to resent this invasion.

"Have a nice promenade?" she asked.

"Very nice. I came to question you on a certain subject, Madame Frontenac."

Madame regarded her for a moment with her jet black eyes, and pushed back her untidy hair.

"What subject, mademoiselle?"

"Our being here. You must know that we are being kept here against our will?"

"That is foolish. My 'usband say you have some business with Mistaire Grogan, and that you wish——"

"No," said Anna. "You are too intelligent to believe that. We have been kidnapped, and in holding us you and your husband are committing a breach of the law."

"But that is nonsense. Are you not free to go anywhere you like? Do we not feed you properly and attend to your comfort?"

"We are not free to leave this island, and you know it."

"How can I help it? We have no petrol left. That is unfortunate, but soon Mistaire Grogan will be back with a supply, and then——"

"We do not wish to wait until he is back. Listen, Madame, this business can only bring you ill-fortune. We need your help, and will pay you well for it."

"But how can I help?"

"You must have some idea where your husband has hidden the petrol. He would not be so stupid as to run out of petrol, which is one of your vital needs. Tell us where we can find petrol enough to get us to the mainland and we will give you fifty pounds. Your husband need know nothing about it, and we will pay a man to bring the boat back when we have landed."

Madame now became very flustered. She swore that

Anna was wrong, and that she and her husband had acted innocently. As for the petrol, her husband had told her it had all been used up.

"Sixty pounds," said Anna. "That is a nice lot of money."

"But I tell you——!"

"Seventy pounds, and my word of honour that your husband will never know."

Madame was now faltering. Anna could almost see her converting the pounds into francs.

"Come, be sensible, and do us a great service," she begged.

Madame protested no longer. Her quick brain was thinking and Anna knew that the battle was won.

"If," asked Madame in a whisper, "if I tell you, how do I know that you have the money and will pay me?"

Anna thought for a few moments. It was clear that the plan could not be carried out that night, for to make the crossing in darkness would be perilous to any but those who knew the coast.

"I will show you the money after dinner," she said. "I will plead sickness and ask you to bring a glass of milk to my room."

"And then?"

"At daybreak you must get up quietly and take me to where the petrol is hidden. Then I will hand you the money and you can steal back to bed. I promise you we will keep faith."

Madame nodded her acceptance, and Anna left the kitchen and went through the house to the front where Brading arrived a few minutes later.

"Couldn't keep him talking any longer," he said. "Or he might have become suspicious. What has happened?"

"I've settled for seventy pounds, but she insists on seeing the money first. I've promised to show it to her in my bedroom after dinner. Is that all right?"

"Yes, but can we trust her?"

"I'm sure we can. No one has ever offered her so much money for so little work. This is what I have planned."

Brading listened while she outlined the procedure and could find no fault with it. He handed Anna the money, which she took to her bedroom and locked it in a drawer. Then she came back to him, her eyes bright with excitement. They sat and watched the sunset until they were called for the evening meal.

After that things went according to plan. With the meal over, Anna retired to her room, pleading sickness. Madame brought her the glass of milk, and Anna showed her the mixed notes, which she fingered lovingly while she counted them.

"All correct?" asked Anna.

"*Oui*. I will come again at dawn. My husband is a heavy sleeper. You will be ready?"

"Yes."

Brading stole into the room a little later to find Anna sitting by the window staring out to sea.

"All set?" he whispered.

"Yes. She is to come at dawn. You had better go down just before that and pull the boat inshore, so that we can get away immediately."

"No. She might trick you at the last moment. I'll certainly go and anchor the boat close in, but then I'll wait for you under that window."

"All right. Go now, or Frontenac may wonder where you are."

"Can't you come downstairs?"

"I am supposed to be unwell. It is better I should stick to that fiction."

"Okay. Don't oversleep."

"I've no intention of even trying."

He touched her hand and then crept out of the room.

§ 14

ANNA's intention not to sleep was not carried out to the letter. She did sleep, sitting up in the chair, but only in snatches, after which she would stare out at the moonlit ocean and move restlessly. But at last, away to the east, she saw a lightening of the horizon and knew that the great moment was arriving. Hearing a very slight sound from below, she leaned out of the window and saw Brading beneath it, his face a pale blob in the semi-darkness. At sight of her he clambered on to a garden seat, so that his head came only a few feet from hers.

"Suitcase," he whispered.

Guessing his intention, she picked up the packed suitcase and lowered it until he could reach it. Without a sound he took it and vanished in the gloom. A few minutes later he was back again, and she knew that the suitcase was in the boat.

Then came Madame, as silently as a ghost. She was clad in a dressing-gown and slippers, and carried an electric torch in one hand, while the fingers of the other were placed on her lips to enjoin silence. There was some dumb play on Anna's part to indicate that the suitcase had already gone through the window. Madame looked through the window, saw Brading and motioned him to go round to the yard door. Then she pointed to the drawer from which Anna had previously produced the money. Anna opened it and this time thrust the packet into her coat pocket.

They went down the carpeted stairs in silence, passed through the passage and out into the yard where Brading was now waiting. Madame led the way to a broken-down barn on the left of the wide yard. Here the torch was necessary, for the place had no windows. In one corner were a number of farming implements, and in the other a great pile of baled hay. With Brading's help she began to move the heavy bales, and finally, stacked well back, they came upon two bidons of petrol.

"There!" said Madame. "One will be enough——"

"One will be more than enough!" said a rasping voice.

Brading swung round and saw at the open door the figure of Frontenac, with a double-barrelled sporting gun in his hands. His face was livid with rage as he brought the weapon to bear on his wife.

"Gaston!" she cried. "Put that down!"

"Get into the house!" he snapped. "You, Louise—go!"

His frightened spouse passed him and was lost to view. Brading drew Anna behind him and faced the dangerous-looking man.

"Let's talk sense," he said.

"I will do the talking. I have treated you both well since you came here——"

"We didn't come here," said Brading. "We were brought here against our wishes. You know that quite well or you would not have gone to such trouble to hide the petrol."

"I was well advised, as it turned out. I was told you are desperate criminals wanted by the police."

"Can it !" snapped Brading. "It's the other way round. It is we who want the police, and quickly."

He moved round them with the gun levelled and drove them towards the door. Brading was now looking for an opportunity to overpower him, but Frontenac never let his eye wander. Anna, clinging to Brading's arm, feared that at any moment he would break loose and risk the gun, with disastrous consequences.

"It's no use, Neville," she whispered. "Let's get out."

He nodded grimly and walked with her out into the morning sunshine. Frontenac emerged a few moments later, carrying the two bidons in one hand and the gun in the other. He placed the two bidons on the ground, close together, then stood six paces away, and fired one of the barrels at them. There was a loud report, a ripping of tin, and from a dozen holes the petrol spurted out of their containers.

"I told you there was no petrol," he shouted. "Well, now there is none, and that is a load off my mind. Now I have a few words to say to my wife—in private."

He strode off towards the house, leaving them to their reflections. Brading stared for a moment at the spurting petrol. It was useless to attempt to salvage any of it, for many of the shots had gone through the bottoms of the cans.

"Cunning Mr. Frontenac !" said Anna. "And his wife told me he was a heavy sleeper."

But Brading scarcely heard her. He was now staring down at the cove, where the motor boat was straining at its anchor.

"The tide's turning," he said. "Anna, this is it. Your scheme was worth trying, but in failing it has lost us many valuable hours. Thank goodness the fine weather still holds."

"So you're back on the old plan ?"

"Yes. It's that or nothing. Come round to the beach on the other side of the headland, where we won't be seen."

Soon they were at the spot where Brading had bathed the previous day. The usual low morning mist hung over the smooth sea and veiled the opposite shore. The tide was now running out at a good speed and there was scarcely a breath o. wind.

"Everything exactly right," said Brading. "I'm going Anna."

"You mean—now?"

"Why not? In a few hours there may be a howling gale. Please don't argue, for my mind is absolutely made up."

As proof of this he sat down on the sand and quickly removed his shoes and socks.

"The coat will be an encumbrance," he mused. "That had better go, too. Will you take care of them for me?"

Anna nodded, realizing that nothing she could say would now deter him.

"What about money?" she asked. "You will need some when you get ashore."

"Yes, that's a little difficult. It might be reduced to pulp in my trousers pocket. That scarf you are wearing might solve the problem. May I have it?"

"Of course."

He took the scarf and quickly fashioned it into the semblance of a swimming cap, knotted at the corners. Some adjustments were necessary before it made a tight fit, but at last he was satisfied.

"You have the unused bribe?" he asked.

Anna produced the wad of notes, and he extracted fifty pounds, mostly in Canadian dollars, and put the remainder with the notes which remained in his wallet, before returning the latter to the pocket of his discarded coat. Then, taking of the cap he placed the wad of dollars inside it, and donned it.

"That ought to keep them dry," he said. "Wal, here we are, all set to go."

Anna was breathing heavily. The whole situation had changed so rapidly she was at a loss for words.

"What—what am I to say to the Frontenacs?" she asked huskily.

"Say nothing. Let them find out for themselves. You can put my coat and shoes into your suitcase, and take it back to your bedroom. With any luck I'll be back in twelve hours, in a boat to take you away. It can't be more than four or five mile across that bit of water, and the sea is like a lake."

Suddenly she grasped his hand, staring at him with misty tearful eyes.

"Neville, are you sure ? I don't want you to risk your life for me. If anything should happen to you I should never forgive myself."

"Nothing's going to happen to me except a bit of exercise and getting wet. I may even pick up a small boat before I get there and save a lot of time."

He stood up, and she walked with him down to the edge of the sea with her heart beating wildly. Here he held out his hand and gripped hers.

"I'll be back," he said.

Then, as he seemed about to relinquish her hand, he drew her to him and kissed her on the lips.

"You'd better know," he said. "I love you, Anna. Perhaps I oughtn't to say this, but in case of accidents I should like you to know. Good-bye and God bless !"

Then he went striding out into the deeper water until it was breast-high and he began to swim with a powerful side-stroke. Anna stood still for a long time, watching him draw farther and farther away from her, and never once did he turn his head to gaze at the forlorn figure on the desolate beach.

Anna eventually took the discarded coat and shoes and carried out his instructions. In her bedroom she dissolved in tears, but quickly recovered and went downstairs to find Madame, very silent and tearful, preparing the breakfast table.

"I'm sorry, Madame Frontenac," she said.

"I did my best," mumbled Madame. "I did my best."

"I know."

It was very soon apparent to the Frontenacs that something was wrong, but they said nothing until the mid-day meal was served and again Brading was absent. There was much low conversation in rapid French from the kitchen, and finally Frontenac appeared, looking less fierce than when Anna had last seen him.

"It was all very regrettable," he said. "My wife does not hold my views about the sanctity of commitments. But where is Mr. Brading ? Have you quarrelled about something ?"

"No."

"Then why does he not come and eat ?"

Anna hesitated for a moment, and then decided that nothing would be lost by telling the truth.

"He is no longer here," she said.

"No longer—— But I do not understand."

"Mr. Brading by this time may be on French soil."

"But the boat is still there. He could not use it."

"That's quite true. He swam."

Frontenac stared at her incredulously.

"Swam !" he ejaculated. "But nobody can swim across. There are dangerous currents, and it is ten miles."

Now it was Anna who caught her breath. Brading had calculated the distance as four or five miles. That was long enough, but ten ! Was Frontenac lying, to frighten her ?

"Anyway, he swam," she said.

"Madness ! Lunacy ! Louise !" he bawled.

Madame came into the room, drying her wet hands on her blue apron.

"Brading has gone," said her husband. "He is trying to swim to the mainland."

"Mon Dieu !" gasped Madame with wide eyes. "He is doomed. Poor man—poor man !"

Anna waited to hear no more. The fears which she had entertained were now increased a hundredfold. She went out into the sunshine and returned to the little beach from which Brading had started the swim. There she sat, staring at the distant land, and hoping against hope.

§ 15

Two days had passed since McLean had made his call on Mr. Toovey, and during that time all Mr. Toovey's movements had been closely watched by two detectives of the local force, but nothing transpired that was detrimental to that gentleman's reputation, and not a word came from the two missing persons. But in London an enterprising newspaper man had wheedled a lot of information from an employee at the hotel from which Brading had vanished, and the gist of it appeared in bold headlines in a morning newspaper :

'YOUNG CANADIAN VISITOR VANISHES FROM HOTEL . CAR FOUND ABANDONED'

Then followed an account of the stolen suitcase from the bedroom of the missing man just prior to his disappearance. To rub it in, the writer mentioned the names of four other persons who had disappeared during the past month without trace, included in which was Anna Westmoreland. What were the police doing ? Did it not call for a thorough overhaul of police technique ? The number of unsolved murder cases was increasing annually, and the personnel of the police force was decreasing. Was it not possible to induce men of a higher standard of intelligence to enter the force ?

"What do you think, Brook ?" asked McLean, and handed him the newspaper.

Brook's subsequent reply was unprintable.

"Quite !" agreed McLean. "But anyone would think we claimed to be omnipotent as well as omniscient. Take Mr. Lancelot Toovey for example. We know he is a liar, and there's little doubt that he knows we know. But lying isn't a criminal offence in itself, and we have to know a great deal more about Mr. Toovey before we can lay a hand on him. At the moment he seems to be leading a quite exemplary life, with nothing in his mind but the enjoyment of Nature."

At that precise moment the subject of their conversation was reading the same newspaper which had caused Brook's impolite comment, and the article on the missing persons seemed no more pleasing to him than it had to Brook. He flung the newspaper aside and got on with his breakfast. A few minutes later he heard the telephone ringing outside. It stopped, and then his saturnine butler came to inform him that Mr. Magnay was asking to speak to him.

"Are you sure it was Magnay, Paul ?" he growled.

"Quite sure, sir."

Toovey rose and went to the telephone. In a few minutes he was back again.

"It was Magnay," he said. "He should be here in about twenty minutes. When he comes show him into the study."

"Very good, sir. Shall I bring the cutlets now ?"

"No. I shan't want them. But leave the coffee and turn my bath on."

It was nearly half an hour later that Mr. Magnay arrived in a big car, and by that time Toovey had had his bath and was waiting to receive his visitor. Mr. Magnay was remarkable physically. He was about five feet tall, with a curiously flat face, and diminutive hands and feet. His slanting black eyes and his lank, sparse hair gave him the appearance of a doll rather than a human being, and he might have been born anywhere east of Singapore. He bowed ceremoniously, to which Toovey nodded, and then sat in the chair which Toovey offered him.

"I did not expect you, Mr. Magnay," said Toovey.

"I myself did not expect to be in this part of your beautiful country," lisped Magnay. "But I had business not far away, and so I gave myself this pleasure. There was another reason, too. I have heard that I must return to my superiors in seven days, and that means that the present delay cannot continue much longer."

"What delay, exactly?" asked Toovey.

"The business was to have been concluded a week ago. . . ."

"But I explained that to you," interrupted Toovey. "The matter is delicate. There have been difficult negotiations through third parties. These are now practically completed, and at any moment I may hear that delivery may be instantly effected. I am as eager as you are to bring this matter to a satisfactory conclusion. You must be patient, my dear sir. I might remind you that much time was lost in the earlier negotiations, when we might have been able to settle the price matter had your people not haggled over it."

"You should not have asked too much."

"And you should not have offered so little. All this could have been prevented, but for some fool who doubted the authenticity of the goods."

Bland Mr. Magnay smiled.

"We had to be sure, and that was bound to take time. But let us not indulge in mutual recriminations. They merely waste my time and yours. Now let me tell you something : the cat—as you English say—is out of the bag."

Toovey stared at him.

"What do you mean?"

"I mean that we have reliable information that the loss has been discovered, as it was bound to be ultimately. You may see the newspapers full of it in a few days, or you may not. But you may rest assured that there will be action taken through many channels, and the game may be spoiled unless . . ."

"Unless what ?"

"Unless you conclude your business with my people at once by a delivery of the goods. In seven days I shall be gone, and if by then this matter is not satisfactorily settled you will be left to treat with other persons. That will be both difficult and dangerous, as you may well appreciate."

"The matter will be settled—probably tomorrow. Are you going back to London ?"

"Yes. You will find me at the same address."

"And the money ?"

"That is immediately available, in American dollars as you requested."

"Good ! I will see that not a moment is wasted."

Magnay then left. Toovey let him out and watched him enter the big car and drive away. It was then his expression changed to one of great anxiety. He hurried to his study and from there made a call to London, and a few moments later he recognized the voice on the other end of the line.

"Listen, Ed," he said. "Magnay has just called and given me an ultimatum. We've got only seven days. After that he'll wash his hands of the whole business, and I believe he means it. What's the position exactly ? Why didn't you ring me as you said you would ?"

"The man—Winterton—has flown to Canada to see his chief. He is expected back very soon. I'm waiting——"

"We can't afford to wait," interrupted Toovey. "There's an article in the newspaper this morning about his friend Brading. He's bound to hear about it when he returns, and the fat will be in the fire. He won't play when he knows that Brading is missing. Yes, yes, I know that the note is in Brading's handwriting, but that damned journalist fellow has spiked our guns. Don't interrupt. This is what I want you to do, and I want it done quickly. Enter the flat at latest tomorrow night, and take what we want. It may be locked in a safe, so go prepared with material to deal with that. If you are successful telephone me at once, and I will fix a meeting with Magnay. Is that clear?"

The voice at the other end said it was too damned clear. Entering the flat would be extremely difficult in view of its geographical position, but Toovey cut short his protestations.

"I know what I'm doing," he snapped. "This is a time for bold action. You've got your orders. Tomorrow night at latest. Tonight if possible. That's all I have to say. Good-bye, and good hunting!"

It was two hours after this that McLean received the report of the detective whose spell of duty ended at noon. He was a very shrewd and competent officer, well-used to the kind of work he was now engaged in.

"No movement of any kind, sir," he said. "I saw Toovey for a few minutes round about nine o'clock. He was in his dressing-gown and took a turn or two along the terrace. He was then called by his valet—to breakfast I presume. Shortly before ten o'clock a visitor called in a car. He was a little man, dark and dapper, and smartly dressed. He was let into the house by the valet and stayed there only ten minutes, when he came out accompanied by Toovey, who waved him good-bye, and then returned to the house. I did not see him again until Spencer took over."

"Can you give me a description of the car?"

"Yes sir. It was a black Daimler saloon, registration number MUO 309. There was no chauffeur. The man was quite alone. While the car was getting away I got the impression that Toovey was worried. My binoculars were powerful enough to show me every line of his face. He looked rather like a man who had received bad news."

"Nothing more?"

"No, sir."

"Thank you, Bentley!"

There was nothing very remarkable in a man receiving a visitor by car, but since Toovey had had no visitors of any kind since he had been under observation, McLean decided to check the car, and put the enquiry through to London. An hour later the information came back.

"Car owned by the Phantom Hire Service," he said. "At present let out to a Mr. Chelli Magnay, a foreign visitor from Saigon, now staying at the Overton Hotel, Piccadilly. I think

I'll run up to town and see Mr. Magnay. You had better stay on here and take the observation reports."

McLean arrived in London late in the evening, and having had his dinner on the train, he went straight to the Overton Hotel and enquired after Mr. Magnay. After a rather long wait he was informed that Mr. Magnay was in the dining-room, having come back from the country rather late. Did he wish to send Mr. Magnay a message?

"Yes. Tell him someone wishes to see him in the lounge as soon as he has finished his meal. No, no name."

The receptionist looked at him rather suspiciously, but promised to have the message conveyed. Mr. Magnay seemed in no hurry to finish his meal, and half an hour passed before the receptionist brought him to where McLean was sitting.

"You wished to see me, sir?" he asked politely.

"Yes. It is purely a routine matter. I am a police officer, making a check of passports. You may like to see my warrant?"

Magnay shrugged his shoulders as if that was a matter of no consequence, but McLean showed him the warrant.

"You wish to see my passport?" he asked.

"Please."

"Then you must excuse me a moment. It is in my room."

McLean nodded, and he went off, to return in a few minutes with a passport issued by the French authorities in Saigon. It was a very much used document, bearing visas and embarkation stamps galore. It gave his nationality as Indonesian and his occupation as 'Merchant.'

"Are you here on business?" asked McLean.

"Partly business, and partly holiday."

"Do you propose to stay much longer?"

"No. About another week. Then I shall go to Paris, and from Paris back to Saigon."

McLean handed him back the passport, the authenticity of which was beyond doubt.

"Do you happen to know a man named Lancelot Toovey?" he asked quite casually.

Mr. Magnay was shrewd enough not to deny that he did, but he raised his slanting eyebrows in surprise.

"How strange that you should ask that!" he said. "I saw my old friend only this morning. I was in the neighbourhood of Falmouth where he lives, and took the opportunity to make a call."

"A business call?"

"It was intended to be, but he told me that he had retired from business a long time ago and was enjoying his retirement. So he should in that lovely place. Do you know it?"

"Yes. It is certainly a beautiful spot. But I had no idea that Toovey was ever in business."

"Oh, yes. For some time he ran a fleet of small ships, but later he sold out and got into oil. Later still he became interested in culture pearls. That is how I met him, for I represent a Japanese firm trading in cultured pearls so like the natural article that even the experts can be mistaken. Here is a specimen."

He took the beautiful pearl pin from his tie and handed it to McLean. McLean knew next to nothing about pearls, but this one seemed to be of surpassing beauty. He handed it back.

"So Toovey traded in pearls?" he asked.

"Yes. He would trade in anything which produced good results, and who can blame him? I was sorry to hear that he was no longer interested in any sort of business. Perhaps when I have enough money I shall follow his example and build myself a nice house above the sea, but not here in England where the sun shines so seldom."

"There are compensations."

"Indeed there are. I have spent a most enjoyable time here, and shall leave with great regret."

"Well, I wish you a good voyage," said McLean. "Sorry to have troubled you."

"My pleasure," said Magnay. "Good night, sir!"

McLean left the lounge, his mind full of doubt about the wily Indonesian. It seemed to him strange that this man, having located an old friend in the person of Toovey, should have limited his call at Toovey's house to a few minutes. It looked as if he had gone there with a definite message, and having delivered it had left without much further parley. That was consistent with the detective's report on Toovey's reaction. He was about to pass the manager's office when he stopped and knocked on the door. A voice told him to come in, and he entered to find the manager busy checking some accounts.

"What can I do for you, sir ?" he asked.

McLean produced his warrant and the manager became all attention as he waved his visitor into a chair.

"You have a guest staying here—an Indonesian named Magnay ?"

"That is so. He has been with us quite a time. I think about seven weeks."

"What do you know about him ?"

"Not a great deal. He stayed here before, about a year ago. I think he is a business man."

"Has he any friends in the hotel ?"

"I think not—except of course certain people he has met here."

"Has he some connections in the West Country ?"

"That may be possible. I seemed to remember certain long-distance telephone calls charged on his account."

"Can they be checked ?"

The manager looked down his long nose, apparently embarrassed by the question.

"If you ask for them I can't very well refuse," he said.

"I do ask. It is necessary that I check up certain statements made to me by Mr. Magnay."

"Very well, Inspector."

He picked up the telephone receiver and pushed one of the numerous buttons on the panel.

"Oh, Helen," he said. "I should like particulars of telephone trunk calls charged to No. 98 since he has been here. Can you dig them out fairly quickly ? Good. Send them in to me when you have finished."

"I'm sorry to give you all this trouble," said McLean.

"Not at all, Inspector. I don't think the girl will keep you long. She's a very competent person. As for Mr. Magnay—he's quite a charming man. Occupies one of our best suites, and is well-liked by the staff."

"Meaning he tips well ?" asked McLean with a smile.

"There may be something in that. So far, unfortunately, he hasn't attempted to tip me."

McLean laughed and accepted a cigarette. It was not long before a boy arrived with a slip bearing dates, telephone numbers and charges. He handed it to the manager, who passed it to McLean, to whom it was most illuminating, for with the exception of three calls to Paris and one to Rome, the rest, spread over the period of six weeks, were all to the same telephone number at Falmouth, and that number, McLean had not the slightest doubt, was Mr. Toovey's.

"You don't happen to have heard of a man named Lancelot Toovey?" asked McLean.

"Why, yes. I'm sure I have. I'm almost positive he stayed here about a year ago for a few nights. I have the old registers here, and think I can find the date. It was just about this time of the year."

He took a large register from the file and turned over the pages, running his fingers down the names. Finally he gave a little cry of satisfaction.

"Here it is," he said. "Lancelot Toovey, The Sanctuary, Falmouth. Yes, he stayed three days."

"And was Mr. Magnay here at that time?"

The manager turned back the pages.

"Yes. He arrived two days before Toovey."

"Splendid!" said McLean. "I am very grateful to you for the information. I won't keep you any longer."

It was now half-past nine, and McLean had to decide whether he should spend the night in town or under his own roof in the heart of Surrey. It was not remarkable that he chose to do the latter, and about an hour later he surprised his lovely young wife by suddenly appearing in the sitting-room of the cottage, where she was wrestling with the last few clues to a crossword puzzle.

"Robert!" she gasped. "I thought you were in Cornwall."

"I was until noon. But what a way to welcome a husband! Even the prodigal son had a warmer reception."

Valerie put down the pencil, slipped into his arms and took his warm kiss. Then she straightened his tie.

"Eternal enigmas—women," he said. "I believe you would prefer my eyes to be crooked than my tie."

"The first cannot be remedied, the second can. Oh, but I'm glad to see you. I've had the rottenest sort of day. The woman didn't turn up, just when I had made all preparations to spring-clean our bedroom."

"Perhaps she had a notion what was in your mind."

"Anyway, I had to do it myself. I think you'll like it. I've turned the beds round. Oh, have you eaten?"

"Yes—on the train."

"Good! Now tell me all the news. Is that stupid case in the bag?"

"It's neither stupid nor in the bag, and mark this, my precious, this is but a fleeting respite. I go back to Cornwall tomorrow."

"You would—you brute! But tell me, is it a really big case, or just one of those things?"

"I love you when you make things so crystal clear. If 'one of those things' includes the kidnapping of two persons, with the possibility of murder thrown in, then you might apply that ghastly phrase. But let's not talk about that. I'm not proud of my achievements so far, although I've had a little success this evening. Suppose you get me a drink?"

"On one condition. That you tell me exactly what you have been up to."

"All right."

Valerie produced the drinks, and McLean told her briefly what had happened since he last saw her. Valerie hung on his words, for not yet had she grown blasé about her husband's occupation and activities.

"So you haven't really got very far?" she said, when he had finished.

"Only as far as establishing that Magnay and Toovey are associates, and almost certainly behind the kidnappings. At least Toovey is. Exactly where Magnay comes into it I have yet to discover."

"And you've never seen the girl at all?"

"No, nor the Canadian who befriended her. But I've got a photograph of the girl. Like to see it?"

"Yes."

McLean produced the photograph, and Valerie quizzed it critically.

"Quite pretty," she said. "And a beautiful figure. Wish I could get myself down to those proportions."

"You're very nice as you are."

"You're just an old Turk. You like your women plump."

"Yes, but in the right places. Now let's go to bed. I'm tired and so are you."

"I'll just get the eleven o'clock time signal," yawned Valerie. "My watch has gone haywire, and I doubt that bracket clock."

She went to the radio and switched on the Home Service, but the pips had gone and the announcer was giving a brief summary of the news.

"That means it's past eleven," said Valerie, adjusting her watch.

"I could have told you so. It is exactly two minutes past. No, don't switch off. What's he saying?"

". . . escaped from a working party," said the announcer. "He attacked a warder, causing him grievous injury. His name is Harold Besterling, and until this incident he was very well behaved. The prison officials believe it will be impossible for him to get away from the island, around which a cordon has been placed. That is the end of the news. The Home Service is now closing down."

"It must be Parkhurst, in the Isle of Wight," said McLean.

"How exciting! Do you know the man?"

"Besterling! The name seems to ring a bell, but at the moment I can't place him. Anyway, it isn't my pigeon, thank goodness! Now come to bed."

§16

THE next day was one of surprises for McLean. He had planned to call at Scotland Yard to see if any message had come from Brook, and in the absence of any such message to go back to Cornwall on the early train, but things worked out quite differently.

He had an early breakfast, said goodbye to Valerie, and caught the local train to Waterloo, beguiling the time by reading the various reports about the escaped convict in the several newspapers which he bought at the bookstall. The latest news was that the man was still at large, but the police had little doubt that he would be captured very soon.

Arrived at the office he found no message from Brook, and presumed that Mr. Toovey was continuing to live his ostensibly quiet and uneventful life under the watchful eyes of the two detectives. His thoughts turned to the man he had seen the previous evening, Mr. Magnay, and it seemed to him highly desirable that Mr. Magnay should not suddenly vanish into the blue, and so two plain clothes men were detailed to treat him as Toovey was being treated. He was checking up the time of his train back to Falmouth when Inspector Drewe blew into his office to get some information on a private matter.

"Actually I thought you were in the West Country," he said. "But Rowlands told me you were back. How are things?"

"Fair to middling, as the farmers say. I'm just going back."

"Wish I was. Could do with a breath of fresh air. Did you read about the escaped convict?"

"Yes. Have they picked him up?"

"Not yet. He was one of my pigeons, too. I arrested him over a year ago while he was on the run. I can't understand him slugging a warder. I remember him asking me how long he would actually be in prison with a three years' sentence. I told him he would come out in two years and three months if he was a good boy. He said he meant to be a very good boy. Yet he goes and does a thing which will put him back for a further five years or more. Shows you can't trust those quiet-looking guys."

"What did he do to get in jail?"

"Stole some money from the man who employed him, and it wasn't his first offence by a long chalk. I knew him before he got that basinful. A slick guy, with a B.B.C. accent, and a darling with the ladies. A man of good family who went all wrong. Never did an honest day's work in his life. Married quite a decent type of girl, too. When we pulled him in we tried to find her, because we thought that he had handed her some of the money he took, but she had packed up and decamped overnight. Poor kid! She must have got a raw deal. I could have told her a few things about him."

"Who was she?" asked McLean.

"I don't know, but she was a real beauty. Rather long, oval face, with high cheekbones, and a sad sort of expression. May have been an actress of sorts, but she wasn't half so good an actor as he was. 'My Anna,' he boasted, 'could knock half the beauty queens into a cocked hat,' and he wasn't far wrong."

"Anna," mused McLean. "I'm always falling foul of Anna's. Here's another one of them."

He produced the photograph of the missing girl, and Drewe gave an involuntary start.

"That is the girl," he said. "Anna Besterling. Taken years before I saw her with Besterling, and looking happier. I'll put my shirt on her being Mrs. Besterling."

"I know her as Anna Westmoreland."

"The girl who is missing?"

"Yes."

"Then why the blazes didn't you publish it?"

"I did, but you were probably too busy finding out the winner of the two-thirty to notice it."

"Well, I like that," snorted Drewe. "Certainly I've been busy, but not backing horses. If I were to back any horse it would drop down dead at the starting post. Anyway, glad to be of service. Make the most of it."

McLean did make the most of it. He delved into the files and found the records of Harold Besterling, with his photograph, fingerprints and physical description. He had been to prison three times and the last occasion was a year ago, when he had been found guilty of stealing a sum of money from his employer, a Mr. Edwin Grogan, of Cedar Avenue, Streatham.

McLean stared at the handsome and somewhat cynical features of Besterling. There was culture in that face, but something of cruelty, too. He was not so surprised as Drewe had been that this man had resorted to brute force when his personal interest was at stake. Now he was free temporarily, but penned up in a comparatively small island where the police and the prison warders were optimistic about his recapture.

Was it possible that Besterling knew of his wife's disappearance and had some inkling of what had happened to her? If so it might well have started him on his wild and desperate course. On the other hand, it might simply be the impulsive act of a man tired to death of prison life and ready to risk everything on a most hazardous venture.

But, anyway, the new information seemed worth following up, and McLean resolved to pay a visit to Mr. Edwin Grogan, who might possibly contribute something to the solution of the mystery. He was about to leave when to his amazement Sergeant Brook entered the office, looking tired and travel-worn.

"What on earth are you doing here?" asked McLean.

"I couldn't get in touch with you. There was no time. Something happened last night just as I was going to bed. Sinclair came to the hotel and told me that Toovey had caught the night train to London. He had followed Toovey's car to the station on his motor-bike and saw him board the train. The man at the ticket office confirmed that Toovey had bought a first-class ticket to Waterloo. I looked up the time-table and found that the train was a slow one, and didn't reach Waterloo until 8 a.m. There seemed only one thing to do."

"Beat the train ?"

"Yes. Luckily the car was full of petrol, so I got aboard and let her go. I had plenty of time in hand, but darn me if I didn't get a puncture right in the middle of nowhere and had to change a wheel. But worse was to come. Some idiot had left the spare wheel with an unmended puncture in it, and I had to do a puncture repair. Getting that big tyre off the rim was hell. It took me ages. Well, I got away at last, and then had to go hell for leather. I reached Waterloo five minutes after the train was due in, but fortunately the train was late too. I waited for it, close to the bookstall. Not many people were travelling, and I had no difficulty in spotting Toovey. He was carrying a small suitcase, and I followed him to the taxi queue. He was third in line, so I had to hurry to the car in case he should get away and leave me stranded."

"Go on," said McLean. "You're doing well."

"I trailed him to a small hotel near Lancaster Gate. It's called the Dorset, I gave him a few minutes and then went in and found his name in the register, with Room 26 marked against it. I reckoned he was safe for a bit and then had a bite of breakfast and came here."

"Good work ! I suppose you haven't seen the morning newspapers ?"

"Not yet."

"Then take a look at that."

McLean handed him a newspaper across the front page of which was splashed the news of Besterling's escape from jail. Brook read it and then looked up at McLean uncomprehendingly.

"Harold Besterling is Anna Westmoreland's husband. After her husband's arrest she appears to have used her maiden name, for fairly obvious reasons."

"What does it add up to ?"

"I don't pretend to know, but I've been looking up the Besterling case. There's a man named Grogan who might be worth visiting. He was the plaintiff in that affair. He lives out at Streatham, and I propose going out there now. Toovey can wait for a bit. I expect you need sleep after your night on the road?"

But Brook was used to missing a night's sleep, and within a few minutes he and McLean were in the car making towards Streatham. Cedar Avenue lay well away from the centre of the town. It contained about a dozen commodious, but rather ugly, Victorian houses, all lying back in spacious gardens, and McLean had to enquire twice before he discovered that Edwin Grogan occupied No. 8.

A semi-circular drive passed round a dense shrubbery and soon revealed the main entrance porch. Here McLean stopped the car and rang the bell at the front door. There was some delay, and finally a middle-aged man opened the door and peered at the visitors.

"Does Mr. Edwin Grogan live here?" asked McLean.

"Yes sir, but he is not at 'ome now."

"Will he be home later?"

"Not for some time. He is abroad. Maybe he will return next week, perhaps later. I cannot say."

The accent and the slight gesticulation suggested a French origin.

"Are you a member of the family?" asked McLean.

"Oh no. I am chauffeur-gardener here, and my wife is housekeeper. We look after the house while Mr. Grogan is abroad."

"Can you tell me where he may be found?"

"I think he is at Nice. We had a postcard a few days ago, but there was no address on it. He said he would be away two or three weeks, but so far he has been gone only ten days. Will you leave a card?"

"No, it doesn't matter. I will get in touch with Mr. Grogan when he returns. Sorry to have troubled you."

"Not at all, sir. Good day!"

When they were back in the car McLean lighted a cigarette reflectively.

"Telling untruths successfully is an art," he said. "Some people never learn it."

"You think that chap was lying?"

"Didn't you?"

"Well, I had my doubts. But why should he lie?"

"I rather wish I knew. But stop at that garage in the drive."

Brook started the car, but stopped when they were round the bend and near the private garage. McLean got out and put his hand on the sliding door. It was not locked and moved back easily. The place was empty except for some oddments, and on the concrete floor were some oil drips, obviously from a crankcase. He went inside and investigated the oil patch. It was quite wet.

"I'm willing to bet that a car stood there within twelve hours," he said. "Yet we are told that Grogan went abroad ten days ago. What do you say to that?"

"The chauffeur may have made a few bob on the side by letting the garage to someone else."

"Quite a reasonable theory," said McLean. "But I still cling to my own conclusion—that Grogan is not on the French Riviera, and that for reasons of his own he does not want to be questioned about Besterling. Alternatively he may have been scared by the newspapers' announcement of Besterling's escape."

"But Besterling wouldn't dare show up here," protested Brook. "Grogan would have him back in prison in a twinkling."

"He might, or he might not. We know far too little about their relationship to be sure of anything. But I'd like to settle this little problem of the car. We might do worse than come back here this evening and see if the garage is still empty. Now you'd better get home and have some sleep."

It was at half-past six in the evening when Brook turned up at the office, looking refreshed and eager. McLean in the meantime had satisfied himself that Toovey and Magnay were still at their respective hotels and that no contact had taken place between them, unless it was by telephone.

"But it's all very significant," he said. "Toovey didn't come to London for the good of his health. We have to find out just why he did come so hurriedly."

"Are we going down to Streatham again?" asked Brook.

"Yes, in a few minutes. I warn you there is more than a

slight breeze blowing at top level. Certain persons do not think much of our progress so far. A man and a woman missing—the possibility of murder not ruled out—and you and I chasing phantoms. Why don't we get a real move on?"

"G-r-r-r!" growled Brook. "Well, I'll go and see about the car."

It was some minutes later when McLean, hurrying along the corridor to join Brook, ran into Inspector Drewe, who seemed to be in no less a hurry.

"What's the latest news of the escaped convict?" asked McLean.

"Besterling? The swine has made it. Damned smart of him to get away from the island, but there's a motor boat missing from a mooring, and that says a lot."

"I thought they had him in a ring?"

"So did I. Now it appears he's got a gun. One of his prison pals blabbed that much. So if you see him, watch out."

"I should like to see him as much as you would. He's the point where our trails cross."

Drewe gave a grunt and went on his way. A few minutes later McLean and Brook set off again for Streatham, and here, on this occasion, good fortune came his way, for as he entered the drive he saw a broad-shouldered man close the door of the garage and then walk the short distance to the house. McLean passed him in the police car and then waited for him outside the main entrance to the house. As he came forward McLean scanned the dark, clean-shaven face, with its strong jaws and large nose.

"Mr. Edwin Grogan?" he asked.

"Yes."

"Good! I called here earlier today, but was told you were abroad."

"I was, but I arrived home this afternoon."

"In your car?"

"No. I came by train. But who are you, may I ask?"

"Police officers. I should like to ask you some questions about a man named Besterling whom, I think, you knew very well."

"Very well indeed, to my sorrow. He is now serving a sentence in some prison."

"Not now. He escaped last night."

Grogan regarded him with incredulity.

"The devil he has!" he said. "But please come inside. I don't like this cold wind."

He conducted them into the hall and from there to a well-furnished sitting-room, where he helped himself to a whisky and soda from a tray on a low table.

"Would you care to join me?" he asked.

McLean shook his head and Grogan drank deeply from his glass, and then lighted a cigar.

"I suppose you know it was I who put Besterling in jail?" he asked.

"Yes. I read up the case a few hours ago. I thought you might be able to tell me more about him than appears in the records. Did you know his wife?"

"Very slightly. Rather a superior type, I thought, but then Besterling had quite a good background. I gave him a job when he was hard up, but never dreamed he would finish up by robbing me."

"What happened to his wife after he was arrested?"

"She vanished completely. Only part of the money which Besterling stole was found on him, and it was assumed that he had handed the rest to his wife. The police went to the flat which they occupied, but they were too late. She had packed up and gone. It was only a furnished flat."

"Do you know any associates of Besterling with whom he might possibly make contact?"

"No. He kept his private life very much to himself. After the trial I was very much surprised to learn that he had been convicted before."

"Do you still run the business?"

"No. After Besterling's arrest I had a good offer for the premises and decided to accept it and retire here."

"Did you know Mrs. Besterling before she was married?"

"No. He had been married about a year before I met her."

"Then you do not know that Mrs. Besterling has been kidnapped?"

"No. When did that happen?"

"Only a week or two ago. It was in the newspapers, but her name was given as Anna Westmoreland."

"Yes, I saw that, but did not connect it with Besterling's wife."

"There were photographs of her."

"Certainly not in *The Times* or the *Financial News*, which are the only two papers which interest me. But is the kidnapping proved? She had good reason to disappear without being kidnapped."

"It was proved."

"How extraordinary! Afraid I can't help you there. It's possible that she was no better than her husband turned out to be, and got herself mixed up in some racket. What are the chances of Besterling being recaptured?"

"Very good, I should think. By this time every police force in the country will be looking for him and——"

There was a rap on the door and the chauffeur-gardener entered and gazed with surprise at McLean and Brook.

"What is it, Leon?" asked Grogan.

"You're wanted on the telephone, sir."

Grogan looked at McLean.

"Excuse me a moment," he said.

"Certainly."

As soon as he had left, McLean went to some magazines which were lying on the couch. Underneath were some newspapers. They were journals of the popular type.

"And he only reads *The Times* and the *Financial News*," scoffed McLean.

"You think he's a fake?"

"I think that anything he may say about Besterling and his wife should be treated with suspicion, and that goes for his manservant, Leon. This case bristles with liars, and it's anybody's guess who is the greatest. To hear some witness tell the obvious truth would be a pleasant experience."

He went to the door which Grogan had closed behind him, and opened it a few inches. Outside there was dead silence. He closed it again and came back to Brook.

"I even doubt the telephone call," he said. "Leon may have seen us when we were outside the house, and took the opportunity to entice his employer away from us, to get fresh instructions in case we should question him again."

"You know, sir," said Brook. "I can't help thinking I've seen that fellow before. This morning that thought crossed my mind, but I can't place him."

"That's curious. I had the same feeling. That little scar

shaped like a crescent on the right cheek seemed familiar. It could have been in a photograph somewhere, at some time——"

McLean stopped as the door opened and Grogan returned. He apologized for the interruption.

"Where were we exactly?" he asked. "Oh yes, you were saying that in your opinion Besterling hadn't much chance. I wish I could be as sure.'"

"You think you may possibly be in some danger?"

"Well—he's a curious type of man. Charming when everything goes the way he wants it, but an awkward customer when things go against him. I shall never forget the look he gave me when he was in the dock. If looks could kill I shouldn't be here now."

"I shouldn't worry," said McLean. "He's probably safely back in a cell by now. By the way, did your chauffeur ever meet Besterling?"

"I think he may have seen him once or twice when he drove me to the office, as he sometimes did. But I doubt if he's ever spoken to him."

"How long has the chauffeur been in your service?"

"About four years. He's useful to me because he is Anglo-French, and France is a country I love visiting."

"But you left him here on your recent trip," said McLean swiftly.

"Yes. I didn't want to take the car. It uses so much time."

"I think I should like a word with him, in private."

"Certainly. But I doubt very much whether he is able to give you any useful information. I will call him."

He pushed a bell, and a few moments later Leon knocked and entered.

"Oh, Leon," said Grogan. "This gentleman, who is from the police, would like to ask you a few questions. I will leave you with him."

Leon nodded gravely, and Grogan then left the room. McLean referred to his note-book, with the object of keeping Leon on tenterhooks. He turned over the pages in leisurely fashion while keeping an eye on the obviously nervous man.

"What is your full name?" he asked ultimately.

"Leon Jacob Vigny."

"Where were you born?"

"Aix in Provence—1921."

"French ?"

"My father was French, my mother English."

"Do you know a man named Besterling, who for some time was in Mr. Grogan's employ ?"

"I have seen him a few times, but never spoken to him, except to say 'good-morning'."

"Did you ever meet his wife ?"

"No, sir."

"Do you remember the time when Besterling was sent to prison ?"

"Oh, yes. Mr. Grogan was very upset about it."

"Did you read the newspapers this morning ?"

"No, sir. I never read the newspapers until the late evening when Mr. Grogan has finished with them."

"So you do not know that Besterling escaped from prison yesterday ?"

"No, sir."

"Have you taken out naturalization papers in this country ?"

"No, sir, but I am thinking of applying for them."

"Then you must have a French passport ?"

"Yes, sir."

"I should like to see it."

"I'm afraid I can't find it at once," said Vigny. "I looked for it some weeks ago when I thought Mr. Grogan would be taking me with him to France, but it seems to have been mislaid."

"When did you last have occasion to use it ?"

"Last year, when we went to Cannes."

"You think it is somewhere in the house ?"

"It must be."

"Then you must find it and send it to me as soon as possible. Where and when was the passport issued ?"

"Paris—August I think—1950."

"What was your occupation before you entered Mr. Grogan's employ ?"

"I was a taxi-driver."

"Address ?"

"Number 24 Rue Malines, Montmartre."

"Your wife is housekeeper here ?"

"Yes."

"Is she French or English?"

"English. I met her in Paris, before we came here."

"Is she in the house now?"

"No, sir. She went to the cinema at six o'clock."

"Well, that's all," said McLean. "But don't forget to send me that passport. Here's a card, with my address on it."

Vigny took the card, nodded his head, and went out. Brook, who had taken shorthand notes, closed his book and put it back into his pocket.

"Very convenient to lose one's passport—at times," he ruminated. "Shouldn't be surprised if he's lost it for ever."

"In that case we'll see what Paris has to say."

Grogan then entered the room, smiling and unperturbed.

"Is there anything else I can do?" he asked.

"No, thank you. Vigny doesn't seem to know much about Besterling, as you said. Sorry to have troubled you."

"Not at all."

McLean drove back to Scotland Yard with the features of Leon Vigny still in his mind's eye, but try as he might he could not remember where he had seen that face before. He looked up the criminal files, but failed to find the name there.

"I'll sleep on it," he said to Brook.

"Me, too," said Brook.

§17

It was on the following morning that McLean received a surprise. He found on his desk a note from an Inspector Howe from another division, asking him to see him as soon as he arrived, and he went along to Howe's office, to find Howe waiting to go home, as he had been on night duty.

"You're on the Westmoreland case, aren't you, Mac?" he asked.

"Yes, but her real name is Mrs. Besterling."

"Mixed up with a fellow named Brading?"

"Yes. What do you know about him?"

"Nothing. But last night a man was caught leaving a flat

at Graham Mansions in suspicious circumstances. Actually there were two men, but the first had time to get away. The constable on beat got the second man, who was coming down from the second floor by a drainpipe. We've got him here. He refuses to give any name or address. No booty of any sort on him, but he appears to have entered the flat of a Mr. Charles Winterton, who is away from home. The place was ransacked, but it's impossible to say what is missing until we see the tenant. He is London representative of the *Toronto Sentinel* and we are informed that he is now on his way home from Toronto, by air."

"Where does Brading come in ?" asked McLean.

"Give me time. On searching the chap this note came to light. It is signed by Neville Brading. Can it be possible that he is the man you are looking for ?"

McLean took the note and read it aloud :

"Dear Charles,

I am wanting that parcel I left in your charge, but can't get up to town. Will you kindly give it to the bearer, and take his receipt for it ? Will drop in and see you some time next week.

Neville Brading."

On the reverse side was Winterton's address, written in a different handwriting.

"It's certainly the same man," said McLean. "But I've no means of checking the handwriting. The parcel he refers to plays a very large part in this case. At what time was the man caught ?"

"One o'clock this morning."

"I should like to see him."

"I thought you might. I'll get him up."

A few minutes later the arrested man entered the room, with a constable bringing up the rear. McLean could scarcely suppress a cry of surprise, for the prisoner was none other than Leon Vigny.

"You know him ?" asked Howe.

"Oh yes, I know him. I saw him as recently as last evening, when he told me his name was Leon Vigny, which I have good reason to doubt. May I question him ?"

"Go right ahead."

"Now, Vigny," said McLean. "How do you come to be in possession of this note ?"

"I have nothing to say," said Vigny.

"Then you are very foolish. If Mr. Brading gave you this note it might make things a little easier for you, but did he?"

"Yes."

"When and where?"

"I can't tell you, but if you doubt the handwriting you can check it with the entry in the register of the hotel where he stayed."

"Thank you for the information, but that is not what I asked. Where is Mr. Brading?"

"I do not know."

"You know where he was when he gave you the note, if that is true."

Vigny said nothing more. He seemed to have realized that any sort of reply to McLean's questions would only lead him deeper into the mire.

"Very well," said McLean. "But it might be well if you considered your position. Brading is missing, and for all we know may now be dead. It's in your interest that he should be found alive. Think that over."

Vigny still remained silent, and at a sign from Howe he was taken away.

"Well, there it is," said Howe. "I've questioned him about the man who was with him, but he won't budge. The question is—did the other man get away with the parcel they were after? The constable who made the arrest believes there was a car in the offing, for he heard an engine start up while he was grabbing Vigny. It looks as if they hoped to get that parcel from Winterton, but when they discovered the flat was empty they decided to burgle it. Any idea what's in the parcel?"

"None at all, but it must be something of great value, for they have gone to endless trouble and expense to get hold of it. Do you want this note?"

"No. You'd better keep it."

McLean returned to his office to find Brook there. He told Brook what had transpired, and caused that worthy to raise his eyebrows in amazement.

"Doesn't make sense," he protested. "The note can't be genuine. If Brading had had the parcel he wouldn't have told me about the suitcase, which was stolen from his bedroom.

Why should he have handed it to the man Winterton, and then sent someone else to collect it ? All along he has behaved like an innocent man. I think the note is a fake."

"We can soon settle that point. I want you to run along to Brading's hotel and make an exact tracing of his entry in the hotel register——"

He was interrupted by the buzzer. Brook picked up the receiver and then stared at McLean.

"It's Winterton downstairs—asking to see you."

"Splendid ! Go and get him."

A minute or two later Brook returned with a lanky man of about forty years of age.

"Mr. Charles Winterton ?" asked McLean.

"Sure !" replied Winterton in a strong Canadian accent. "I've just arrived by air from Canada. Stopped at my flat to park my grips and found the place in an unholy mess. I was given a note by the hall porter asking me to contact Inspector Howe, but downstairs the Inspector had left a message to tell me to see you, if he should be out. Funny thing that burglary. So far as I can see there's not a thing missing."

"Are you a friend of Neville Brading ?" asked McLean.

"Yep. I've known him since we were kids. He looked me up just before I was called back to headquarters."

"He's missing."

Winterton stared incredulously.

"I don't get it," he said. "I thought he was back in Canada by now."

"He was kidnapped. I suppose you would know his handwriting ?"

"Sure. We wrote to each other once or twice a year."

McLean produced the note and handed it to Winterton, whose face became blank with astonishment as he read the message.

"Nev wrote this all right," he said. "But I don't know what he's talking about. He never left any parcel with me."

"You have no doubt about the handwriting ?"

"None at all."

"That helps a little," said McLean. "I think it means that Brading was playing for time. Did he know of your impending trip to your head office ?"

"Yes. I told him."

McLean's mind worked swiftly. He thought he could see the situation. Brading had been kidnapped because of his association with Anna. The gang believed that he had handled and disposed of the mysterious parcel. Probably under threat he had written the note, knowing that days must pass before Winterton could receive it—precious days during which he hoped some aid would come to him. Now the truth was out and the subterfuge exploded. It looked rather bad for Brading, wherever he was, and for Anna, who was doubtless in a similar plight.

"There's no need to go to the hotel, Brook," he said. "Mr. Winterton has settled that matter for us."

"Say," interjected Winterton. "Where did that note come from ?"

"It was taken from the man who was arrested."

"Then he must know where Brading is ?"

"Yes, but he won't talk—yet."

"You think he may—later ?"

"It's possible, but by no means certain. He's given us a name, but I rather doubt if it's his real name. If we can establish his identity it might help a lot. At the moment he believes in the old adage that silence is golden. As a matter of interest— had you possessed the parcel would you have handed it to anyone on the strength of this note ?"

"No, I wouldn't. I should have suspected the absence of any address on the notepaper. Brading's a businesslike guy. He wouldn't act that way. He wouldn't expect me to hand over any property of his without being certain it was on the level."

"I agree entirely," said McLean. "Well, by some means or other we've got to get the prisoner to talk."

"Wal, I guess I could make a few suggestions," drawled Winterton.

"I'm sure you could," laughed McLean. "But we happen to be in England."

The buzzer sounded again and Brook took up the receiver.

"Mr. Grogan waiting to see you, sir," he said, as if the matter was completely trivial.

"How interesting !" said McLean. "I was about to ring him, I'll see him in a minute."

Winterton took the cue, and said that unless McLean had

anything more to ask him he would go back and try to get his flat in some sort of order.

"That's all at the moment, Mr. Winterton," said McLean. "Thank you for calling."

A minute or two later Grogan was shown into the office. McLean offered him a seat which he took.

"Now, Mr. Grogan, what is the trouble ?" McLean asked.

"I've been robbed. Last night I went to bed about eleven o'clock, leaving only Vigny to do the locking up. This morning I discovered that he and his wife had gone, and presumably in my car. I never heard a sound, but then, as you know, the garage is some distance from the house."

"Have they taken anything else ?"

"Not so far as I can discover. The curious thing is that their wages are due this morning. One would have expected they would have waited to draw their wages."

"It may have been due to my demand to see Vigny's passport," said McLean.

"But why ? His passport is in order."

"How do you know ?"

"Well, he has been to France with me several times, and his passport was never in question."

"He told me he had lost the passport. But there may be other reasons. If you will give me details of the car I will see that the information is circulated."

McLean handed Grogan a sheet of paper and a pen, and Grogan wrote down the relevant details, which McLean scanned and placed in a clip.

"Now I have a surprise for you, Mr. Grogan," he said. "Vigny is in custody."

"In custody ? But how did you know——?"

"We didn't know—about the theft of the car. He was caught leaving the premises of a man named Winterton, which he had entered with a second man with felonious intent."

Grogan expressed extreme surprise.

"Incredible !" he said. "I would never have believed it—at least not until he took my car. I suppose you have the car ?"

"Not yet. But now we have the details it shouldn't be long before we pick it up. Do you know any friend of Vigny's who might have joined him in this affair ?"

"No."

"How did you come to meet him and take him into your employ?"

"It was in Paris, about four years ago. I had no car and used to employ him to drive me about. He mentioned that he would like to come to England with his wife, who was a good housekeeper. I had just bought my present house and needed someone to run it for me, so we came to terms. He did not come with me at once, but followed when he had obtained the necessary permit. All this time he and Helen have been most satisfactory."

"Did he supply any references?"

"Yes, but I can't remember exactly what they were. At any rate they were satisfactory."

"Is she an Englishwoman?"

"Yes, but she had been employed in France before Vigny met her."

"Do you know if she has any living relatives here?"

"I don't know."

"Have you a photograph of her anywhere?"

"No."

"Do you wish to see Vigny?"

Grogan reflected for a moment and then shook his head.

"It would serve no good purpose," he said. "He's made his bed. Let him lie on it. But I do want my car back as soon as possible."

"You shall have it—when we find it."

"Thank you, Inspector. Just one more question. That fellow—Besterling—is he still at large?"

"Yes."

"A pity. It seems that I am making a habit of employing people who finish up by robbing me."

"It does indeed, but there is some satisfaction that they also finish up in jail."

"It would be if only you could keep them there."

"You win," said McLean with a laugh. "Well, I'll keep in touch with you, Mr. Grogan."

When he had gone McLean leaned back and breathed a deep sigh.

"I think he's dropped a brick," he said. "A nasty brick which may trip him up."

"Can't say I noticed anything," said Brook.

"It stuck out a mile, if what I believe is true. That passport of Vigny's—Grogan has vouched for its authenticity by saying that Vigny travelled to France on it several times. It could be true, but if so why didn't Vigny produce it ? I'm convinced that the passport is a fake one, or that Vigny never had a passport at all. If we can prove either case, then Mr. Grogan is very much in the soup. Get me through to Paris—the passport authority."

The priority call was put through, and within a matter of minutes McLean was talking in French to the official at the other end of the line. There was a wait of about ten minutes, and then McLean was assured that no passport had been issued to anyone of the name of Leon Vigny.

"Good !" said McLean to Brook. "Now we are making a little progress. I want the Sûrèté—Inspector Legros of the Records Department."

The subsequent conversation which passed between McLean and Legros was spread over a lengthy period, for Legros had to delve into old files and documents, but finally McLean gave a little whoop and hung up the receiver.

"Our memories are getting rusty, Brook," he said. "Does the name Roger Hachette ring any bell ?"

"Hachette . . . Hachette ! Why, yes. We had a communication about him years ago, from Paris."

"We did. The man with the scar. It's all in our files, along with photographs. Get thee hence, and do something about it."

Brook was soon back with the document. It dealt with two men, Hachette and another, both of whom had escaped from a prison at Nantes over four years ago. Hachette was undoubtedly the man who called himself Vigny, but his accomplice in crime—Gaston Vassier—was unknown to McLean. Both had been convicted of manslaughter and sentenced to twelve years each.

"That settles Mr. Vigny," said Brook gleefully.

"Yes, but it doesn't settle Mr. Grogan. We cannot yet prove that he knew he was harbouring an escaped convict."

"But if Hachette talks ?"

"Why should he ? He has nothing to gain by it. He might be tempted if I could promise him immunity from extradition, but you know that is out of the question."

"But don't we make anything out of this discovery?"

"Quite a lot. It brings Grogan right into the picture. It links up Grogan with the kidnapping, for undoubtedly Hachette was acting for him when he went to Winterton's flat to get that parcel, which was never there. What I don't understand is why Grogan's car was not driven back to Streatham afterwards."

Two hours later McLean had the answer to this question. The car was found abandoned a few miles out of town. It suffered from a petrol choke, which a mechanic speedily put right, and was then driven to Scotland Yard. In the meantime McLean had got a specimen of Hachette's handwriting and compared it with that on the reverse side of the note. It was identical.

"A pity," he said. "I thought it might have been Grogan's. Well, we mustn't expect too much. We have a nice little crew lined up—Grogan, who is undoubtedly after that parcel; Toovey, who I believe, supplied the motor cruiser to take Brading, and perhaps Mrs. Besterling, to some other place from the house near Falmouth; sinister Mr. Magnay, sitting quiet in his hotel, like a spider in a web; and Besterling himself, who I believe could supply the answers to all our queries."

"But what do we do next?" asked Brook.

"Wait and watch. Sooner or later these ringleaders must get together to decide what next they will do, for their position is as vexed as ours. All the signs are that they are in a desperate hurry, and men in a hurry are liable to make mistakes. We've got to be on the spot if, and when, they make that mistake."

§18

It was growing dark before Anna left the little cove from which Brading had started on his hazardous swim, and whither she had returned in the faint hope that she might sight him on his way back in a boat of some kind to take her away. But now her hopes were at zero, for nothing could explain his long absence but disaster, although she strove to find other reasons. He might have got safely ashore, but had trouble in finding a man with a suitable craft. He might have been picked up by some boat, from which he could not be put ashore for some time, but her logical mind did not for long entertain this wishful thinking against the far more obvious alternative.

She crept into the house, but came upon Madame in the hall, looking almost as anxious as she did herself, but for very different reasons.

"I came to look for you, but could not find you," said Madame. "There is food waiting for you."

"I am not hungry."

"You must eat or you will be ill. That Mistaire Brading—he throw away his life, but——"

"Whose fault is that but your husband's?" asked Anna angrily. "He knew we were being kept here against our will. He lied about the petrol. . . ."

"But he had promised——"

"Yes, he had promised Mr. Grogan to hold us here. For that service he must have been paid well. Both he and you are liable to imprisonment for aiding and abetting. I will eat no more of your food, nor rest until——"

She stopped as Madame suddenly burst into tears and looked the picture of misery. Her grief seemed so sincere that Anna took her by the arm and soothed her.

"I'm sorry," she said. "You certainly tried to help us, but that does not excuse your husband. He knew what he was doing when he took us over from that arch scoundrel——"

It was unfortunate that Frontenac appeared on the stairs just in time to hear this bitter rebuke.

"I shall be glad to be rid of you," he said. "I never wanted you here, but while you have been here you have had the best we can offer—roast fowl, which we cannot afford to eat ourselves. You could not have been better treated in a first-class hotel. And how do you repay me? By bribing my wife to be disloyal to me. Mr. Brading acted like a fool. If he was drowned you are more to blame than I, for you could have stopped him."

"No one could have stopped him," retorted Anna. "He was a brave man who came to my help when I was in great trouble, and he risked his life that I might be free from persecution and your friend Grogan clapped into jail. Even now he may have succeeded—perhaps on his way back here with the police."

Frontenac shook his head.

"I know what is possible and what isn't," he said. "Now be sensible and eat some food."

"No," said Anna. "I'll take nothing from you. If need be I'll die on your hands."

Frontenac shrugged his shoulders and passed down the passage and into the kitchen. Anna went upstairs to her room and flung herself on her bed. Madame then went into the kitchen where she found her husband seated before the meal which she had served up. He gave her a glance and went on eating.

"Gaston," she pleaded. "I must talk to you."

"You seem to prefer to talk to her," he snarled. "I can't forget the dirty trick you tried to play on me."

"It would have been better had it succeeded. If that man should make the mainland and come back with the police. . . ."

"He won't."

"But he's big and powerful, and desperate. It would be the end of everything if he succeeded——"

"For God's sake, shut up !" he snarled.

"I won't. You've got to listen. You can get to the mainland and if you take her——"

"I've no petrol. You saw what happened to that."

"You were mad to destroy it, but there's the sail, which you hid. You've done it before and can do it again. Go and tell her that you will put her ashore tomorrow."

He stopped chewing and stared at her incredulously.

"Are you sane ?" he asked. "And what do I tell Grogan when he returns ?"

"Tell him they escaped—without your assistance."

"How ? He would find the boat here."

"You have no imagination. Tell him they sighted a fishing boat and signalled it, and were taken off."

"He would never believe it."

"Then let him disbelieve it. We have ourselves to think about. He wouldn't dare do anything about—about that other matter."

"Wouldn't he ? I know him better than you. He wouldn't hesitate to put me back in that terrible place for the rest of my life. Do you want that to happen ? Do you ?"

"You know I don't. But, Gaston, we are in great danger."

"Not if Brading is dead."

"There's still Mrs. Besterling. You could win her over now by an act of kindness."

"And Grogan—could I win him over by a similar act?" he asked sarcastically.

"We might leave here before he came back."

"Leave here!"

"Yes, for good. Sail the woman across, and get some petrol. Within hours we could be at sea, with all the things we value most packed in the boat."

"Do I pack my cows and chicken in the boat?"

"It is no joking matter, as you may find out, Gaston. I will not be laughed at."

"Then cease to make stupid suggestions. I am certain that Brading is drowned."

"But——"

"No more, Louise. I will deal with real trouble as it arises."

Anna, in her bedroom, found sleep impossible. She rose from the bed and sat by the window, watching the play of the moonlight on the moving waters, with her thoughts racing round her tired but active brain. She saw no beauty there—nothing but death and disaster. With Brading gone she felt absolutely alone in this cruel, mocking universe. No longer was there any need to conceal from herself that she loved this man from a far-away land who had come to her at a time when she needed a friend more than anything else in life, and his last words to her hung in her mind. Why had she not the courage to have told him then and there that on her part, too, friendship had developed into something far more binding and joyful?

Why should she consider the man who had tricked her into marriage—a man convicted of robbery, with numerous other convictions to his discredit? What was left of that marriage now but shame and disillusion? She had undertaken to carry out Besterling's last instructions before she had had time to consider the situation, but it needed only a little time for her to become suspicious of his behaviour. If he had nothing to hide, why had he not told exactly what the box contained and how it had come into his possession. Grogan had given her his own version, but no one but an idiot would have believed his story. She had prated to Brading about loyalty to her husband when, in fact, there had been precious little of that quality. She had lied, too, in a sense, for while it was true that she had in the first instance carried out Besterling's instructions, on reading the details of his earlier criminal record, after he had been convicted, she had taken steps to safeguard the parcel not only against his enemies, but against Besterling himself. It was not that she mistrusted Brading, but that she was reluctant to admit the weight of her suspicion against her husband. In a sense that was loyalty, but how utterly misplaced !

When morning came she was faint with hunger. She went downstairs and found her untouched evening meal still on the table. It was too much for her resolution, which to her now seemed a mere piece of infantile bravado, since Frontenac probably didn't care whether she lived or died, and might in the circumstance actually prefer the latter alternative. So she ate the food and drank the big mug of milk.

Outside a strong breeze had got up and the sea was broken into millions of small wavelets. She crossed the headland to the cove where she had spent most of the previous day. Above the high-tide mark in the dry sand were the impressions which she and Brading had left behind. The sea was a vast emptiness except for the far-away dim outline of land. The sight disturbed her, and she moved along to the cave and then up over some rocks where the spindrift from the breakers salted her lips. She could have enjoyed it all in different circumstances.

It was on clambering down the rocks on the further side that she became aware of something lying in the long grass beyond the beach itself. It looked very much like a human body, and she clutched at her heart in an agony of fear. Then, drawing nearer, she recognized the pale blue shirt, and around the half-buried head was the scarf which he had tied to conserve his money—her scarf.

"Neville !"

She tried to speak the name, but no sound came. Then she ran forward at great speed, the long grass swishing round her ankles. His head was cushioned on his arms, and fearfully she touched one of the hands. A little cry escaped her, for the hand was warm, and as she held it the eyes opened and regarded her as in a stupor.

"An-na," he muttered. "I thought—I thought. . . ."

Her arms were now enfolding his neck, and he dragged himself into a sitting position, cushioned against her breast which was heaving under her deep emotion.

"Oh, thank God!" she said. "I thought you were drowned. But are you hurt?"

She was gazing at the congealed blood on his left bare foot, which appeared to have come from a long abrasion.

"No. That's nothing. I hit against a rock. Didn't see it in the darkness."

"How long have you been here?"

"A long time. It was all a ghastly failure. I got away well on the outgoing tide, but after a few hours I struck a strong cross-current. It was hell after that. I swam and swam, but all my progress was in the wrong direction, and the mainland never got any nearer. I realized that I was beaten and that my only chance was to try to get back here. Well, I got back—round about midnight I guess—but all I could do was stagger out of the sea and lie down here to rest for a while, but I fell dead asleep until just now when you came along. I'm sorry, Anna."

"Sorry! You needn't be sorry, and you've nothing to reproach yourself with. Frontenac told me that the mainland is ten miles away—not the four or five which we imagined. Oh, it's good to have you back!"

"It's good to be back, but for one thing—Grogan."

"Nothing is worse than your being drowned. Are you hungry?"

"More thirsty than hungry. My head aches a bit. Must be the scarf."

Anna untied the skull-cap. Inside the notes were damp, but not actually wet. She handed them to Brading, who put them into the pocket of his shirt, which the wind had dried.

"What's the position at the house?" he asked.

"They are both certain that you were drowned. I waited until you got well away before I told them what had happened. Now come back to the house and have some food."

Brading stood up, and rubbed his limbs for a few moments. Then he stood in a state of deep reflection.

"What's wrong now?" she asked.

"Anna, I've got an idea. Why not let the Frontenacs continue to believe that I was drowned?"

148

"But how would it help ?"

"It can only be a day or two before Grogan and his gang come back to put us on the rack again. Frontenac will tell them what he thinks happened to me, and you can back up the story."

"But what will you do in the meantime ?"

"Hide in that old cave, and see you at intervals. You could bring me some food."

"But I still don't see how it would benefit us."

"It would, because Frontenac is certain to replenish his stock of petrol from the ship's storage tank. With me out of the way he will get his boat into use again, and that will be my opportunity."

"But Grogan may remove me from here ?"

"That's possible. But with one of us free to tell the police all we know, Grogan would be for the high jump. There is no other alternative which is half so promising. You must see that."

Anna did see it, but the thought of being separated from Brading after this glad reunion was far from pleasant. Brading, appreciating her indecision, and emboldened by her changed attitude towards him, took her in his arms.

"I'm sure it's best, darling," he murmured. "If he took us both he wouldn't allow us to be together, and I should be unable to help you in any way. The only way to beat Grogan is by cunning, for he holds all the cards."

"Whatever you say, Neville," she said.

"Good ! Let's get down to the cave. It's dangerous to stay here too long."

They stayed together until nearly noon, and then Anna went back to the house, looking as dejected as she had when Madame had seen her last. She dallied with the mid-day meal, but contrived to slip some home-made rolls and some sliced ham into her handbag. The drink question was a little more difficult, but after the meal she found an empty wine bottle in the yard and filled it with water from the pump. Half an hour later she was back with Brading, seated on the sand just outside the cave entrance, watching him eating his sparse meal with gusto.

"The best I could do," she said. "The shoes are a difficult proposition. I dare not risk being caught with them, and they won't go into my handbag. Do you really need them ?"

"I'll say I need them, but you're right about the risk. Look
—leave them under the seat beneath your window late tonight.
I'll creep along and pick them up."

"All right. Anything else ?"

"Yes, when you come again bring my cigarette case and
lighter from my coat pocket. I'm dying for a smoke."

Anna laughed and produced the articles from her handbag.

"You're an angel," he said. "Gosh, only six left !"

"Can you smoke French cigarettes ?"

"I can smoke anything in an emergency."

"Frontenac has a good stock of them. I saw them on a shelf
in the kitchen. I might become a thief in an emergency."

The plan seemed to be working out very well, but in
Anna's mind there was always the vision of Grogan arriving in
the cruiser, to put an end to this pleasant interlude. She
wanted Time to stand still, but contrarily it seemed to pass at
remarkable speed.

"Anna !"

"Well ?"

"Suppose we get out of all this mess, as we shall, what are
you going to do ?"

"Do ? Get a job, I suppose."

"That's not what I mean. What are you going to do about
your husband ?"

Sooner or later Anna knew that question would be asked,
and here it was plain and unequivocal.

"I don't know," she said, after a long pause.

"You know I love you ?"

"Yes, I know that."

"Then what's to prevent your coming back to Canada
with me ? I've got a good business there. The wheels are so oiled
it almost runs itself. I could make you happy, Anna. Do you
believe that ?"

"Yes, I do. But it's all a dream."

"Not on your life. Where's the hitch ?"

"The husband you mentioned. He's in prison, with two
more years to serve. I've promised to wait for him."

"Yes, you told me that before. I could understand it if you
had any love left for him, but you haven't."

"I've never said that," she protested.

"Not in words, but it's in your eyes whenever he's mentioned. Tell me that you love him, that you mean to take up where you left off when he comes out of jail, and I'll never mention the matter again. You can't say that truthfully, can you?"

"No, I can't say it truthfully, but I've got to give him a chance to clear himself with me. There was no time for that when—when we parted."

"But you don't doubt he was guilty, do you?"

"He could be innocent. That money may have been planted on him by someone who hated him."

"But, Anna, if he was guilty and that was his first offence, he wouldn't have been given so harsh a sentence. There must have been previous convictions."

Anna averted her eyes. She dared not look at him and deny that, but Brading was quick to draw the obvious conclusion.

"So there were previous convictions," he said. "Anna, you're fighting in a bad cause, aren't you? He tricked you into marriage by posing as an honest man. He comes to you with a mysterious parcel which he asks you to hide for him, without offering the slightest explanation. Can you doubt that he stole that parcel as well as the money, and is directly the cause of all this trouble? You can't seriously believe that he can explain everything to your satisfaction when he has a chance. He'll simply lie, as all thieves lie. Think how happy we could be—you and I. He'd give you a divorce when he realized——"

"No—no. He'd never do that. Whatever he may be, he loves me passionately and is madly jealous. He would follow me to the end of the earth, and is quite capable——"

She did not complete the sentence, but Brading had a shrewd idea of what was in her mind.

"So you're afraid of him, Anna," he said quietly. "Afraid of what he might do to anyone who might make an attempt to take you away from him."

"I want an understanding."

"Even though it means waiting two years?"

"Two years isn't long in a lifetime."

"It's an eternity when one is in love."

Anna said nothing, and Brading got the impression that he was hurting her by his impulsiveness.

"Forgive me, Anna," he said. "I guess I can be more than a bit selfish and inconsiderate when it suits my book."

Anna's response was to grip his hand tightly and gaze at him with her wide, deep eyes.

"If I obeyed my heart I would go with you tomorrow if it were possible, but the heart isn't always the infallible guide to decent behaviour. Be patient, Neville."

By mutual agreement they did not meet that evening, lest the Frontenacs should become suspicious of Anna's craze for roaming, but after the evening meal Anna put some more food into her handbag, and when darkness had fallen she wrapped this in paper and concealed it in one of Brading's shoes, which she finally left under the seat as arranged. Although she sat long by the window she did not hear him come, but the next morning she found the shoes gone.

At breakfast she put on her expression of deepest gloom, and Madame tried, with some success, to console her. She hinted that her husband was regretting his behaviour, and might in a day or two take her to the mainland.

"How can he?" asked Anna. "He has no petrol for the boat."

"No. But he has an old sail, and is a good seaman. I will do what I can, *cherie.*"

"Thank you," said Anna. "You are very kind."

Whether or no Madame really was working this miracle Anna could not make up her mind, but she was anxious that Brading should know, and after slipping some rolls into her handbag she walked over the headland and came down to the beach on the southern side. Here she had the surprise of her life. Making towards the place where she stood was a trim-looking motor boat. She could just see the pilot's head over the cabin roof, but he was too far away for recognition even had she known him. The boat slowed down a little, and she got the impression that he was looking for some place where he could get ashore. She waved her arm to the right, and her signal was understood and answered.

With her heart thumping she raced up over the headland to the cove. There was no doubt in her mind that this was not Grogan. He certainly would not come in so small a craft, and alone. It meant that salvation was at hand. Breathless, she reached the descent on the further side, to see the motor boat enter the cove and move slowly to the narrow quay, with its few broken steps. The engine stopped and finally the craft was moored to a stake thrust between the stone slabs. The pilot, bareheaded, tall, and with a scrubby beard, stood on the quay lighting a cigarette. She drew nearer to him, and then suddenly halted. Something in his attitude—the way he stood, hands on hips, and lips parted, brought back the past.

"Anna !" he shouted.

Slowly she approached him as if hypnotized, and then she knew beyond all doubting.

"Harold !" she gasped.

It was he now who approached her in a few long strides. She put out her arms defensively, but he broke through them with a laugh and hugged her tight.

"No—no !" she cried.

"Not a very warm welcome," he protested. "Well, that can wait. Where's Frontenac ?"

"So you know him ?"

"Yes, but by another name. I've got a few things to say to him, also to Grogan when we meet."

Anna freed herself and stood regarding him with pallid face.

"You—you've escaped ?"

"Obviously. I always meant to escape, and it looks as if I chose the right moment. Who's the man you're with ?"

"What man ?"

"A man named Brading, who seems to have taken an interest in my affairs."

"He—he's dead."

"How do you mean ? Did someone bump him off ?"

"No. He tried to help me. Grogan brought us both here, and Brading tried to swim to the mainland. He failed."

"You're lying."

"You can ask Frontenac, for here he comes."

Frontenac came hurrying down the path from the house, and Besterling stood waiting for him with a smile on his face. At a few yards distance Frontenac stopped.

"Paul !" he gasped.

"I've changed my name since those days, just as you've changed yours, Vassier. It is now Besterling, and Anna is my wife. Why the hell have you been keeping her here ?"

"I had no option. Grogan brought her, and a man named Brading."

"Where is Brading?"

"He was drowned trying to swim to the mainland."

"How do you know he was drowned?"

"Well, he never came back. He'd have come back if he had got ashore."

"Is that your house up there?"

"Yes. But how did you know where to find me—and your wife?"

"I still have a friend or two. Let's go to the house. I'm hungry and thirsty and have a lot to say."

Anna's state now was one of complete bewilderment, for the whole situation seemed to be out of control. She had lied about Brading because it had seemed the easiest thing to do in the circumstances, and now her overwhelming desire was to see Brading and tell him what had happened. But at the moment that was impossible. It was, too, perhaps premature, for not yet had she any idea what Besterling's intentions were.

On reaching the house Madame was at the door, waiting to discover the exact meaning of this unexpected invasion. She gazed at Besterling as one does at a complete stranger, and Frontenac did the introduction.

"My wife," he said. "Louise, this is Mister—Besterling, whom I knew a long time ago."

"You mean—Anna's husband?" quavered Louise.

"Yes. He is hungry. Bring some sandwiches and wine. We will go into the sitting-room."

The mystified woman gave Anna a quick glance and then hurried along to the kitchen. Frontenac led the way to the sitting-room, where Besterling surveyed the furnishings with appraising eyes.

"Very nice," he said. "Better than I have been used to. I have often wondered what had become of you, Gaston. Now tell me about Grogan. When did he come here?"

"A week ago—in a motor cruiser. He is due back again at any moment."

"Why did he leave my wife and the man here?"

"I don't know. He didn't tell me."

"But you knew damn well it wasn't for the good of their health, didn't you?"

"I knew nothing." Frontenac wrung his hands together. "I was not in a position to refuse. I had no idea that this—lady was your wife."

"What about the man—Brading? Did he and my wife live together here?"

Anna's face grew scarlet with indignation, but Besterling seemed quite unaffected.

"Did they?" he repeated.

"No," said Frontenac. "You do your wife a grave injustice. There was nothing like that—absolutely nothing. They tried to get away in my boat, but I stopped that. I had to. When Brading was drowned my wife pleaded with me to take Anna back to the mainland. I had destroyed the petrol, but I have an old sail. I had practically consented to do so. . . ."

"Yes, you say that now."

"But it is true. This has been a most unhappy experience for me. My wife threatened to leave me."

Madame then entered the room with various tit-bits of food, and a bottle of wine and glasses on a tray. She did not linger an instant.

"I'll see you later, Gaston," said Besterling. "My wife and I have some talking to do."

He poured out a glass of wine and offered it to Anna, who shook her head.

"Not thirsty, not hungry, not thrilled with joy at my most opportune appearance? Well, I don't wonder in the circumstances."

"What circumstances?" asked Anna.

Besterling gulped down the full glass before replying, and then munched a meat sandwich. Suddenly his eyes grew hard.

"That night—when I was arrested I handed you a parcel, with instructions what to do with it. Did you carry out those instructions?"

"Yes."

"That's a lie. I went there to get the parcel. It was gone."

"I left it there, at first," said Anna.

"At first? What do you mean by that?"

"After the trial, when I read the newspaper report and learned that you had been convicted three times previously, I went to the hiding place and took the parcel away."

"Why?"

"Because I realized that you had lied to me all through our married life. All that money you used to squander—where did it come from? You told me you had a private income, but I don't believe it. All that time you were working for Grogan— eating out of his hand. I'm not love-blind any longer. The parcel is safe, but I'll not tell you where it is until you explain where you got it and what it contains. Grogan told me you stole it from him when you took the money, and that it contains private papers belonging to him. That's why I was kidnapped. He knew you had handed the parcel to me and was determined to get it back."

"Did you admit it?"

"Yes, but he doesn't know where it is."

"Then why did he leave you here?"

"We tricked him—Mr. Brading and I. When I believed that Brading had gone back to Canada I told him that I had left the parcel in a suitcase, which Brading had collected from my lodgings when I was locked out because I couldn't pay the rent. Brading took the suitcase to his hotel, after paying my landlady the rent which I owed. He meant to give it to me, but Grogan had already got hold of me. Later the suitcase was stolen from Brading's bedroom. That was Grogan's doing. Of course he found no parcel, so his next move was to kidnap Brading. But Brading refused to say anything, sensing that I was in trouble. But finally Brading said he would tell them where the parcel was if he could see me first. Grogan agreed, and then we hatched our plot."

"Get on with it," said Besterling impatiently.

"Brading demanded a reward to make it all look genuine. Grogan agreed to pay him a thousand pounds when the parcel was in his hands, so Brading gave him the name and address of a friend to whom he said he had given the parcel for safe keeping, and wrote a note authorizing his friend to hand over the parcel. Grogan said he would have to keep us here until he had the parcel. Then he would come back and set us free and pay the reward. That's all there is to tell."

"Did you tell Brading where the parcel was hidden?"

"No. He never even asked me."

Besterling took another glass of wine and finished up the food.

"All right," he said. "Now I'll tell you the truth. I did steal

156

that parcel from Grogan's office, and the money. But he owed me the money as commission on a business deal and wouldn't pay up. My intention was to cut adrift from him for good, because his business wasn't on the level and I didn't want to get involved. I took the parcel because I knew it contained documents which would tell against him in a court of law. I didn't do it for blackmail, but because I wanted to protect myself—and you."

"Then why didn't you mention them at your trial?"

"They were not relevant. I wanted to hold them against him in the future—our future. I was planning to go abroad with you and start a new life elsewhere. Don't you believe me?"

"No," said Anna. "You are now playing Grogan's game. That box must contain articles of more value than mere documents. Grogan wouldn't have wasted all the time and money for scraps of paper. He is ready to commit murder for it."

"Very well. It is easy to prove. We'll get the box and you can see for yourself. Will that satisfy you?"

"No."

"Then what in God's name do you expect me to do?"

"Just tell me the truth," said Anna stubbornly. "I shall know it when I hear it."

The strong wine was now beginning to have an effect upon him. His eyes shone with a curious light, and his rather fine big hands were closing and unclosing.

"You're trying me too far, Anna," he said. "I've taken great risks in breaking out of prison, and I'm not going back whatever happens. Our lives lie together, and if you trust me I'll make things comfortable for you. But Grogan stands in the way of happiness. I must have some defence against him, and those documents are the best weapon. I'll take you away from here. I've got a boat——"

"Where did you get the boat?" asked Anna sharply.

"I've still got a few friends. One of them lent me the boat, and some money, and this clothing."

He spread out his arms to display the suit he was wearing, and in doing so the sleeves rose a little, to reveal an inch or two of clean white shirt cuff. But the cleanliness of the right-hand one was marred by a deep red smear. Anna's gaze went to it, and terror struck at her heart, for the smear looked like blood. He did not seem to realize the real cause of her frightened expression.

"Come, be sensible," he pleaded. "Where did you hide the parcel ?"

"I—I must have time to think," she stammered. "My—my head is swimming. I must get some fresh air. No, don't come. I'll think it over."

"That's right," he said. "That's a good girl."

She staggered from the room, out into the sunshine. The strategem had succeeded. Gazing behind her to make sure she was not being followed, she took the shorter land route to the cave, avoiding the more open beach walk.

§19

BRADING had heard the unmistakable throb of a marine engine as he sat just inside the cave eating the food which he had found concealed in one of his shoes. To him the significance was plain. Grogan had returned. He crept into the open, with a view to confirming this, but no vessel was in sight, and he realized that any ship coming from the English coast would approach the cove from the other side of the island.

There was nothing he could do now but wait for Anna, who would surely lose no time in coming to him before the actual landing of Grogan. Failing that, he resolved to creep across to the cove, to weigh up the situation.

Time passed and there was no sign of Anna. His natural conclusion was that Anna had not had sufficient warning of the ship's arrival and was now unable to make contact with him. He gave her a few more minutes, and then climbed the slight cliff and began to make his way cautiously in the direction of the cove. He had not gone more than a hundred yards when Anna came to view, running across the boulder-strewn ground with the speed and grace of a young deer. She waved him back as she saw him, but a few moments later overtook him, panting speechlessly.

"Take it easy," he said. "I heard the boat's engine."

"The—cave," she panted. "Tell—you—there."

Soon they were under cover, Anna with her face even more tense than the circumstances seemed to warrant.

"Now," he said, "sit down and rest for a moment."

"No. I'm all right. Neville, it isn't Grogan."

"Not Grogan!"

"No. Worse. It's my husband. He's escaped from prison. It alters everything."

Brading looked at her incredulously.

"Have you spoken to him?" he asked.

"Yes. But he doesn't know about you. I had to lie to him. I told him you were drowned, and Frontenac confirmed it."

"Go on," he said.

Now in complete control of her breath, Anna told him exactly what had transpired at the house, not forgetting that terrifying crimson smear on Besterling's borrowed shirt.

"Yes, it alters things," he mused. "But not necessarily for the worse. Did you learn his intentions, apart from his desire to know what you did with the parcel?"

"They were plain enough. He wants me to go back with him. I pretended I wanted to think it over, and there isn't much time because if I'm not back quickly he is bound to come and look for me."

Brading paced up and down in the confined space. Here was the ultimatum, and it had to be faced.

"It's amazing that he should want to return," he mused. "Having got safely out of England, one would think he would be content to stay here for a bit. Anna, there is only one thing to do."

"What?"

"Take his boat and sail it to England. This is a chance that may never come again. You won't be able to take anything with you. We must go just as we are, and now. What do you say?"

Anna never hesitated for a moment.

"I'm ready," she said. "I never want to see him again. He's horrible, somehow. So changed. He frightens me. Oh, Neville, thank God you're here."

They took one look to make sure that the beach was clear, and then hurried up the steep path and through the sunken tracks by which Anna had come. Arriving near the cove, Brading realized there was a chance they might be seen from the house when they left their present cover.

"We ought to be able to make it before they can get down here," he said. "It means a sprint. Ready ?"

"Yes."

"Come on then !"

They broke across the curving cove, running at great speed, then climbed onto the narrow jetty and made for the place where the boat was tied up. Brading pulled it in close to the quay and Anna went down the steps and clambered aboard. A moment or two later Brading followed her, casting off the mooring line as he did so. He then went to the engine, and there he suffered a shock. The starter was equipped with a locking device and could not be moved.

"Blast !" he exclaimed. "He's ditched us !"

"Can't you start it somehow ?"

"Not a hope. Lord, she's drifting out !"

He seized a boathook and just managed to get a grip on the mooring stake. Slowly the boat was pulled in close to the quay and safely moored.

"What do we do ?" asked Anna anxiously.

"Our one hope is to find some tools. I might be able to free the starter. What's in that locker ?"

Anna opened one of the lockers under the seat. It contained only a baler and some mops. She then tried the locker on the other side, and found a box of tools and two full cans of petrol. Instantly Brading changed his mind.

"There's a better way," he said. "If we stay here any time we are bound to be seen and that would ruin everything. We'll take the petrol and hide it. Tonight we'll get away in Frontenac's boat. What do you say ?"

"Yes."

He handed Anna one of the cans, taking the other himself. The locker was closed, and then they stole away, casting anxious glances at the house as they hurried past it. At a short distance from the cove, and out of sight of the house, Brading scraped a hole in the loose sand and buried the cans.

"You must go back, Anna," he said.

"But what shall I tell him ?"

"Tell him a lie, unless you prefer to tell him the truth."

"No. He cannot know the one from the other. But suppose he wants to take me with him?"

"I don't think he'll risk that. If he should be that bold, you can refuse and promise to wait for him here. If he should leave today come to me later and we'll get Frontenac's boat into action. If he should decide to stay here the night, our plan holds just the same, only you will have to take greater care in getting out of the house."

Anna nodded grimly. She hated the task which lay before her, but the situation offered no other promising alternative.

"He—he might miss those two cans of petrol," she said.

"Yes, but we have to risk that. Now go, my darling, and keep your chin up."

"What about food? You've had so little."

"I'll be all right until tonight, but then bring all you can carry."

Anna nodded, smiled a little wanly, and then, of her own accord, reached up and kissed him. The next moment she was gone over the rocks, finally to enter the house by the back door. Madame saw her from the kitchen and beckoned her.

"My 'usband—he is with yours," she whispered. "He ask for more wine and is drunk. Maybe you do not wish to go with him, eh?"

Anna shook her head.

"I am ver' sorry," said Madame. "I tell my 'usband he must not let you be taken away by force. He say he can do nothing. If that man do not take you, Grogan will, and one is as bad as the other."

"Yes, one is as bad as the other," agreed Anna.

Madame gave a little hiss of warning, and Anna left the kitchen and met Frontenac in the passage looking tense and uncomfortable.

"He is asking for you," he said in a hoarse whisper.

Anna entered the sitting-room, to find Besterling reclining on the sofa with his feet up on a stool. His eyes were bleary, and on the table beside her were two empty wine bottles and innumerable cigarette butts.

"You've been a long time," he hiccoughed.

"I'm sorry, Harold," she said meekly. "But it's all very difficult."

"It needn't be. Maybe I haven't been all I should be. I've

made mistakes, but I've paid for them. Grogan's been my downfall. When I get what I want I'll be free of him for ever. Do what I ask you and you'll never regret it. After all, you made a vow, didn't you ? Swore it on the old book. I'm only asking you to keep that vow. That's not unreasonable, is it?"

"No," she said, after a pause.

"Then where is it ?"

"It's in a pond—down in Surrey. You know the place—that farm where we stayed on—on our honeymoon. It's down only the depth of my arm, two feet to the left of the grill which takes the overflow down the watercress beds on the other side of the path."

"I know it. But what a risk ! Someone might see it."

"No. The pond is always covered with pond weed and water-lilies. It's so heavy it won't move."

"The sooner we get it the better. I want to get some provisions from Vassier."

"Who ?"

"I mean Frontenac. Be ready in a few minutes."

Anna stared at him.

"You mean I'm to come ?" she asked.

"Of course. Do you imagine I'm going to leave you here for Grogan to play about with? Besides, when I've got the parcel we can go off together."

"But I don't want to go at once."

"Why the hell not ?"

"There's a wind getting up, and I'm not a very good sailor. Besides, you need a rest. You must have been up all night. Make it tomorrow morning, Harold," she pleaded.

"Won't do, old girl. If Grogan should suddenly descend on us a fine mess I should be in. Nothing he'd love better than to shove me back in prison. I'm going to see Frontenac now about the food."

He got up from the chair and staggered a little, but he recovered himself and laughed at her consternation.

"Maybe you think I'm too canned to sail the boat, eh ? Well, you'll soon find out. Get your bag packed."

Anna was now in a grave dilemma. She had foreseen the possibility of his wanting to take her away, but had not bargained on this frantic haste. She heard him stumping along the passage, bawling for Gaston. By some means she had to put off this instant departure, which would ruin the plan agreed upon by herself and Brading, but how to achieve it was the problem. She was quite sure that mere argument would have no effect upon him. She could feign illness—throw a faint and pretend to be in great pain. But a moment's reflection convinced her that it would be unavailing. Already she felt she was under suspicion—that he was taking her not because he feared to leave her to Grogan's tender mercy, but to have her on hand just in case she was lying.

Should she run back to Brading and put the new situation to him ? He might decide to act at once rather than wait until nightfall, and take the risk of being seen from the house. But if she made this attempt there was the chance that Besterling would miss her immediately and search for her. The one thing to avoid was any meeting between him and Brading, for that might be the end of all her hopes.

She made to slip out by the front door in order to get a few more minutes to make up her mind, but as she reached the door Besterling came out of the kitchen and saw her.

"Hey !" he called. "What's the idea ?"

"It—it's suffocating in here."

"You'll soon have all the fresh air you want. Get that bag packed. Here, I'll lend you a hand."

He caught her by the arm, but she threw off his grip and moved towards the stairs.

"I don't want any help," she said. "You wait here."

"Well, make it snappy. I'll go and have a wash. It will freshen me up. Is there a bathroom here ?"

"On the half-landing."

She continued up the stairs and entered her bedroom, where she sat down on the bed and racked her brain for some solution to this pressing problem. The desire to escape from Besterling was now an obsession. Anything was better than to go alone with him in the boat. The only way now to avoid him was to run back to Brading and induce him to put into operation immediately their scheme to escape. There was danger in attempting this in broad daylight, with the boat in full view of the house, but she could see no other way out of her plight and the precious minutes were passing.

She peeped out of the door and saw that the bathroom door was half-open. To go past that would be risky, but there was the window, with the seat beneath it. She looked out, and then swiftly shoved a few things in the suitcase and dropped the case on to the seat. Then she clambered through the window, hung by her hands from the narrow cill, and dropped on to the seat with very little noise. The next moment she was staggering under the weight of the suitcase towards the spot where Brading had buried the petrol cans. Here she dumped the suitcase, and relieved of its weight she went flying down the sunken track towards the cave.

Breathless she reached it, to find Brading bathing his face and arms in a pool left by the tide just below the cave entrance. He stared at her in astonishment.

"We—we've got to leave at once," she panted. "He wants to take me away immediately. Nothing will stop him. Neville I can't go with him. I'm terrified of him. I've brought my suitcase and dumped it where we left the petrol. Are you ready?"

"It's going to be dangerous," he said. "If we fail we'll never get another chance."

"But it's our only chance. Neville, you must realize that."

"Yes, I do."

"Then come now. In a few minutes he may be looking for me."

"All right. Here we go."

They moved up over the cliff at great speed, and down the track which led to the cove by way of the petrol dump. Here Brading climbed up a sand-dune and looked towards the cove. The two boats were there, Frontenac's afloat in the deep water, with its anchor thrust into the shelving beach. No living person was in sight.

"Okay so far," he said. "Now for those cans."

The petrol was swiftly brought to the surface. Brading took one of the cans and the suitcase, leaving Anna with the second can.

"We'll go as far as that big rock just above the cove," he whispered. "Then rest a couple of minutes to get our breath, before the last rush in the open."

Anna nodded, and very soon they were under the shelter of the rock. From there to the anchor was less than two hundred yards.

"As soon as we reach the anchor, drop the can and give me

a hand on the mooring line. We've got to pull the boat in as close as possible, and then wade."

"Will there be enough petrol to take us to England ?"

"No. It will have to be France. Are you ready ?"

"Yes."

They went off at full pelt, Brading outpacing Anna only with the greatest difficulty. Reaching the anchor, he dropped his burden and hauled on the rope, and a few seconds later Anna added her weight. Very slowly the craft came round.

"It's the wind," grumbled Brading, "keeping her out."

Anna turned her head for a moment to gaze at the house, and a hoarse cry broke from her lips. The cause was not at the house, but at the headland. Coming down from the crest was Besterling at breakneck speed. Anna's worst fear had materialized.

"It's too late, Neville," she moaned.

Brading took one look at the approaching man. He ceased to haul on the rope and stood dead still.

"I suppose it had to come some time," he said. "We'll have it out right here."

Besterling came to a halt about six paces away. He was very much out of breath and his eyes blazed in a strange way.

"Who the hell are you ?" he panted.

"The name's Brading, if that means anything to you."

It appeared to mean a great deal, for Besterling's expression was now one of murderous hate.

"My wife's boy-friend, eh ? Who got drowned while going for help. And now off again for more help, but not alone. Where did you get those petrol cans ?"

"Out of your boat," replied Brading calmly. "We happen to need it as badly as you do."

"Well, you're going to be disappointed. Anna comes with me, and now. Anna, come here !"

Instead of obeying Anna drew even closer to Brading, who saw no possibility of avoiding a brawl. But still he made the attempt.

"Hadn't you better go," he said to Besterling. "Anna appears to have made up her mind."

"I'm the one to make decisions. Very gracious of you to offer to take her off my hands, but I've other plans for her future. Anna, will you come here, or do I have to drag you ?"

"It's no use," said Anna. "I'll never go with you willingly—anywhere."

Besterling glared at Brading, who was all tensed for action. "I'm warning you, Brading," he said. "If you butt in on my personal affairs you'll be sorry. Stand away from my wife. Go on ! Beat it !"

Brading stood dead still, ready for battle. He was at least two inches taller than Besterling, and built like a gun. Anna, hating violence of all kinds, was as pallid as a sheet. She had no doubt about the outcome of a physical encounter, but dreaded it notwithstanding.

Brading was gently pushing Anna away from him when Besterling whipped an automatic from his hip pocket and levelled it at Brading.

"Get away !" he growled, "or I'll kill you."

Anna uttered a little cry of horror and made to place herself in front of Brading, but he held her off.

"I wondered why you were so courageous," he said to Besterling. "Now I know. Hitherto I had some doubts about you, but now I know the sort of creature you are. Put down that gun or I'll come and take it from you."

"Neville !" pleaded Anna. "Take care !"

Besterling made a sudden dive at her and managed to clasp her arm with his free hand. With a wrench he pulled her sideways with such force that she tripped and fell. Brading leapt at him and struck him full on the jaw. Besterling staggered back, but managed to keep his balance. He pivoted round, raised the pistol and fired three quick shots. Brading gave a little groan, sank to his knees, and then fell flat on the sand with blood streaming from his hip.

"You—you cruel murderer !" cried Anna.

"He asked for it. Didn't I warn him ? Oh, no, you don't!"

This as Anna dropped on her knees beside the still form. Pocketing the pistol, he pulled her to her feet while she tore at his face with the nails of her free hand. With a curse he lifted her bodily and carried her to his motor boat, where he locked her in the cabin and then returned for the petrol and suitcase. As he was leaving, Frontenac came running from the house.

"What have you done ?" shouted Frontenac. "Who is he ?"

"See for yourself," snarled Besterling, and made away.

20

FRONTENAC approached the prone form and gave a little cry of amazement as he saw Brading's face. Two bullets had entered the body and the bleeding was considerable. He leaned over Brading and spoke to him, but Brading was beyond speech. Then came the sound of an engine, and Frontenac stared across to the jetty and saw Besterling's boat moving out to sea, with Besterling alone at the helm.

Louise now came running across the sand from the house. She took one look at Brading and uttered a cry of astonishment, then brandished her clenched fist at Besterling.

"Assassin !" she hissed.

"Save your breath, Louise," grunted Frontenac. "We have to get this man to the house or he will die."

"Yes—yes, but where did he come from ? I thought he was drowned."

"Anna may be able to explain."

"But where is Anna ?"

"In her bedroom, isn't she ?"

"No. I looked in her room just now. Her suitcase was not there either."

"Then he must have taken her to the boat. They must have planned to get away on that boat, but he intercepted them and shot Brading. No more now. You take his feet."

Together they carried Brading up the steep path and into the house. Louise ran to get a waterproof sheet before they placed him on the couch in the sitting-room.

"There are two bullets inside him," said Frontenac. "I must try to remove them, or he will die."

"No, no. It is too dangerous. We will plug the wounds and bandage him. Then you must get the sail and go to the mainland."

"What are you saying !"

Louise looked at him fixedly.

"You will go to the mainland and bring a doctor, or I will sail the boat myself. What is it to be ?"

Frontenac stared through the window at the moving clouds. The wind was favourable, and the sea comparatively calm.

"All right," he said. "I will do as you say as soon as I have plugged——"

"I can do that as well as you. Go now, Gaston. I will make him comfortable."

Frontenac nodded, and went out at once. Louise then got to work on Brading, and within a quarter of an hour she had stopped the worst of the bleeding and made bandages by tearing up an old sheet. She placed pillows under his head, and finally covered him with a blanket and stole away to attend to her manifold duties. When she came to look at him half an hour later his eyes were open.

"That is better," she said.

"Where is Anna?" he asked in a weak voice.

"Gone—with her husband."

"In the boat?"

"Yes. We found you wounded and brought you here. You must lie still, and soon the doctor will come."

"What doctor?"

"My husband has done to the mainland. He had an old sail, and is a good sailor. He will bring the doctor."

"Thank you, Madame. I expect that was your doing?"

"No. He wanted to do it. Gaston is not without his good points. He did not want to keep you and Anna here, but there is something in his past which he wish to conceal, and that man Grogan knew all about it."

"I understand," said Brading. "You're very kind. I knew your heart was not in this business. Did you bandage me up?"

"Yes."

"What is the damage?"

"You have two bullets inside which must be removed. Now you must not talk any more. If you want me, knock on the wall with that stick and I will come."

She crept out of the room and Brading was left to his reflections. Very sober reflections they were, too, for he could imagine Anna's state of mind now that all illusions about the man she had married were irrevocably shattered. He had not imagined that Besterling would go to such lengths as to take with him by force any person who could betray him to the police. It all went to show that Besterling by no means trusted his wife's statement and was taking no chances with her. By some means or other he would keep her out of contact with the police and the public until he had got what he wanted, and that suggested the possibility of the most extreme cruelty.

Every movement of his body, even the act of breathing, caused him pain, but the physical discomfort was nothing compared to the mental agony born of his failure to prevent this situation from arising. Why had he not suspected the presence of that pistol ? It should have been obvious to him that Besterling would not have engaged in a rough and tumble without the backing of a weapon. Why had he innocently set himself up as a target ?

Time passed and Louise came again to have a look at him. She satisfied herself that the bleeding had stopped, and then suggested that he should take some thin broth which she had made. Brading, who badly needed sustenance, said he would try, and she brought a bowl of broth and fed him with a large spoon, most satisfactorily.

"That was good," he said. "I think I might be able to sleep now."

"Yes—try," she begged.

He did succeed in snatching a little sleep, and some time later—he could not guess how long—Louise came into the room and brought him to full consciousness.

"The doctor has come in my husband's boat," she said. "He will be here in a few minutes. I do not know what my husband has told him. Perhaps he will say it was an accident, because—because. . . ."

Brading's mind was clear enough to know what she was driving at. What was troubling her was the possibility that the doctor might consider it his duty to inform the police if the whole truth were told, and the police might come and learn more than was good for Frontenac.

"I understand," he said. "You may rely on my discretion."

In her unspeakable gratitude she clasped his hand for a moment and then raised it to her lips. A little later the doctor entered, with Frontenac close behind. He was a diminutive man with spectacles and a bald head, and it was soon clear he spoke not a word of English. He undid the bandages and examined the two wounds. Then he stuck a thermometer in Brading's mouth and talked to Frontenac while the instrument was working. After a minute or two he took out the thermometer and consulted it, muttering a few words.

"What does he say?" asked Brading.

"There is no fever. You are not in danger."

"Good!"

After calling for warm water and swabs, the doctor got to work with his forceps. The bullets were fairly deep, and the pain was excruciating, but in due course the two bullets were extracted and dropped into the gory bowl. Brading, near to fainting, closed his eyes and went into another world. When he became fully conscious of what was happening there were fresh medical bandages round the wounds and the doctor was writing something in his book. Best of all, the pain which had racked him had vanished. The doctor came to the couch and smiled for the first time.

"*Ca va bien, eh?*" he asked.

Brading at least understood that, and nodded his head. Then Frontenac, looking very serious, came forward.

"The doctor wishes to know how you got the wounds," he said. "I told him—it was an accident. Is that right?"

"Correct," said Brading. "I was cleaning an automatic and didn't know it was loaded. Very silly of me."

Frontenac interpreted, and then there was a long conversation between him and the doctor which Frontenac again translated for Brading's benefit.

"He says you were lucky, and that if one of the bullets had been an inch higher you would be dead by now. You will be able to go to the mainland in a few days."

"A few days! But I must get back to England at once, if I have to go on a stretcher."

"It is no use. He says you must lie quiet. But I will take you to the mainland as soon as you are fit to travel. Perhaps you would like to send a message to someone?"

Brading reflected, and then shook his head. He wanted to dispatch his own messages, and without a moment's unnecessary delay. But it was no use arguing while the doctor was present. He asked Frontenac to pay him for his services, and this Frontenac did from a well-packed wallet.

The two went out, and after a few minutes Frontenac came

back again looking very relieved. Through the open window Brading could hear the throb of an engine in the distance.

"So he came in another boat ?" he asked.

"Yes. He had to get back. I was lucky to be able to bring him at once. He is very expensive. He charged me three thousand francs."

Brading smiled at the Frenchman's idea of expensiveness, and reached out for his trousers which contained his wallet.

"Will twenty dollars settle it ?" he asked.

"It is too much."

"No. Cheap at the price. Now about me. You've got to take me across tomorrow morning. It's best from every point of view. I don't want Grogan turning up here, and I must put the police on the track of Besterling. Was there a name on that boat he was using ? I didn't see one when I went aboard."

"There was a name, but it had been painted out. I could make out the first letters. They were A-L-B-A. There was more of it, but it was not visible."

"Might be Albatross."

"Yes, it could have been that. Oh, there is another thing. When I saw Besterling taking away the petrol cans his face was bleeding badly. Anna must have scratched him when he took her by force."

"Good ! That may help. Now about tomorrow. Is it a date?"

"Is it wise ?"

"More than wise. It's imperative."

"I will do what you wish. But there will be trouble to land you at the port unless you have a passport."

"There must be a Canadian consul somewhere——"

"There is a better plan. I have brought a good supply of petrol with me. I might be able to land you in England if the calm weather continues."

"Now you're talking good sense. Land me in England and I'll pay you a hundred dollars."

"The money isn't all that important, M'sieur. I have caused you much trouble against my better judgement. My wife has been right from the start. Tomorrow I will land you in England unless there is a full gale, and all I ask is your silence about me."

"You have my word on that."

"Good. Now sleep, and then eat well."

21

IN the meantime McLean, in London, had been keeping a close watch on the three chief suspects—Toovey, Magnay and Grogan. It was in the nature of things an extremely difficult business, for even the best detectives could slip up in the tricky business of shadowing a particular individual in a densely crowded city, and in restaurants and 'tube' subways with their jostling thousands.

"I can't afford to lose touch with any one of them," complained McLean. "Yet the Chief is talking about taking away some of my observers when I could do with two or three more."

"What about the arrested man—Hachette ? Can't we put a bit more pressure on him ?"

"Not a hope. Then there's Besterling, still at large. What he's doing is anybody's guess. But the newspapers will carry his portrait again tomorrow with the offer of a reward of a thousand pounds for information leading to his capture."

"I wouldn't mind winning that," said Brook.

"You are not eligible, my dear Brook. See what that is ?"

Brook picked up the telephone receiver. It was Dyson on the other end of the line, one of McLean's watchers. He had something to report. Brook handed the receiver to McLean, who took it with some eagerness.

"All right, Dyson," he said, after a pause. "Keep after him."

Brook stared at McLean as he replaced the receiver.

"At last Toovey has made contact with Magnay," he said. "He went from Streatham to Magnay's hotel, and is now having lunch with him."

"You don't think that's important ?" asked Brook.

"Not from our point of view. They admit to knowing each other. Lunching with an old friend is quite an innocent relaxation. Now if they should decide to go off together after lunch it would be a different matter. But I don't think they will."

"Why not ?"

"They must know they are being watched. You may watch

an innocent man and he will never know it. He has no need to look over his shoulder every few steps. Grogan, too, knows, but he would have no excuse for visiting the other pair. Yet I feel that somewhere, and very soon, they must meet, and not only meet but act in some way."

The next day McLean received the blow he expected. Four of his watchers were detailed for other duties, and he was told to do the best he could with what he had. He accepted this situation with good grace, but Brook was furious.

"I'll bet Inspector Drewe has got those chaps," he said. "Helping him to nail Besterling, who's probably in Jericho by this time. They must want him badly to offer a thousand nicker. But it's like locking the stable after the horse has gone."

"They do want him badly, because the warder he slugged is seriously ill. We want him, too, so in a sense Drewe is working in our interest."

"But what do we do about Grogan ? He's now free to go where he likes."

"Not where he likes. He can't leave the country by boat or 'plane. I've seen to that. And I can still keep a limited watch on Toovey and Magnay."

It was later in the day when the gloom of the morning was relieved by a most astonishing telephone message from the Southampton police to the effect that a man believed to be Neville Brading had been given admission to the hospital. He was suffering from gunshot wounds, but was in fair condition, and was asking to see someone from Scotland Yard immediately in respect of the missing woman, Anna Westmoreland.

"Manna from Heaven !" said McLean. "Get the fastest car we've got."

Within an hour and a half McLean and Brook were in the private ward of the hospital where Brading was sitting up in bed, looking a little worse for wear, but otherwise full of life. He recognized Brook at once, and Brook introduced McLean.

"You've been giving us a very busy time," said McLean. "Tell me in your own words what happened to you ?"

Brading recounted his experiences up to the time when he and Anna were taken away from the house in Cornwall by the launch, and then stopped.

"Continue," said McLean.

"We were taken to a place, but I don't want to tell you where."

"Why not ?"

"Because the people there had nothing whatever to do with our being kidnapped. That was the work of a man named Grogan."

"Ah !" said McLean. "That let's in some light. We have had Grogan under observation. But please continue."

"We were foisted on these people, who treated us well, but were afraid to let us go because Grogan had some pull over them. But finally they repented and actually helped me to escape. For that reason I don't want them subjected to any publicity or questioning. They are not British citizens."

"In that case you need not tell me anything more about them. But what happened to you and Miss Westmoreland—I mean Mrs. Besterling ?"

"So you know about that ?"

"Yes."

Brading then related the rest of his story, McLean listening intently to every word of it until it concluded with Brading's landing at the port only two hours previously.

"So Anna never told you where she had really hidden the parcel which plays such a big part in this business ?"

"No. I did not even ask her. She may have told Besterling before he took her away, but whether it was the truth or not I am unable to say."

"You don't know how much petrol he had in the boat ?"

"No. But he had those two spare cans. I'm pretty sure that his intention was to come back to England and get the parcel, and that he took Anna only because he thought she might be double-crossing him."

"Can you describe the boat he was using ?"

"Yes, and there's something else I forgot to mention. I have a good clue to the name of it, which was imperfectly painted out. The first four letters were A-L-B-A. There were other letters which could not be made out. I thought it might be 'Albatross'."

"Quite a reasonable guess. What about the boat itself ?"

Brading gave the details, which Brook wrote down, and then he remembered Frontenac's statement about Besterling's badly scratched face. McLean nodded appreciatively.

"Oh!" said Brading. "Did the gang do anything about that note which I sent to my friend Winterton?"

"They did. They decided not to wait until Winterton's return from Canada, and two men broke into his flat, but found nothing because, according to Winterton, there was nothing to find. Fortunately one of the men was caught, and is in custody. His name is Leon Vigny."

"Leon! He's one of Grogan's men."

"Yes. He poses as Grogan's chauffeur. But nothing will make him talk. I should like you to see him later."

"It will be a pleasure," said Brading. "I owe him something. But about Anna, Inspector. Is there any hope of finding her?"

"Every hope. How long do they propose keeping you here?"

"Only a few days, as they badly want this bed. I shall then go back to my hotel and rest a bit. What about my car?"

"You can have it whenever you want it. Now I have to hurry back to procure a warrant for the arrest of Grogan. That's a nice thought for you to sleep on. When there is any news of Anna I will let you know."

"Thanks a lot."

McLean went back to Scotland Yard extremely pleased with the new development.

"Find Besterling and we find Anna," he said. "But that only holds good temporarily."

"You think they'll part company soon?"

"I think it's a certainty. Once he lays his hands on what he wants he'll abandon her. To stay with her a moment longer than is absolutely necessary would be madness, and he's clever enough to realize that. Somewhere he's got that boat hidden up, with his wife a prisoner in it."

"But he may not go back to it, once he gets the parcel," said Brook.

"I think he may. It's his best means of escape. He must know that we have all other bolt holes blocked. His best plan would be to put Anna ashore late at night and then get across to the French coast. There he could sink the boat and possibly get clean away."

"The fool to come back at all," said Brook, "when he was already halfway to freedom."

"It's the lure of wealth in some shape or form. He's so tied to that parcel that he is incapable of thinking or acting logically. Now I want to have a word with Inspector Drewe before I see the Chief about that warrant."

Drewe, wrestling with messages that had come over the telephone in response to the appeal in the morning press, and looking none too happy about them, was amazed by what McLean had to tell him, and a little huffed that McLean had got in first.

"I think I should have been told about this," he said.

"You are being told. Brading was my case, and I had no idea that Besterling would be mentioned until I saw him. Now we both seem to be in the same boat."

"I wish we were in Besterling's boat," growled Drewe. "Anyway, thanks for the details. I'll get them circulated at once."

"Any luck with your newspaper announcement?"

"Lot of rubbish chiefly. Nothing really worth following up. Besterling has been seen in Liverpool, Manchester, London, even Scotland, in places where only an escaped lunatic would show his face. But this is different. We ought to be able to find that boat. What's your own angle exactly?"

"I'm applying for a warrant for Grogan's arrest. It cuts across my previous plan, but I can't afford to leave him at large. Keep in touch."

"Okay."

§ 22

MR. EDWIN GROGAN, now alone in his house at Streatham, was not completely innocent of what was going on at police headquarters. He was like a man walking a tight-rope over Niagara. The slightest mistake now and he would be swept to his doom. Quick at sizing up men, he made no mistake about McLean. A very astute officer that, working patiently and efficiently, behaving as if he believed every word that was told him, while all the time his brain was busy seeking out inconsistencies. Just how much did McLean know ? What strings was he pulling behind the scenes ?

One string at least was obvious to Grogan. McLean had set a watch on his movements. Everywhere he went he was followed, and he knew there were at least two men employed. They never so much as looked at him, but he was too old a bird to be deceived. He also suspected that his telephone calls were intercepted, or at least recorded, and so he was very careful what persons he spoke to on his own telephone.

Things had gone all wrong. Anna had lied. Brading had lied. Now he wanted to get back to them and force the truth out of them, but he dared not take that risk. Then there was Leon in prison. He had implicit faith in Leon, but—one never knew. The situation was tense in the extreme, for Mr. Magnay would not wait for ever. There was the possibility that Magnay might wash his hands of the whole business, in which case it would mean fresh negotiations. He saw his dream castle of great wealth and luxury breaking up before his eyes.

On this particular morning something happened, or to be more correct did not happen. He left the house on foot, caught a bus and went into the centre of the town. It was soon clear to him that no longer was he being followed. He went into a café and ordered some coffee, watching the entrance door for those now familiar faces. But neither of them put in an appearance. When finally he went home, on foot this time, he felt like a man out of a cage. Of course it might be a trick to lure him into some indiscreet act, and for the shadowing to be suddenly clamped on again. On the other hand he might have fooled them after all.

The point now was—should he get away while he could, and make one last desperate attempt to wring the truth from Anna or her boy-friend ? He dared not think of taking the same boat, but there were other means.

He was rapidly coming to a decision when a miracle happened. A bell rang, and he knew it was the bell at the tradesmen's entrance. Cursing at the absence of his late domestics, he went through the passage to the back door. Outside stood a man in a mackintosh. He was wearing glasses and consulting a thick accounts book which he held in his hands, and his impression was that it was a man come to read the gas or electric meter. As he opened the door the face came up, a face on which were two long scratches. Then the glasses were whipped off and he uttered a cry of amazement.

"Besterling!"

"Yes, your old friend. Get inside."

"You must be mad to come here."

"Get inside! I want to talk business."

Grogan hesitated for a moment and then opened the door wider. Besterling entered and closed the door.

"Who's in the house?" he asked.

"Nobody but me. What the hell do you want here?"

"I'll tell you when you get me a drink. Go on, into the sitting-room. We can talk there. It's a matter in which you are more than a bit interested. But don't try any tricks, because I'm not in the mood to enjoy them."

In the sitting-room Besterling drew the curtains a little closer, although the room was some distance from the road. Grogan produced some whisky and soda and poured out two glasses, watching Besterling like a lynx.

"Mud in your eye!" said Besterling, raising his glass. "Seen the newspapers this morning?"

"Of course I've seen the newspapers. But I thought you were out of the country."

"I was—with Anna."

Grogan almost choked over his drink.

"You've seen Anna?" he asked incredulously. "Who told you where Anna was?"

"An old friend of yours. I admit I had to use a lot of persuasion, which he'll remember for a long time. But I found Anna—and her boy-friend."

"Where?"

"So you don't believe me, eh? Well, when next you see Gaston Vassier. . . . Ah, you believe me now?"

Grogan was breathing heavily. He seemed not sure that this unexpected visit, on the part of the man he had sent to prison, had either a peaceful or a business motive. Besterling, sensing his doubt, uttered a little laugh.

"Not interested in that nice little reward of a thousand quid, I hope?" he said.

"Don't be a damned fool. You robbed me—you can't deny that. I had to do something about it, didn't I?"

"You didn't have to beat up my wife."

"That's not true. You took that stuff, as well as the cash. Can you blame me if I took steps to recover my property? What would you have done had it been the other way round?"

"All right—all right. But if you had played fair this wouldn't have happened. You promised a pay-off for my assistance and what did I get? Practically nothing."

"I told you that I would settle in full when I had disposed of the stuff. That was no easy matter. But you wouldn't wait. You wanted the whole works, and you darn nearly got away with it."

Besterling lighted a cigarette, and helped himself to another whisky, neat this time.

"In spite of everything I'm ready to do a deal with you, Edwin," he said.

"What sort of a deal?"

"Delivery of the stuff—for a consideration."

"When you find it."

"I mean now—within an hour."

Grogan was all attention, but he eyed Besterling suspiciously.

"Are you sure where it is?" he asked.

"Dead sure. Anna told me."

"She told me, too, but it happened to be untrue. She'd tell you anything to get rid of you."

"She didn't get rid of me. I took her away from that place where you marooned her."

"Indeed. What did Brading say to that?"

"He said a whole lot, but I took her, and am going back to her when I have settled this business."

"Well, what's the proposition?" asked Grogan, endeavouring to conceal his immense interest.

"Five thousand pounds in used one-pound notes, in exchange for the parcel intact. That's chicken-feed compared to the value of that stuff."

Grogan shrugged his shoulders. The whole situation was fantastic. Immediately he laid his finger on the incredible part of the offer.

"If you know exactly what Anna did with the parcel why don't you go and get it?" he asked.

"You're a bright boy, Edwin, but not bright enough. Anna

lodged that parcel in a place where I dare not go without running the risk of being recognized."

"Why should you be recognized—at dead of night, for example ?"

"It can't be got at dead of night."

"Then why didn't you send Anna ?"

"Anna's not co-operative."

"But you believe her word ?" said Grogan, with heavy sarcasm.

"I tell you I know where the parcel is, without a shred of doubt. I have proof of it."

"Produce your proof, and then we'll talk seriously."

Besterling hesitated for a moment, and then produced a small notebook from his pocket. Inside was a thin piece of paper, folded very small. He opened this out, and held it up for Grogan to read. It was a receipt from the left-luggage office at Waterloo station for one package, and it was dated some three weeks previously.

"It—it could be a fake," said Grogan.

"It could be, but it isn't. I got Anna to admit she deposited the parcel there, and she kept this receipt in the back of an old watch which her father had given her when she was a kid."

"You could still have taken a chance," said Grogan, not yet completely satisfied.

"No. There are two men in that office who knew me in the past. That's the hell of it."

Grogan paced up and down. If Besterling were speaking the truth, all his previous misfortune could be righted, for Magnay was still in the market. It seemed to him that Besterling would not have risked this visit to him without solid reasons. True, he was asking for a comparatively large sum of money, but no one but an idiot would imagine that he would part with such a sum without seeing what he was buying.

"I shall have to consult my partner," he said finally.

"Meaning Lance ?"

"Yes."

"There's no time. This deal has to go through. . . ."

"It won't take much time, for Lance is in London."

"Then ring him up now."

"Not on this 'phone. I'm not sure that my calls aren't

being intercepted. I'll have to go to the public box on the corner of the street. You'd better wait here."

Besterling stared into Grogan's eyes.

"Be sure it is Lance you ring up," he said. "You may be in need of a thousand quid."

"Use your brains," snapped Grogan. "What would I get out of giving you away to the police ? I want that stuff, and I want it as quickly as you want your rake-off. Stay here, and I'll be back in a few minutes."

Besterling nodded, and Grogan left him, pointing to the whisky as he closed the door behind him. He was back again in a very short time, to find the whisky nearly all gone.

"Well ?" asked Besterling.

"Lance is agreeable, but he wants to talk first. I couldn't go into details on the phone."

"Haven't we done enough talking ?"

"No. He's arranged a meeting place in an hour's time."

"Where ?"

"At Jan's filling station."

Besterling's eyes opened wide. He seemed to have objections, but finally he shrugged his shoulders and nodded.

"How do we get there ?" he asked. "I can't risk taking a public conveyance."

"I'll drive you there. The car can be driven into the garage and we can talk in the back room."

"But there's an assistant there in the daytime."

"He'll be got rid of. In the meantime Lance will go to the bank and arrange about drawing the money."

"Why arrange ? Can't he bring it ?"

"He may, but sometimes banks need a little time to meet a sudden demand for a largish sum in old notes. You've no need to worry. Later we will draw the money before the bank closes. But no payment until delivery of the goods. That's fair enough, isn't it ?"

"Yes. When do we start ?"

"In half an hour. No, it may be safer running around in the car than staying here. I'll get it right away."

Grogan came back with the car. He gave a little toot outside and Besterling was quickly in the back seat. They drove around the streets aimlessly for some time, and then took the road for Jan's Garage, which was near Hampstead Heath.

It was quite a small place, with a row of pumps outside and a long brick building where presumably running repairs were carried out. Grogan saw Jan by the pumps, gave him a sign, and ran his car deep into the garage, where there was a small office beside a staircase which led to a store-room above.

"We shall be all right here," he said to Besterling. "I think we'd better talk upstairs. That office is a bit too public."

Besterling got out of the car as Jan came in. The latter stood staring at Besterling as if he could not believe his eyes. The spectacles which Besterling had donned was no disguise from Jan's point of view.

"Remember me?" asked Besterling ominously.

"Never seen you before," replied Jan.

"Good!"

"We're going upstairs," said Grogan. "When Lance comes tell him we're there."

"Okay!" said Jan.

The two men had scarcely reached the upper room when a taxi drew up outside and from it stepped Mr. Lancelot Toovey, neatly dressed as he always was. He paid off the driver quickly and looked at Jan.

"They're here," said Jan. "Upstairs. Want me to lock up now? I've told the boy he needn't come back."

"I think that's a good idea. But stay around."

"I'll be in the office."

Toovey mounted the stairs and entered the stockroom, where Besterling and Grogan were sitting on a low bench amid rows of tyres and what-not.

"Good to see you, Harold," he said. "You've given the police a nice run. I've been to the bank and arranged about the cash. It will be ready in an hour."

"Then what have we to talk about?" demanded Besterling.

"Quite a lot. If you are telling the truth, which I believe you are, I don't want to muck the thing up by inadequate precautions. For instance, I don't want you running around for the next few hours, and that goes for Edwin, too. You will both stay here until nine o'clock. Then bring the car to Waterloo station and meet me outside the left-luggage office, say at nine-thirty."

"Why wait all that time?" asked Besterling.

"Because by that time it will be dark, and the job is best done in darkness."

"But there's no risk," argued Besterling. "They are bound to hand over the parcel on demand."

"If the receipt is genuine."

"Of course it's genuine. Do you think I could fake a thing like that ? What would I gain by attempting it, since it's understood you pay me nothing until you handle the stuff."

"May I see it ?"

"No. Your brother has already seen it, and is satisfied."

"But it is I who am putting up the money."

"You don't put up any money until you have the goods."

"But I take risks. I take one when I meet you and do not inform the police. I take another when I go to that office and tender a receipt which may be spurious. Anna is rather a clever woman."

"Good heavens ! Do you think Anna could fabricate a railway receipt form ?"

"No, but the receipt might cover some quite valueless article which she chose to leave at the office. My time is valuable."

"Mine is even more valuable," said Besterling. "But here's the receipt. You can look at it, but not touch it."

He produced the paper, and Toovey put on his glasses and examined it from a distance of about two feet. Then he produced from his pocket an exactly similar receipt.

"I took the precaution of getting a specimen," he said. "Yes, they are identical. All right. The deal stands, but it must be tonight. I'll bring the notes in an attaché case, and we can swop parcels in the car, and then land you safely somewhere. But be punctual. You can't afford to hang about that station."

"Thank God that's settled," said Grogan. "But have we really got to stay in this dismal hole all that time ?"

"You have," replied Toovey, authoritatively. "To take any chances now would be madness. I'll tell Jan to bring you a pack of cards and you'll be surprised how quickly time will pass."

Downstairs, Toovey had a word with Jan. He, too, was to stay on the premises until Grogan and Besterling had gone. He was not to use the telephone on any account. Then he left by the side door and walked briskly up the road to the taxi rank.

IT was one o'clock when McLean finally got his warrant for the arrest of Grogan, and he and Brook drove over to Streatham to put it into effect. They found the house closed, also the garage. McLean peered through the small garage window and saw that the car had gone.

"That would have to happen," said McLean. "The moment we take off our men he is gone. That was a bad mistake. They should have given me the warrant when I first suggested it, but the official view was I hadn't provided sufficient grounds."

"What do we do now—wait?" asked Brook.

"One of us certainly, and that means you. If he returns, hold him, and use his phone to ring me at the office. I'll go back and put out a message for his car to be stopped if it is seen. Fortunately we have his car number. Here, you had better take this—just in case."

He produced an automatic which he had drawn prior to leaving headquarters, and Brook slipped the weapon into his pocket.

"Don't tell him anything," said McLean. "Just hold him until I come along."

McLean got back into the car and drove himself back to the office. There he sent out the message relative to Grogan's car, and was about to take a bite of lunch when the man who had been on observation at Toovey's hotel entered the office.

"I thought I'd better come and report personally, sir," he said. "Just after one o'clock Toovey left the hotel, carrying an attaché case. I'm certain he didn't see me, but he was very cautious. He walked to Harrods and went inside. Wandered through several departments, and finally took the lift to one of the upper floors. Rather than wait for the next lift I dived up the staircase, and there he was coming down. I had a newspaper in my hand and pretended not to notice him. But I found him again, in the street, getting on to a west-bound bus. His back was towards me, and as he got into the lower portion I went up the stairs. From where I sat I could see the passengers leave the bus, but he never got off until we reached Pall Mall. The bus was just starting again when I got off, and Toovey was crossing the road. I halted behind a car and saw him enter a bank."

"What bank?" asked McLean.

The name of the bank was given and McLean wrote it down.

"I now had plenty of time to hide-up," said the detective. "He was in the bank six minutes; when he came out he wasn't carrying the attaché case."

"You're sure he had it when he went in?"

"Quite sure."

"Well, what next?"

"I trailed him successfully for some time, and then he dived into a narrow alley in Seven Dials. I had to wait until he got to the other end, but when I got there he was gone. I think he must have jumped a passing taxi, for I looked everywhere and saw no sign of him. I'm sorry, sir."

"That's all right," said McLean. "I know the difficulties in that area. Better go back to the hotel and get a fresh hold of him. Ring me when you make contact."

McLean took a very brief meal and then telephoned to Grogan's house. He was informed there was no reply, and from that he assumed that Brook was still waiting for the absent man. Intrigued by the detective's story of the suitcase, McLean went to the bank in Pall Mall and saw the manager.

"What can I do for you, Inspector?" he asked.

"I believe you have a customer named Lancelot Toovey, who lives near Falmouth?"

"Toovey? No, I don't think so. Just a moment."

He pushed a button and a clerk knocked and entered.

"Have we an account in the name of Lancelot Toovey?" asked the manager.

"No, sir."

"Well, I know that this gentleman called here less than two hours ago," said McLean. "He was carrying an attaché case, which apparently he left here."

"Oh, that was Mr. Lance Grogan," said the clerk.

"Yes, of course," said the manager. "He does live near Falmouth, but has only a drawing account there. His main account is at this branch."

"Can you tell me the nature of his business this morning ?'

The manager looked at his underling and told him that would be all, whereupon the young man left the room.

"Do you ask this in your official capacity, Inspector ?" asked the manager.

"Absolutely. This man is under suspicion, and also under observation."

"In that case I suppose I have no option. He called here to cash a cheque for five thousand pounds, and he wanted the money in used one-pound notes. We do not usually have to meet sudden demands of that nature, so he was informed that it would take us an hour or so to get the necessary notes. He called back about half an hour ago and took away the notes in the attaché case which he had previously left with the cashier."

"Has he ever before drawn considerable sums of money— in used one-pound notes ?"

"No. His cash drawings are most modest. In fact we see very little of him here."

"Have you any idea at all why he should want that large amount of cash ?"

"None whatever."

"There appears to be another member of the family, named Edwin Grogan, who lives at Streatham. Do you happen to know him ?"

"No."

McLean thanked him and then left. There seemed little doubt now that Lance and Edwin were either brothers or cousins. They were certainly not father and son, for there was too little disparity between their ages. Toovey—so called— was probably ten years the older, but bore no resemblance at all to Edwin. That they were hand-in-glove in this business was obvious.

The drawing of the money was highly significant. A payment had to be made to some person who did not want the notes traceable, and McLean could think of one such person— Besterling. It was Besterling who had taken great risks in forcibly removing his wife from the place where Edwin Grogan had left her. Was it out of love for her, or because she alone knew where the mysterious parcel was ? Had Besterling managed to extract from her that vital information ? If so, had he sold that information to the elder Grogan for the sum of five thousand pounds ?

There seemed to be a flaw in this train of reasoning, for if Besterling was able to lay his hands on the parcel, why sell the secret to another person who would obviously pay only a fraction of its real worth ?

He went back to the office deep in thought, and the more he thought the more he was convinced that the parcel had been found and that the pay-off was about to take place, or had indeed taken place already. Again he telephoned the house at Streatham, only to find no change in the situation. Then came Inspector Drewe, hot and excited.

"Important news, Mac," he said. "A body was taken from the Solent early this morning. It was that of a man named Selkirk. He had been on holiday in a cabin motor cruiser named *Alma Mater* !"

"That explains a lot," said McLean.

"Yes. The body was almost naked and had a serious head wound, although he actually died from drowning."

"So Besterling must have knocked him out while he was aboard the boat and then taken his clothing ?"

"That's it. Previously a small boat was missing, but that has now been found. Presumably it didn't suit Besterling's purpose, so he went after bigger and faster game. It is a sea-going craft, and equipped with a capacious tank. He could be anywhere by now."

"I don't think so," said McLean. "He's not far away. Did you put out that SOS ?"

"Yes."

"Then we've got to act swiftly——"

McLean stopped as Drewe put his hand to his stomach, groaned a little and sat down.

"My damned ulcer working again," said Drewe. "That would happen when I'm up to my ears. Mac, you may have to take over the whole boiling. I've simply got to lie up. After all, Besterling is as much your case as mine. Now it's murder, and you'll get all the help you want."

A little later McLean heard that Drewe had been given leave of absence on medical grounds, and that the whole case was now in his hands. The precious hours passed and nothing fresh came in. Grogan had not returned to his house, and

Toovey was still absent from his hotel. It was tantalizing to reflect that somewhere, not very far away, the *Alma Mater* was lying up, possibly with Anna aboard, trussed up and incapable of action, while her murderous spouse was gathering in the harvest.

His mind turned to Magnay. Of the four miscreants he was the only one apparently available, for no news had come from the lone detective who had been watching him since early morning. Presuming that he was involved, which seemed beyond doubt, the probability was that the wily Indonesian's role was that of receiver, and the odds were against the Grogans holding the booty a minute longer than was necessary. A report was due from the watching detective in an hour, but McLean was not prepared to wait so long. He went to the hotel where Magnay was staying, and found the detective waiting in a parked car where he had a good view of the hotel entrance.

"Things are at boiling point," he said. "Is he still in the hotel?"

"Yes, sir. This morning he went to the National Gallery and spent an hour there. This afternoon he went for a walk in Regent's Park. He was alone all the time. But on his way back he went into a public telephone box. He spent four minutes there, and there was nothing I could do about it."

"Of course not. I'm going inside to see him. It may come to nothing, but I'll see you when I come out."

"Very good, sir."

McLean entered the hotel, and was told that Magnay had been seen going down to the American Bar a few minutes earlier. McLean went down the steps to the bar, which was packed with people. He pushed his way through the crowd, and then saw Magnay in a recess talking to a well-dressed girl. As Magnay's back was towards McLean he could not possibly have seen him enter, and McLean took up a position where it was almost impossible for Magnay to see him if he looked that way. He ordered a drink, and watched the couple in the recess. The Indonesian was most attentive to his attractive companion, and they were both drinking what appeared to be champagne cocktails. A few minutes passed and then the loudspeaker over the door bellowed:

'Attention, please! Mr. Magnay wanted on the telephone. Mr. Magnay wanted on the telephone in the inner hall. Thank you!'

Magnay apologized to his girl-friend and went out of the door at great speed. McLean finished his drink, walked in leisurely fashion to the door, but then sprang up the stairs three at a time. He saw Magnay disappear into the telephone box in the inner hall. McLean walked to the box as if he were unaware that it was being used. He saw Magnay with his back towards him talking to someone, but not a word was audible from that sound-proof cubicle. McLean suddenly opened the door, and Magnay's head came round.

"I beg your pardon," said McLean. "I didn't realize——But what a coincidence! I was just about to enquire after you?"

"On the telephone?" asked Magnay.

"Oh, no. At the desk. But please go on with your conversation."

He shut the door. The ruse had been partly successful, for he had heard the words 'I shall be waiting . . .' But where would Magnay be waiting, and for what? A few moments later Magnay emerged.

"You wish to see me?" he lisped.

"Yes, but not here. What I have to say would be better said in your apartment."

"But——"

"In your apartment, please."

"Very well."

They went up in the lift to a very luxurious suite on the first floor. It comprised a bedroom, bathroom, and sitting-room. In the sitting-room there was a pile of suitcases, apparently ready for transport, but not yet did they bear any labels.

"I have a friend waiting for me downstairs," said Magnay, "so would you please expedite your business."

"Yes. You have, I believe, seen your friend Toovey since you have been in town?"

"Yes. He telephoned me from his hotel to say he was in town for a few days, and I invited him here to lunch."

"Have you always known him as Lancelot Toovey?"

"Yes—always."

189

"Have you completed your business in London ?"

"Yes. I am leaving tomorrow morning."

"For Paris, I think you told me ?"

"Yes, for Paris."

McLean gave a glance at the suitcases.

"All your personal belongings ?" he asked.

"Yes. The things I came with, excepting a few presents."

"I should like you to open those cases, Mr. Magnay."

"But that is a most unusual request. Surely only the Customs officials have the right to demand that ?"

"In normal circumstances, yes. But this is a different matter. I don't demand it. I am merely making the request."

"But for what purpose ? It has taken me some time to pack the cases."

"It will not take me long to look through them."

"And if I decline ?"

"Then I shall have to ask you to come to police headquarters, with your luggage, where the proper authority will be issued."

Mr. Magnay shrugged his shoulders.

"You have the last word," he said. "But please hurry. The cases are not locked."

McLean started on the suitcases, and was a little disappointed when he found nothing but clothing and a couple of cases containing culture pearls which according to Magnay was his particular line of business.

"I hope you are satisfied," said Magnay, with a smile.

McLean nodded, but then went to the wardrobe in the bedroom and opened it. It was empty except for a pair of slippers and a dressing-gown. He then pulled open the drawers in the dressing table and found them all empty except one which refused to open.

"This one is locked," he said. "Have you the key ?"

Mr. Magnay hesitated for a moment, and then produced the key from his pocket. McLean opened the drawer and found a large leather satchel inside. It was equipped with a zip-fastener and also a small lock.

"This also needs a key," said McLean.

"Oh, yes. It contains money, and I know better than to leave money lying about in a hotel, no matter how respectable."

He handed McLean another small key and the satchel was then opened. Inside was a solid block of new American bills of very high denomination. McLean counted them meticulously.

"Two hundred and fifty thousand dollars," he said. "That is a lot of money to carry around."

"Yes, it is rather."

"Did you bring these dollars with you?"

"Yes. They were for business purposes, but the business didn't materialize."

"What was the nature of the business?"

"I think we will leave it at that, Inspector. I have been very patient."

"So have I," said McLean. "I should like to see your passport again."

On this occasion Magnay had the passport in his pocket. He handed it to McLean, and McLean perused it for a moment.

"I am afraid I shall have to check this up," said McLean.

"But tomorrow morning——"

"You shall have it back early tomorrow morning. I am sorry to cause you all this trouble. Better take care of that money."

Magnay said nothing. He watched McLean leave the room, and only then did his suave demeanour change. The slant eyes blazed with anger, and frustration, and he sat down on the bed and stared into space.

McLean was pleased by the outcome of his visit, but by no means satisfied. He had for the time being put a check on Magnay's movements, but that was but a drop in the ocean. The other members of the gang were still at large, and Besterling might have completed his part of the dishonest business and be hareing back to the stolen boat. He hurried to the watching detective.

"Magnay has some appointment this evening," he said. "He may keep it or he may not. It is absolutely imperative that we do not lose touch with him. I will send you two men as soon as I get back to headquarters. But you will have to stay on to identify Magnay if he should leave."

"That's all right, sir."

"I want reports every half-hour."

"Very good, sir."

Back at the Yard McLean dispatched two men to aid the

man covering Magnay. As no word had come from Brook or the man who was watching for Toovey, he concluded that the situation in both cases was unaltered. He weighed up the probabilities. The Grogans must have got possession of the parcel and paid off Besterling. They had then telephoned Magnay and made some appointment with him, at which meeting, no doubt, the grand coup would be accomplished. But would Magnay part with his dollars while McLean held his passport ? It was a nice question and one to which McLean did not know the answer.

§ 24

WHILE McLean was sitting in his office, depressed by the dead silence on the part of Brook and the reports of no change from his other watchers, Grogan and Besterling in the stock-room at Jan's Garage sat playing their last hand of cards, amid a welter of cigarette ends and in a thick cloud of suffocating smoke.

It was a fortunate hand for Besterling, for he had doubled the stakes, and held a beautiful run of 'spades.' He called 'nap' and spread out his cards on the table. Grogan took one look at them and threw in his cards.

"Five bob !" said Besterling. "You're no good at this game, Ed."

"I'm good at others," growled Grogan as he paid the money. "Now we've got to get going. Hope Jan's fixed that new registration plate. Come on !"

They went down the stairs into the garage, where Jan had positioned the car for an instant getaway. Grogan looked at the new number plates and grunted his satisfaction.

"I'll drive," he said to Besterling. "You'd better sit in the back and put on those spectacles."

Besterling did this, and Grogan took his place at the driving wheel.

"Will you be coming back here?" asked Jan. "Or can I go home?"

"You can go. I'll bring the car tomorrow morning and you can swop over the plates then."

"Okay!"

The car moved out and was soon in thick traffic making towards the rendezvous. Grogan looked a little nervous now, but Besterling appeared to be as cool as a cucumber, as he stretched himself out in the long seat, smoking another of his interminable cigarettes.

"You'd better step on it," he said. "This is like a funeral procession."

"I'm driving," snapped Grogan. "Nice jam we should be in if I had an accident now."

At the top of Charing Cross Road a policeman who was directing the traffic waved his hand and stopped. From the back Besterling could see Grogan's grim face in the driving mirror.

"My goodness, you're in a flap," he said. "I thought you were a tough sort of guy."

Grogan made no retort, but he breathed an audible sigh of relief when the constable changed his position and gave them the road. Besterling laughed.

"I'm enjoying this," he said. "Any one of all these people could pick up a thousand quid as easy as kiss my hand, and they haven't a clue."

"Shut up!" snarled Grogan. "You can be comic later on, but not now."

"The trouble with you, Ed, is that you've got no faith in yourself. Now that precious brother of yours is different. No flies on Master Lance. He knows all the answers. Steady! You can't cross the bridge here. You've got to go all round the houses."

Grogan's nervousness was now intense. So much was at stake and the outcome lay only a few minutes ahead. Yet there was nothing to worry about if Besterling was telling the truth, and that he must be telling the truth was obvious by his presence in the car.

At last they came to the entrance to Waterloo Bridge with the traffic lights in their favour. The car moved across the wide even surface, turned into the station entrance, and finally came to a halt in the parking area. The great moment was at hand.

"Dead on time," said Grogan. "You'd better stay in the car. Give me the ticket and——"

"Not me," said Besterling. "I'm coming with you. There are lots of ways out of this station."

"But it's dangerous."

"That's my worry. Come on, let's see if Lance is on time. Don't look so damned scared. It's going to be as easy as falling off a log. You'll see."

It was clear he meant to have his way, and Grogan went with him on to the platform and from there to the left luggage office. Outside the office was Lance, with an attaché case in his right hand. He showed no sign of excitement or worry.

"Got that ticket, Harold?" he asked.

"Sure!"

"Give it to me then."

"When I've had a peep inside that case," said Besterling.

"Well, be quick!"

Lance opened the case, and Besterling saw inside it the many packets of banded used one-pound notes, each one marked '100' in blue pencil.

"Okay!" he said. "Here's the ticket."

Lance took the small ticket and walked into the office. It was a slack time, and two minutes later he reappeared with a wrapped parcel under his left arm.

"To the car," he said. "Don't hurry."

They entered the car, Lance beside his brother, and Besterling in the back seat.

"Now I'll take my cut," said Besterling.

"Not here you won't. I want to have a look inside the box, and that's best done elsewhere. Where do you want to be dropped?"

"Down river. I'll direct you."

Edwin had now got his nerves right. The streets eastward were almost deserted, and before very long they had left the vast built-up area and were rolling along a secondary road in the open country in fading light.

"Open up now, Lance," said Edwin. "Here's the key."

He felt in his waistcoat pocket with his left hand, and then passed a diminutive key to his brother, who had already removed the string from the heavy package. Removal of the waterproof wrapper brought to view a lead box fitted with a brass lock. Lance inserted the key and pulled up the lid. The dashboard light shone into the box. There were two cylindrical objects, wrapped in thin sheet metal. He peeled the wrapping off one of them, gave a little grunt of satisfaction, replaced the wrapping, and closed the box, putting the key into his own pocket.

"Satisfied?" asked Besterling.

"Yes."

"Then hand me that attaché case, and stop at the next cross-road. That's where I get off."

Lance put his hand down to the attaché case and lifted it over the back of the seat to Besterling, who seized it and planted a kiss on it.

"That's one for the road," he said. "Steady, Ed. We're coming to the crossing."

The car slowed down and Edwin could now see the crossing. He pulled up just short of the corner.

"There you are," he said. "Not a thing in sight. Make it snappy. I want to get back."

Besterling rose and opened the rear door, with the attaché case gripped in his left hand. Then he suddenly threw the case back into the car, and opened the front door on the driving side. In his right hand was an automatic, which he pushed into Edwin's side.

"Get out! Beat it!" he snarled.

"You swine!"

"Did you think I was going to let you get away with that stuff?" said Besterling. "Get out, Lance, and leave the package where it is. You follow him, Ed. I give you five seconds. One—two—three——"

"Better come, Edwin," said Lance, and stepped out onto the green verge. But the next moment he was round the back of the car, with a pistol in his hand. Besterling ducked as two bullets missed him by inches and crashed through the bonnet of the car. Then he wheeled and fired, and Lance coughed and fell to his knees, with blood streaming from his mouth.

Edwin, seeing the starting handle at his feet, picked it up, leapt out of the door, and took a swing at Besterling's head. Besterling saw the action in time, and again the automatic spat fire, and Edwin crumpled up and fell not far from his brother. Besterling picked up the fallen pistol and the starting handle, and trundled the two bodies into the ditch on the other side of the verge.

"You asked for it," he muttered insanely. "Never paid your debts, but I pay mine."

Pocketing the two automatics, he got back into the car and pressed the starter. There was a low whirring, but no throb from the engine. Again he tried with the same result. With a curse he got out of the car and raised the bonnet, staring at the two holes which Lance's bullets had made. Then he discovered that one of the bullets had smashed the distributor. The car could not be started. An avalanche of foul invective left his lips. His neat little plan had only partly succeeded.

In the distance he saw bright lights on the telegraph lines, and realized that they came from an approaching car. Quickly he seized the attaché case and the heavier wrapped parcel, slammed the door of the car and went running down the cross-road. Farther on there was a stile leading across a field. He mounted it and was soon in the shadow of tall elms which grew in the hedge. Looking back, he could see that the car had stopped. He ran on the soft turf across one field, then another, until finally he was swallowed up in the darkness.

§ 25

McLEAN's vigil at Scotland Yard was, for a long time, most unrewarding, but at half-past ten there came a message from a small police station at East Hornden to the effect that a Mr.

Ward, who lived in the neighbourhood, had seen a man who answered the description of the escaped convict, with the exception that he was wearing glasses. This man behaved most suspiciously. He lingered for a while outside a public house, which was just about to close, and then took a cycle belonging to a man in the pub. He had some difficulty in riding it as he was carrying an attaché case and another parcel. But finally he went eastward.

This sounded interesting, and McLean lost no time in getting the information radioed to the scattered police cars in the district. But the more dramatic news came ten minutes later, from the police at Upminster. A saloon car had been found abandoned two miles from the town. There were bullet holes in the bonnet, and in the ditch near the car were two severely-wounded men. One of them had died on his way to hospital and there was no clue to this man's identity. But the other carried a letter addressed to Mr. Edwin Grogan. He had been given a blood transfusion, but was not in a state to answer any questions.

McLean had scarcely time to think when again the telephone rang. It was Brook, who stated that nothing had happened at the house, and were there any fresh instructions ?

"Indeed there are," said McLean. "I have just heard that Grogan and his brother have been shot up. The brother is dead, but Grogan is in hospital at Upminster. I'm going there at once. But get a taxi and I'll pick you up on the corner of London Bridge. I think I have news of Besterling, but we shall have to move quickly."

To McLean's great joy Brook was waiting for him when he reached the meeting place, and he took over the wheel to permit McLean to have a perfectly free mind.

"You know the way ?" asked McLean.

"Yes."

"Then let it rip. We can't afford to waste a minute. I'll bring you up to date as we go."

Brook forgot his hunger and thirst as McLean related what had happened since he had last left Brook.

"There's no doubt at all," he concluded, "that Besterling has the parcel. He cashed in on it to the tune of five thousand pounds, and finally decided he would have the parcel as well.

The report of the man who said he saw Besterling steal the cycle has the ring of truth about it, for the car was found about two miles west of the place where the cycle incident took place. I suspect two areas—the waterways round about Canvey Island, and those in the neighbourhood of Rochford. I've concentrated all cars in those two areas, and I've got a speed-boat blocking the exit from the River Crouch. But I must see Grogan first. If he's able to talk he may be able and willing to tell us something useful."

The car went at great speed through the darkness, and was soon at Upminster. At the hospital McLean saw the house surgeon, who told him that Grogan was still in great danger. It was no use at all seeing him. If the blood transfusion was successful Grogan would doubtless be able to make a short statement in the morning.

McLean was disappointed, but got back into the car and told Brook to stop at East Horndon. Here he was taken by the local police to the damaged car, where a constable stood on guard. The vehicle corresponded in every way to Grogan's car with the exception of the number plates. On the road and the grass verge the blood was still wet and plentiful.

"No wonder we couldn't trace the car," mused McLean. "Well, we'd better get on."

"Which way now, sir ?" asked Brook.

"To Rochford. We'll try the reaches of the Crouch, and then run across to Burnham."

While Brook knocked off the miles, McLean studied the map and kept in touch with a number of the radio-equipped police cars, but none of them had anything to report. Finally they reached Rochford, to find the place sunk in slumber. McLean used the wireless and called Car 24, which he knew was in the vicinity. An answer came back. The car was two miles along the small river and two men had gone farther on foot. They had seen a number of small craft on the river, but nothing bearing any resemblance to *Alma Mater*.

"Carry on," said McLean. "I'm going to slip over to the Burnham area. Watch out for a man on a cycle carrying two parcels, or an abandoned cycle."

A little later a report came from Car 19 to the effect that a cycle had been found about two miles above Burnham. The reason for the abandonment appeared to be a deep dyke, which the rider was compelled to wade across.

"We're doing well," said McLean. "If it's Besterling he can't be very far from his destination or he would not part with the machine. There's a track which leads to the ferry just above Burnham. If we get there first we shall have him in a trap. Step on it."

They were now on very indifferent roads, and the car bumped and slithered as Brook drove within the narrowest margin of safety. When they reached the ferry the tide was at the full and there was a great deal of low-lying mist.

"That's in his favour, if he's already gone down-river," said McLean. "With the mist to help him he might get clean away. Leave the car here. We'll have to proceed on foot."

"What about using the ferry boat?"

"He'd run us down if he had the chance."

* * * * *

A mile or so up the tortuous waterway, at a place where the reeds grew high on either side, Anna lay in a bunk inside the cabin of the *Alma Mater* with her arms and legs tightly bound and a bandage round her mouth. The boat was on a short anchorage, and the two portholes of the cabin were screened by curtains.

Since early morning she had lain thus, suffering all the torments of the damned. Nor were her bonds the sole cause of her anguish. Constantly before her mind there arose that vision of Brading, writhing on the sand of Frontenac's island with two bullets in his body. What the future held she dared not think. Finally she had told Besterling the truth about the hidden parcel, and a nearly dislocated right arm was the price she had paid for her earlier stubbornness. He had never believed the lie she had told him, doubtless because he could not credit that she would go deep into Surrey to hide the parcel when she could have done it equally well nearer home. That was the sole reason he had brought her with him. He backed himself to force the truth from her where Grogan had failed, and he had succeeded after the most inhuman treatment and because she was sick of the precious parcel which had brought so much suffering to her and the man she now loved dearly. All she wanted was to be free of him for ever. But was it freedom which awaited her when he came back with the booty ? She had seen him as he really was, and had no illusions left. She had seen him shoot a man down in cold blood, and that made the future—her future—a matter of great uncertainty.

As in a horrible nightmare the minutes and hours passed, without hope. She could hear the water rippling under the boat, but did not know what it really was. It was the only sound in that great stillness, and it seemed to build up into a symphony which went round and round endlessly in her tortured mind.

It was some time later that she heard a new sound. It came from outside the locked cabin door, and it signified to her that Besterling was back. Then there came the sound of a turning handle, followed by the shaking of the door itself. This mystified her, but had the effect of rousing her from her semi-conscious state. To complete this process there came a deep voice.

"Hullo there ! Is anyone inside ?"

To her amazement and great joy it was not Besterling's voice. She gathered all her remaining strength together and tried to shout through the bandage. The result was quite inhuman, but it was effective, for the voice came again.

"She's there. Get a tool and force the door, Brook."

There was silence for a few moments and then there were heavy bangs and a sudden inrush of air.

"There must be a switch here somewhere. Ah !"

The electric light came on and she saw two drenched men on the threshold. The taller of them came to the bunk, stared down at her and then removed the bandage from her mouth.

"You are Anna Westmoreland, or rather Mrs. Besterling ?" he asked.

"Yes," she whispered.

"I am Inspector McLean of Scotland Yard, and I've been looking for you for quite a long time."

"Oh, thank God !" she murmured.

McLean and Brook undid the rope which bound her. They lifted her a little higher on the cushion to give her additional comfort, and as McLean touched her arm she gave a little cry of pain.

"Are you hurt ?" he asked.

She nodded and closed her eyes. He unbuttoned the blouse she was wearing and pulled it down from the right shoulder, wincing as he saw the terrible swelling at the two joints.

"Did your husband do this?"

"Yes. Could I have some water, please?"

Brook produced a cup of water, but she was unable to hold the cup, and McLean held it to her lips and heard her sigh as she drained it.

"When did you last see your husband?" he asked.

"This morning—very early. He went ashore."

"How did he get ashore? Had he a small boat?"

"Yes. I think he hid it in the rushes somewhere."

"We could see no boat. We had to swim. Feeling better now?"

"Yes, but I must tell you—about the parcel. . . ."

"There's no need. He has the parcel and is on his way here. Now lie quiet. I have to make some arrangements."

He beckoned Brook out to the cockpit, where they stared up and down the river. Nothing was in sight.

"You'll have to do a bit more swimming, Brook," he said. "I want you to go back to the car. Use the radio and tell Car 19 what has happened. Tell the men to work in this direction. If you should run into Besterling don't take any chances with him."

"I won't. What about you, sir?"

"I've got a pistol. When you've sent the message come back here."

Brook nodded and went over the side. McLean watched him swim to the bank and then went back to Anna, who had got one arm into action and was gently rubbing her legs.

"It shouldn't be long now before we have him," he said. "I shall be interested to see what is in that parcel. Have you any idea?"

"No. It was a very heavy metal box, but it was locked."

"And where did you hide it?"

"At the left-luggage office in Waterloo Station. I lied to him at first, but he forced the truth from me, and took from an old watch the receipt that was issued to me. But I must tell you about Mr. Brading——"

"There's no need. I know the part he played in this drama."

"But he was shot. He may be dead. . . ."

"He is very far from dead. As soon as you are fit enough I will take you to see him. He is in hospital, and doing very well."

Anna stared at him incredulously, and then burst into tears. But they were tears of enormous relief, and he went out into the cockpit. The mist had lifted and the bright stars were reflected in the still water. Looking upstream he could see the faint outline of a small boat and could hear the creaking of oars in the row-locks. The great moment had come.

He crept back into the cabin and closed the door. Then he lifted a finger to enjoin silence on Anna's part, and switched off the electric light. In the darkness he took the automatic from his pocket. It was wet from its recent immersion, but he knew that would make no difference to its efficiency.

Now the sound of oars was much closer. They ceased and a slight bump on the craft signified that Besterling was about to come aboard. The question now was whether Besterling would notice the wet deck and take fright. There was also the matter of the broken lock. That was not so easily overlooked.

He heard Besterling come aboard. He stumbled over something and let loose a curse. From Anna there came no sound at all but her low, tense breathing, and he felt sorry that she would be compelled to witness this last act in the drama.

The footsteps came close to the closed door, and McLean flattened his back against the wooden partition to the left of the door. Then there was silence for a moment. Besterling had presumably discovered the broken lock and was cogitating on the cause. Suddenly the light came on, and simultaneously a hand came through the half-open door, holding an automatic. McLean struck down with his own weapon on the wrist behind the weapon, and it clattered to the floor. McLean then came face to face with the scowling man, who was clutching an attaché case in his left hand. He had discarded the spectacles which he had been wearing, and his eyes shone with the light of madness. McLean kicked the fallen pistol further down the cabin and kept his own weapon levelled on Besterling's body.

"Come in!" said McLean. "And sit down there."

Besterling took one step forward and sat on the foot of the bunk opposite Anna, still clutching the suitcase and breathing heavily.

"Who the hell are you?" he gasped.

"A police officer. I am going to arrest you on a charge of murder."

Anna gave an involuntary cry, but Besterling, with his scarred face, never even looked at her.

"You'll need some help," he said.

"The help will be here in a minute or two. Don't move or I shall shoot you."

Besterling looked at the levelled pistol and then up at McLean's grim face.

"What have you done with the parcel?" asked McLean.

"What parcel?"

"The parcel you collected this evening."

"I don't know what you're talking about."

"You had the parcel when you stole the bicycle."

McLean was simply killing time, for there was little he could do until Brook came back with his handcuffs.

"All right," said Besterling in a quiet voice. "I'll tell you everything. It was like this. Anna told me where I could lay my hands on it. I went ashore this morning in the boat and walked to the nearest bus-stop. I was afraid to——"

In the middle of the sentence his boot shot upwards and kicked McLean's arm. For an instant the pistol wavered, and in that instant Besterling was through the open cabin door, leaving the attaché case on the floor. His back was towards McLean, and offered a fine target, but McLean shot low to miss him and bring him back to his senses. It had no effect, and McLean leapt through the door after him. As he reached the cockpit Besterling jumped overboard. Less than fifty yards away was Brook. He had apparently heard the pistol shot and was running as hard as he could.

"He's overboard!" yelled McLean. "Watch for him!"

Brook ran close to the water and stood on the bank peering at the spot where Besterling had disappeared. But nothing came to the surface. McLean watched, too, thinking that Besterling was making a long swim under water to avoid the pistol. But still there was nothing to be seen of Besterling, though the light from the cabin afforded good visibility for a considerable distance.

"Must be caught up in the bottom weed, sir," shouted Brook.

"All right. I'll get into the boat. You stay where you are."

McLean untied the small boat which Besterling had used and then pushed one of the oars down into the deep water. For some time he felt nothing, but finally the oar touched something solid, which moved away a little but did not come to the surface.

"He's here, Brook," he said. "But there appears to be no weed of any kind. You'll have to go back to the town and get a grappling iron."

"He'll be dead by then," said Brook. "Shall I try diving? I'm already wet through."

"All right. See what you can do."

Brook divested himself of his coat and boots and then dived neatly into the water, coming up quite close to the boat to get his breath.

"Take no chances. If there's any weed. . . ."

"I'll take care. Here goes!"

Brook's head went down and he disappeared from view. He came up in a minute or two, and then tried again, and again. On the fourth attempt he was successful and appeared in distress, striving to keep another body above the water. McLean propelled the boat closer to the struggling and breathless swimmer.

"He's heavy as lead," gasped Brook. "Got him, sir?"

"Yes."

It took some minutes to get the body aboard the small boat and then into the motor-boat. There they tried artificial respiration, but it was useless. Besterling was dead. It was Brooks' last remark which gave McLean a clue to this extraordinary phenomenon. He opened the mackintosh and felt in the side pockets of the jacket. In each one was a heavy bar of metal.

"What is it?" asked Brook.

"The contents of the lead box. He must have found the box was an encumbrance, so he threw it away and pocketed the contents. When he jumped overboard he didn't realize that he would never come to the surface. It needs very little extra weight to keep a man down, and these two bars must weigh about ten pounds."

"But what are they ?"

"I don't know, but I can make a guess. There are certain rare metals that are kept in lead boxes. There's something stamped on them. We need more light."

He took one of the bars close to the cabin door. On it was stamped '*U*.235. 4000 *grams. Oak Ridge, Tennessee. U.S.A.*'

"There's the secret," said McLean. "Pure refined uranium."

"All that fuss and risk for two metal bars !" said Brook. "Was it worth it ?"

"Presumably it was. At any rate Mr. Magnay seems to have considered it a bargain at a quarter of a million dollars. There are going to be some awkward questions asked when the United States Atomic Energy Commission learns of this obvious theft. But now we've got to get Besterling's body ashore, and also Anna. I think I see some friends of ours coming along the river bank."

Later Anna was told of her husband's strange death. She did not pretend to be grieved, for the love she had borne Besterling had long since been shattered by Besterling himself.

"Providence works in strange ways," she said. "He risked everything to get possession of that stuff, and in the end it caused his death."

§ 26

ON the following morning it was reported to McLean that Magnay had left his hotel at eleven o'clock the night before and had been successfully trailed to a night club in the West End. He appeared to be waiting for someone, but after an hour he went back to the hotel and was still there.

"I'm going to run up and see him," said McLean. "I have his passport and he would like to have it back."

"Don't we do anything about him?" asked Brook.

"What can we do? He certainly had nothing to do with the kidnapping. That he was acting for another Government is obvious, but there's nothing we can really charge him with. The sooner he leaves this country the better."

Mr. Magnay was as impassive as ever when McLean saw him and handed him his passport.

"This means I can leave?" he asked.

"Yes. The goods you were waiting to receive are not now available. Your old friend Toovey, so-called, is dead, and his brother Edwin was near to death when I last saw him. If I were you I should stick to selling your culture pearls, but not in this country. I hope you understand?"

Mr. Magnay bowed.

"Yes, I understand," he said. "I shall catch my plane in a few hours."

Back at the office an important personage who had just arrived by air was waiting to see McLean. His name was Sargood, and he represented the F.B.I.

"It's about a man named Grogan," he said.

"Which Grogan?" asked McLean. "There were two of them."

"This man's name was Lance. There has been a serious loss of United States Government property, which has only just recently come to light. Certain officials are implicated, and one man has made a confession."

"Two bars of U.235?" asked McLean.

"Yes. How did you know that?"

"It came to light early this morning. Lance Grogan was shot by an accomplice, who got away with the bars."

"Is he dead—Grogan?"

"Yes, and his brother, who worked with him, is too ill to make a statement."

"And the bars?"

"We have them here."

Sargood opened his eyes in surprise and relief.

"That sure is good news," he said. "We've certainly got to hand it to you Scotland Yard people. By this time we thought they were behind the Iron Curtain."

"They very nearly were," said McLean. "As a matter of interest, what were those two bars worth?"

Sargood screwed up his face. The question seemed to cause him some little trouble.

"There's no open market for that stuff," he said. "But I reckon production cost today is close on five hundred thousand dollars a pound."

McLean gazed at him incredulously.

"Are you serious ?" he asked.

"Sure !"

"How disappointed Mr. Magnay must be," mused McLean.

"Who ?"

"Oh, just a little dealer whom I sent packing just now. It's a long and complicated story, but now I'll take you to the Superintendent."

An hour later McLean heard over the telephone that Grogan had died without regaining consciousness. That was a little disappointing, since he had hoped that Grogan might tell him just what part Besterling had played in the theft. But he was satisfied that the whole case was closing on a happier note, and that note was Anna, who came to the office by appointment the following morning. She had been resting at a hotel and having treatment for her injured arm, which was now in a sling. But there was a new look in her eyes.

"You're looking much better," said McLean.

"Yes. I've slept and slept and slept. Are you sure it's quite convenient to take me to Neville—I mean Mr. Brading ?"

"Quite sure. The car is waiting now."

Her face beamed, and very soon they were in a fast car making for Southampton, with Brook at the wheel. When they reached their destination McLean took her into the ward where Brading was sitting up in bed, and then went to rejoin Brook in the car.

"Nice girl," he said. "Just unfortunate in her first choice. Those two will have a lot to talk about, so we shall have to exercise patience. Have a cigarette. This is one of our easy days."

An hour elapsed before Anna came out of the hospital, running down the steps with her face aglow. She got into the car beside McLean and sighed.

"Is he going along all right ?" asked McLean.

"Oh, yes. He's been walking around already. In three days he is coming back to London."

"Fine! And you—what about you?"

Anna hesitated and then looked at McLean with her wonderful, expressive eyes.

"He wants to marry me in a short time, and then take me back to Canada. I—I said I would. Do you think I've done right?"

McLean touched her on the hand.

"I think nothing could be more right," he said.